THE DERRINGER

A Western

J.V. JAMES

Classic Old West Tales

for Clive – your words were magic

CONTENTS

PROLOGUE
THE FINGER OF FATE

Cedar Rapids, Iowa.
June 12, 1862

If little Roy Stone had done what his Ma told him to — that fateful day when he was seven — he'd never have known the truth of what happened at all.

He'd never have seen the double-cross, never have witnessed the murders, never seen the killer's blowed-apart finger.

But Roy was excited for the future, so he hid himself in the closet. Poor kid saw the whole rotten thing, beginning to end.

It was musty and dusty in there, and he didn't much like the perfume smell. Almost sneezed, right when his Ma came into the room, but somehow he managed to hold it.

She looked more joyful right then than Roy had ever seen her — and she was leading a man by the hand.

Not in the usual way.

The man she was leading today was a real upstandin' feller. Treated Ma like a lady. Reese Scott was his name, and he was to be Roy's new Pa.

He'd never had a Pa before.

Shoulda touched my left shoe for luck, he thought from inside that dark closet. But somehow, they seemed to be having so much luck, it likely didn't matter, so he didn't.

Closet doors didn't quite join up straight, and as he watched through the crack, he saw his Ma kiss Reese Scott.

Roy wondered then if he should close his eyes, and maybe put his fingers in his ears. This was the room he wasn't allowed in, and kissing was the main reason why.

Then Big Jim clomped in heavy-footed, and it didn't matter no more, 'cause the kissing was over. Ma still held Reese Scott's hand, but her smile was gone, and things took a serious turn.

Sometimes the back of Roy's neck would tingle, and he felt like bad things might happen. Sometimes it turned out he was right. Neck tingled worse now than ever before, and Roy didn't even dare breathe.

Big Jim Starr was the boss of the Lucky Starr Saloon, and Roy had lived here his whole life. He had always been afraid of Big Jim — then again, so had everyone else.

Ma said it weren't nothin' to be ashamed of.

Said it was only good sense to be afraid of dangerous things, and fear was a good natural feeling that would save your life again and again — long as you just paid attention, and didn't let the fear stop you from thinking.

Roy was tiny alright, always had been — even now he was seven, he was barely the size of a five-year-old. Big Jim always referred to Roy as *The Derringer*. Didn't mean it in any way complimentary, always spoke it like it was an insult. There was nothing wrong with the size of Roy's brain though — he was a real clever boy.

He couldn't see Big Jim's huge hairy face now, only the back of him — and the hair that stood out from his head in every direction. He sure was called *Big* for a reason. Wasn't fat though, just taller'n most, and so heavy with muscle it turned strangers' heads in the street. Some folks said he looked like a mountain man, but to Roy, he had the look of a big mean black bear — only bears didn't carry no guns, but Big Jim always did. Huge one it was, and pearl-handled.

Roy looked at that oversize gun now, wished he could reach out and touch it. He held wild fascinations for guns, knives, arrows — even slingshots. But that massive pearl-handled gun, it was the best.

Roy stayed right where he was, hoped this would be over with quick. Sometimes Big Jim talked too long, but no one ever complained to his face.

Thing about Big Jim though, he only ever talked about money — except for when he talked about killing.

Not like Reese Scott, who mostly talked about ponies, or cattle, or what color dog Roy might like once they moved to Colorado.

When he clomped on into that room, Big Jim didn't say nothin'. Just stood there — he liked to stare people down awhile sometimes. No one ever much stared back at him. He looked bigger than ever before, it seemed like to Roy. The quiet was so filled with his meanness, Roy wished he'd stayed outside playing, the way he'd been told to.

Then Big Jim spoke. His voice sounded like a spade diggin' into wet gravel, perhaps on account of all the whiskey he drank. "You got the money, Scott?"

"Yessir," said Reese Scott, taking a thick roll of bills from his pocket and holding it out in front of him. "As agreed, five-thousand dollars."

"Damn new-fangled notes," Big Jim growled.

"Paper currency's the future," said Reese, raising and lowering his palm a little, as if weighing the notes in his hand. "We all might as well just get used to it. We'll be leaving on today's stage, Mister Starr. I guess this is goodbye."

Big Jim snatched the money, put it in his coat pocket, then laughed. "Goodbye? Now hold on a minute," he said. "Five-thousand is just a deposit, she's worth double that and you know it."

Reese Scott stepped forward, raising his fists, but Roy's Ma grabbed his arm and cried, "No, Reese," as Big Jim pulled out that huge gun and pointed it at Reese's chest.

"Please, Jim," said Roy's Ma. "You promised me. Please."

"Now, Ange," said Big Jim, waving the gun around to make Reese step back, "you didn't think it'd be *that* easy, did you? *I own you.* You're my best girl — and clever too, you know the numbers. I can make five-thousand a *year* from you, and you might yet last five more years."

"We had a *deal*, Starr," cried Reese, poking a hole in the air with a finger. "What sorta man breaks a..."

He shut up right quick when Big Jim thumbed back the hammer of his revolver and pushed the end of the barrel against Reese's chest.

"I'm unarmed, Starr," said Reese Scott, putting his hands up to show it.

"Please, Jim," cried Angie, and her own hands came together in front of her, like as if she was praying. "I'm worn out, Jim, I'm done. Almost thirty, you know that. Another year or two's all I got, and no one'll want me at all. Please. If not for me, do it for little Roy."

"You and that damn derringer. You're just lucky I let you keep him. Shoulda been tied in a sack and—"

"Please, Jim. Please."

"Tell you what," said Big Jim — and he pushed the gun up under Reese Scott's chin now, so hard it made the man's eyes bulge as he backed against the wall. "Get me another five-thousand, and I'll let you all leave."

"I don't *have it*," cried Reese, his face twitching in anger. "I sold my ranch and my stock to get that money, you *know* that. It's everything I worked for, every penny I have, *you lowdown double-crossin' SKUNK OF A—*"

Those was the last words Reese Scott ever spoke. The gun in Big Jim's hand exploded, and it seemed to little Roy like a great sheet of flame mixed with blood flew up through the air and painted the wall — then Reese Scott fell down in a heap, all broken and lifeless.

As the smell of burned flesh and gunpowder assailed Roy's nostrils, Angie Stone screamed. Then a smaller flame — Derringer flame — flew from her hand toward Big Jim.

He growled as he turned toward her, the air blue with his cursing, "My hand, oh my hand, you damn whore."

And fire and noise erupted once more, then again.

And now, it was Roy who was screaming, and his dear Ma fell to the floor, as he darted from the closet, threw himself down upon her. "I love you, Roy," was her only words, as she weakly raised up a hand, brushed a lock of hair from his eyes.

She coughed, her hand fell, and her soft eyes flickered a little — then Angelina Stone went to sleep, forever and more, in a pool of bright blood that spread across the uneven floor toward Big Jim Starr, her killer.

And little Roy Stone, he looked up at Big Jim, and he never forgot the way the man looked in that moment — huge and terrible he was, two dark angry eyes and a big spread-out nose and a mouthful of gritted teeth that growled against all his pain. No more face than that, just a beard as dense as dark forest, and a headful of dark hair to match it.

And those dark eyes were staring, shocked and staring at his own hand — the rude bloodied stump that was there at its end now, instead of the pinkie finger that should be.

"I'm going to kill you," little Roy cried in his small voice, and he shook as he said it — not with fear but with righteous anger — but Big Jim only laughed with contempt, then looked back at his hand.

But the thing was, that little boy *meant* what he said — and what was more, he *believed* it.

He would grow up and kill that big man. That was all that now mattered.

CHAPTER 1
UGLY AS A MUD FENCE

Cheyenne Stagecoach Depot, Wyoming.
July 12, 1877

Lot of interesting stories begin with a stagecoach. Roy sure knew that. Four years of ceaselessly traveling the West had left him with a whole lot of stories, a fair whack of money, and an ever-increasing desire for vengeance. Burned bigger and brighter each day, that vengeful desire.

See, that sorta vengeance, it sets a young man to a whole lotta traveling. Nothin' else but revenge'll quench the fire in such a man's heart. Nothin' else'll satisfy his soul, no matter the cost.

The day Roy turned eighteen, he said goodbye to the only home he'd ever known, and set out to find the man who had murdered his mother — and he was twenty-two now.

After four years of travel, what Roy didn't know about stagecoaches wasn't worth knowing.

He'd paid $125 to ride this one from Cheyenne to Deadwood. The cost was outrageous, as stagecoach rates went — but Roy figured it just about right, considering potential for danger along such a route. Triple what it cost to go from Sidney, and ten times the danger. He was happy to pay it anyway, being sure to get an interesting story.

Maybe someday I'll write a damn book. The Stagecoach Chronicles. Got a nice ring to it.

He'd paid for his ticket the previous day, won two-hundred dollars playing poker, had himself a steak dinner, then got a good night's sleep in one of Cheyenne's finest hotels.

He'd considered getting a shave, and the thin wispy beard he'd recently grown was patchy, made him look even younger. But he knew, when hard men looked at him, his failure of beard somehow made him look less of a threat, and that suited him fine.

No shave, he'd decided — but he didn't deny himself anything other than that.

A steaming hot bath, fluffy pillows, clean sheets, and a comfortable bed. Paid the cook a sly twenty dollars to cook him a good hearty breakfast and bring it up to his room nice and early. It had been a most welcome night of luxury — but too much soft living turns a man soft himself, and Roy knew that for a certainty.

Best to balance it out. One night of true comfort's enough, at least for the present.

Roy turned up at the stage station early, made sure he was first into the coach. Took the seat facing forward, next to the right-hand side door.

No getting stuck in the middle for this feller. No facing back where he'd come from neither.

What's up ahead is what matters.

Luggage between his feet, cushion under his rump. Plenty of apples, canteen of water, jerky in case of emergency. Special order Seventy-Three Winchester Carbine between his knees, four-shot Sharps derringer in his inner coat pocket — both well oiled and loaded up full. Business as usual, travel wise.

Didn't stay usual for long.

What soon made it different to usual, was the woman who climbed up inside the coach, smiled and sat down beside him.

Dang it. Not just a woman, but a PRETTY one!

Now, Roy had nothin' against pretty women — truth was, he was all for 'em, in the right situation. Right situation being just about anywhere else.

Last thing you want in a stagecoach is a dang pretty woman.

Problem is, even the stupidest, ugliest, stinkingest of men, confined to a stagecoach with others, will feel himself compelled to compete for the affections of any halfway attractive woman.

Young men, old men, fat men, thin men. Miners, ranchers, horse thieves, and undertakers. Even the most bloodless of men, such as bankers and lawyers, can act almost verifiably human in that situation.

In Roy's estimation, there wasn't a man alive didn't feel the need to impress a pretty woman in a stagecoach — and *pretty* came to be a loose term, in the circumstances of such confined travel.

Most likely a book just in that.

No. Roy knew it for sure and for certain. Rules of stagecoaches always work fine, right up 'til a woman steps on board. Then the whole dang thing goes awry.

Ain't meant to smoke, on account o' their delicate constitutions.

Ain't meant to drink, on account o' their delicate sensibilities.

Ain't meant to cuss, on account o' their delicate ears.

And before long, all that bein' careful not to offend what's delicate, it sets all the men's teeth on edge.

Cain't do *this*, cain't do *that*, cain't do *nothin'* except for be someone you ain't. Not if you hope to impress.

Well, you can only bottle up a man's true nature so long. Before long, the pressure of all that pretendin' blows off the lid.

Leads to fightin' in the end, the force o' men's true natures eventually bubblin' and boilin' out of 'em.

So when that pretty woman climbed through the left-hand side door, Roy took one surprised look at her overly beautiful face; a second, most appreciative look at the generous shape of her curves; and a final, astonished sorta look at the foolish hat she was wearing — had flowers and what looked like a *bird* on it — then he opened the right-hand side door and climbed right on out, cushion in his left hand, Winchester in his right.

"I'll be riding the box seat," he announced then, and Roy always did what he said he would. He threw his cushion onto the box seat, reached back inside, grabbed his bag without looking at the girl, and threw that up on top of the coach.

"Box seat's unavailable," said the driver, after throwing another passenger's luggage up on top. "Not to mention, too dangerous. That's where the guard sits, this route, and the first place road agents aim for."

That driver was around five foot eight, same as Roy, but huge in the arms and the shoulders. Pushing forty at least, and done too many hard miles out in bad weather.

"Heard tell this route wasn't that dangerous now," said Roy. "Maybe I should catch the train down to Sidney, head up to Deadwood from there."

"You'll be safe with me here, kid," said a whiskey-soured voice from behind. "I'm the guard. You want my seat, you can have it."

Roy had turned when the man first spoke, waited for him to finish, then he started to say, "Thank y—"

"Hundred Lincolns," the guard growled, holding out his left hand, palm up. "Or *you* can take *your* chances balancin' on top of all that damn cargo. Mighty long way to fall when the goin' gits rough. Either that, or git yerself back in there with the other stinkin' passengers, where you're meant to sit."

"Aw, Curly," said the driver, eyes wide. "You ain't meant to sell your seat that way, we might get—"

"Shut up, Joe, and mind your business," growled Curly.

But Joe was one of that type who, once he gets talking, doesn't find it so easy to stop. "There's a *real* pretty girl in there, Curly. How about you drive, and *I'll* sit inside."

"Pretty sure I said to shut up, Joe," came the sharp reply from the guard, and this time it worked.

Roy had never once took his eyes off of Curly. The man was ugly as a mud fence. Short and dark, real mean-lookin' up close from having his nose broke in one too many directions. Two inches shorter than Roy, but twice the size of him, muscle-wise. If you'd took away his guns, dressed him all up in a genteel hat and bowtie, give him a pearl-handled cane and had him sit a horse sidesaddle, he'd *still* have looked just like Trouble — capital T. He yet held his hand out palm up though, and that was the main thing.

"How about fifty?" said Roy. "I can't really—"

"You deaf?" Curly growled. "Price is a hundred."

"Leaves me near broke, but I guess it's better than—"

"I seen you jump right on out," Curly laughed, "soon as that fancy filly climbed in. You scared of girls, kid, or what?"

"Scared of a lotta things," said Roy mildly. He put his hand into his pocket, pulled out five of the double eagles he'd won the night before, placed them on Curly's outstretched hand. Then he put his little Winchester up onto the box seat, climbed on up, and parked his behind on his cushion.

"Pleasure doin' business with you," growled the guard. And for the first time in a long while, the hairs on the back of Roy's neck commenced to tingle.

CHAPTER 2
"RUN 'EM DOWN, JOE"

R oy was on edge to start with, but by the time they went through Lodgepole Creek, he'd settled down some.

Musta just been nervy about Deadwood, he decided. *Big chance I'll find him up there. Seems like it attracts the worst kind.*

And Big Jim Starr truly *was* the worst kind.

They'd gone forty miles out of Cheyenne when the hairs on the back of Roy's neck *really* commenced to tingle. Halfway between Bear Springs Station and Chugwater Station.

Fierce bad feeling it was. So much so, Roy bent forward and reached down to touch his left boot for luck.

He knew it was just an old superstition, but he always liked the way it brought his Ma to his mind — the cheerfulness of her whenever she'd told him to do it. Didn't have many memories of her, and that was a nice one.

Gave that boot a good rub while he thought some about her, and thought back on how she had loved him.

Well, danged if that old superstition didn't save Roy's life. First bullet went right through where his head had been two seconds earlier. Tore right through his luggage bag it did, before going into a pine box behind it. Box of shovels maybe, by the ping sound it made.

Thanks, Ma.

"Warned ya 'bout the box seat," cried the driver of the stage as he urged the horses into a gallop, aiming right for the outlaws where they stood in the middle of the trail, maybe ninety yards up ahead.

"Run 'em down, Joe," cried Curly the guard, as he threw his body down flat and commenced with his aiming.

There were three of them outlaws, all with repeaters, judging by the way lead was flying. They wouldn't be easy to aim at neither, as the coach was bumping and swaying and rattling fit to bust wheels, so fast them four horses was movin'.

Roy raised up his Winchester, got a bead on the middle feller, just right — but what was right went all wrong, the way what's right sometimes does — the coach pitched to the left, driver's elbow knocked Roy's Winchester sideways, and his first shot went into the trees. Mighta scared a possum, but that's about all.

Them three fellers up ahead, they sure wasn't scared, and they sure wasn't joshin' about.

Bullets sizzled past Roy's ears as the stage bore down on the outlaws, a mighty cloud of dust rising from the thundering feet of the horses. As he took aim a second time, he saw one outlaw then another bite the dirt, both of 'em shot in the chest by the guard on top of the stagecoach.

Roy took careful aim at the only outlaw remaining and squeezed the trigger — just as a wheel hit a rock and he got jolted sideways. Near went flyin' off the side he did, and again, his shot went awry. Not even no possums where that bullet went. Mighta scared a bird if one had been flying over.

That last outlaw, he jumped off the trail just in time to save himself being run down. But as they went thundering past him, the guard up on top put a forty-four right through that outlaw feller's brain, and the threat was all over and done with.

"Nice shootin', Curly," said the driver to the guard as he reined the snorting horses to a halt a few seconds later.

Curly grunted at Joe the driver and gave a slight nod. Then he looked down at Roy, a superior smile at the corner of his lips. "Better luck next time, young feller," he said. "Least you and your baby-gun tried."

Wasn't much Roy could say, except, "Thank you. Sure wish I could shoot the way you do. However did you learn to shoot that way, Mister?"

"Done a deal with Old Scratch, and you best believe it — I get to shoot this way, and when I'm done he gets my soul."

"Well, you saved our bacon for sure. Only wish I coulda helped."

They both stayed where they were, looking all around, ready to shoot just in case there was anyone left.

"You need a proper rifle, kid, not that toy," Curly

said, then he spat a dark wad on the ground. "Ain't never gonna shoot straight, a baby barrel like that. Some fool's cut it down to nothin', like a poor excuse for a scattergun."

"Yessir, guess you're right," Roy said. Didn't matter to him what Curly thought. Thing was, Roy's Winchester Carbine was a special order from the factory — and while its twelve inch barrel shortened its effective range to about eighty yards, it was more accurate than most full length rifles. Dang site easier to handle as well. Made a heck of a noise though.

Winchester took great pride in their special order weapons, and they knew a twelve-inch would have plenty to prove.

Roy was just the feller to help prove it, too. A man with revenge in his heart is a man who makes sure he has the skills to extract it, for when the time comes.

He'd been taught by the best, and it just wasn't like him to miss.

But in this case he'd fired twice, and both shots had missed by, *oh, about a mile maybe,* he reckoned. *Might as well a'been a mile anyways.*

But that guard feller, Curly, he'd fired three, and every shot killed its man. Downright impressive shooting.

"Best leave the gunplay to us professionals, kid," Curly said. "Maybe ride inside the coach from here on, like we told you before." Then he stepped onto the wheel of the stage, jumped down into the dirt, and commenced walking back to check the pockets of the dead men.

One of the men inside the coach stuck his head out,

looked quickly this way and that, as Roy climbed down to the ground still holding his Winchester.

"All dead?" the man inside the coach enquired. He *looked* a tough sorta feller, but right now, he was nervy as a cat in a roomful of rockers.

Roy knew he must help reassure the folks inside the stagecoach, for they were still two days from Deadwood, and any further panic would make the trip unpleasant. "Looks like we're in real good hands," he said to that nervy feller, while checking his pocket watch. *Eleven-twenty.* "Guard killed 'em all. Three shots, three men all dead, from a fast-moving stage. Best shooting I ever saw. No one injured inside?"

"No, sir," said the feller, after turning around as if to check. "One man has opened a bottle, that should help settle some nerves."

Thing was though, the hairs on back of Roy's neck were still tingling, and long experience had taught him not to relax 'til that stopped. "Somethin' ain't right," he mumbled to himself.

"Some o' you men gimme a hand with these carcasses," Curly growled as he pocketed twelve dollars from the first dead man he came to. "Most likely got bounties out on 'em, and I plan to collect."

"I gotta check out the coach," called Joe the driver, shrugging his mighty shoulders.

There were five passengers inside, Roy knew that much. Hadn't forgot that one was a woman.

No place for a woman like her. And this'll just make it all worse.

Thing was, even if Roy *hadn't* seen her, he'd have known she was a pretty one — every time they stopped to change horses, the loafers at the swing stations kept craning their necks to look inside the coach. The looking inside was followed by much smoothing down of hair, adjusting of hats, and offers of food and drink to be fetched for the "little lady." She couldn't be convinced to "get out'n stretch yer limbs a few minutes" anyplace yet, no matter how many times she was asked.

Seems to like it in there, thought Roy. *Takes all kinds, I guess.*

Even Joe, the grizzled old driver, took every opportunity to look in on the lady, and attempt to see to her comfort — though it was clear he cared not a whit for the rest of his passengers.

In contrast to all the attentions bestowed upon her, the lady had neither been seen nor heard by young Roy since that very first moment. He had made it a point not to lower himself like the others, and had so far ignored her completely.

Even now she stayed put, did not poke so much as her pretty nose out of the window. After some arguments about who should stay with the lady, two of the men from inside the coach got out to help, and Roy went along too.

They dragged the dead men back to the coach and — with considerable grunting and effort — threw them up on top, after laying a tarpaulin over the luggage so it wouldn't get any blood on it. Most of it weren't really luggage, just boxes of shovels and pickaxes and gold pans and such, but they still had to keep the blood off it — some folks were funny about blood.

They soon found the road agents' horses, and Curly made sure no one else but him touched the saddlebags. Looked like he got a good haul from outta them saddlebags. Then they tied the horses to the back of the stage, and all climbed back in — or on — and got moving again.

But Roy, his neck hairs was still all a'tingle. It wasn't because of what just happened — he'd seen death enough in his time, been in tight situations aplenty. No, there was *something* here not quite right.

And he knew, within the next day or two, he was sure to find out what it was, one way or another.

Don't much matter, he decided. *I'm plenty watchful, somewhat fearful, well-enough armed, and expectin' what ain't expected.*

Man like that, he's pretty much ready for anything.

CHAPTER 3
AN UNPLEASANT DANCE

I t was after midday when the stage pulled in at Chugwater Station.

"Twenty minute stop, food's worth partakin' of," cried the driver. "Clean privies too, if you need 'em."

Seemed like most of the passengers *did* need 'em. *Nothin' like a good scare to send folks runnin' to the privies.*

Roy left the privies to the passengers, he didn't need 'em. Went inside, looked at the people — no sign of Big Jim here.

Then Roy looked at what they called food, and just shook his head — walked right on back out without so much as a word.

Glad I brought plenty of apples.

Doors of the coach were both open, he could see there was no one inside it. Curly and two local fellers were unloading the bodies of the outlaws — they'd have to be sent back to Cheyenne for identification.

Roy walked up ahead a ways, stood alone on the trail,

looked to the mountains ahead. Thought about what might be in Deadwood.

About *who* might be in Deadwood.

Four years of searching, every clue leading nowhere. But if the man was alive, someday, somewhere, Roy would find him. He would not rest 'til he did.

He owed that much, at least, to his mother. To Reese Scott as well. To Grampa. And to himself.

If Big Jim Starr was alive, Roy would find him, tell him why he was there, and send that damned skunk off to Hell. Like a thousand times before, he watched that future moment in his mind.

Nothing else mattered, not really.

Deadwood. Maybe in Deadwood.

He heard the other passengers behind him now, as they filed back out to the coach. Half listened to their meaningless talk, whole lotta noise about nothing. So many people just wandering aimless through life. Filling their minutes. He heard the men all falling over each other to be the one to help the lady up into the coach.

Heard her voice then too. First time for that.

"Thank you," she said, "you're all very kind."

Even her voice was pretty. Small though. Soft. Not at all like the women Roy had known. They'd had to fight for everything, the strong, tough women who'd raised him, after his mother was gone. This one here, she seemed more like a child — somehow she sounded all wrong. Like she'd been picked up out of her real life, dropped off somewhere in the wrong place.

It was hard not to turn round and look at her then. He

wondered what her *real* world looked like. What sort of place she belonged in. Wasn't noplace he'd ever seen, he was certain of that.

"You'd best travel inside the coach, kid," Curly said from behind Roy now.

"It was you set the price for the box seat," said Roy, before turning to face him, "and I paid you fair, what you asked. Reckon I'll use what I paid for, the whole way to Deadwood. But I thank you ... for your concern."

"Suit yourself," Curly growled. And again, the hairs on the back o' Roy's neck started dancing an unpleasant dance.

There were no further incidents though, for the rest of that first day of travel. Made good time too, despite the unwelcome interruption — it was pretty much all downhill as far as Fort Laramie.

Seeing the Fort was about the most interesting part — mostly on account of how it didn't look much like a Fort.

Fort Laramie had no fortifications at all — not a blade of grass either, and aside from one massive Cottonwood, the trees all half-dead or worse.

Roy wasn't surprised they didn't stop there — but he'd hoped they would, having heard tell of its pet elk, a most privileged citizen who went wherever he liked, eating up shoes and hats and canteens, even curtains from off people's windows.

There was also rumored to be an old artilleryman in residence, the one man who'd lived there since the Fort's very first day — he too was a celebrated citizen, though for different reasons than the elk. It was said that this man was the ugliest in all of Wyoming, his face all seams and scars, the results of many a battle survived by the old Indian-fighter.

Sure would love to meet that feller. Such stories he must have to tell!

Instead, Roy had to settle himself with a distant view of the Fort as they rolled on by it, and a close up view of the massive new bridge as they crossed the North Platte soon after.

The bridge had only been completed the previous year, and General George Crook and over a thousand of his men had crossed it, on their way to go meet up with Custer to fight Sitting Bull.

Sure hope crossing this bridge works out better for me than it did for them.

The stage timetable had said they would stop at the Fort — but instead, they proceeded over the bridge, and once safely across, stopped at a log stage station owned by John Montgomery. Joe the driver made a flimsy excuse for the change, but the truth was clear enough to Roy — Curly was not keen on being seen at the Fort. Indeed, the guard did not even *look* at the Fort, but in the other direction instead, the whole time they were going by it.

They made good time, stopping every dozen or so miles for fresh horses. When nearing a stop, Joe would blow on his bugle — *untunefully* would be far too kind a word — then he'd urge the horses on faster, make a real show of it as he came in.

Just before dark, as the final remains of the sunset flamed blood-red atop the horizon, they arrived at Rawhide Buttes Station, still right on schedule. No urging the horses on then though — way that whirlwind was blowing, it was all the driver could do to keep the team under control.

Then suddenly, as fast as that wild wind had sprung up, it stopped, at the very moment Joe pulled the brake on out front of the Station.

"Overnight stop," he yelled good and loud, as he climbed down off of the box. "Two to a room, beds got no bugs. Food's eatable, gambling's good, and the painted cats here'll just about rattle yer..."

His voice trailed off as he remembered the lady in the coach. Took off his hat, held it in front of him. Looked right contrite as he opened that left-side door.

Roy waited right where he was, up there on that box seat. Once the passengers started climbing out, he just looked straight ahead, waited there like a statue 'til they all went inside.

It wasn't so much the *words* foolish men used, it was the pleading and whining inside the words — that was what annoyed Roy most of all. Like as if, somehow, they figured the contest for the woman might soon be decided, and they could angle their words for an edge. It was like they actually believed she might choose one of them to spend the night with her.

Her, of all women.

He sat there thinking about it, just shaking his head.

Damn fools. Can't see what's in front of their eyes.

He'd seen her for less than five seconds, and he knew it right off — knew it sure as death, sure as food, sure as whiskey. Sure as blood that pooled on a floorboard — *knew* that she was *not* the sort of woman to spend the night with a man.

Not unless she married him first.

He shook his head again, jumped down to the ground, patted the dust from his clothes.

Looked at his surroundings and laughed.

Bird on a hat. On a stage to Deadwood, no less. If I ever do write that book, I won't be puttin' that in — ain't a soul alive who'd believe it.

"Delicate" just got a whole big brand new meaning.

CHAPTER 4
SNAKES IN THE HENHOUSE

Fools come in all shapes and sizes, that was one thing Roy had learned. Not just in his four years traveling the West, but also throughout his childhood.

Place he grew up, seemed like most of the men all competed to throw their money away quicker'n the rest.

Lucky thing for Roy, that mostly held true all over, wherever he went. And while growing up, he'd had good teachers. Knew a whole lot of ways to part men from their money, and knew never to take too much from any one man.

Other folks mighta thought a saloon a poor place to grow up, but Roy got a fine education there. Once his own Ma was gone, five other women jumped right in to mother him, and he became special to all of them — though one in particular took him into her heart, a dear friend of his mother's called Maisie.

What with being educated by all of those women, as

well as the man he called Grampa, Roy understood words, numbers, and a lot of other things real good. One thing he learned about was women and whiskey — knew that *both* make a man unable to think straight. And a man who ain't thinking straight tends to see gambling as a real good idea — regardless of who's at the table.

That's why gambling places always have whiskey and women. And this here place the stage just pulled up to, it wouldn't be any different.

From outside, it looked like a fort. Old one, from the primitive days. Built of huge heavy logs, all well chinked with mud. Narrow windows everywhere, where defenders could fire at Indians.

At least, Indians was what they wanted folks to think of. Part of a good education is seeing the details, learning to work out the *story*, figure out what folks *want* you to think.

Outside, that building looked plenty old and battle scarred.

Wasn't so old as it seemed though, on close examination. Only scars on this building was from weather, not gunfire. Most likely not yet two years old.

Still, inside had a different feel to it. Almost too nice for a rest stop. A lot better than Roy had expected. Fancy chandelier and everything. It was carefully designed to make travelers feel secure, ease the worries the outside created — seemed like a place to relax, maybe feel you could let down your guard.

Such feelings were likely to make travelers loose with their money.

Roy had planned to sleep on the floor of the main room,

as he usually did in such places. But perhaps — perhaps — this place might even have clean beds and bedding.

Believe THAT when I see it.

Thing was though, real money *had* been spent here — and that meant he'd have to be careful. Whoever invested that money would be keeping a tight hold on things.

Roy decided to do the smart thing — maybe just win enough to pay for his food, and don't get anyone angry. This place seemed a long way from the law.

He avoided the lady of course. The twenty seat dinner table had been hewn from one massive Cottonwood, so was plenty long enough to avoid her — but although he waited until she was seated, then sat himself up the opposite end, it seemed like whenever he dared look at her, she pretty soon glanced his way.

Not unusual. Women's just like cats or horses — mostly interested in whoever shows the least interest in THEM.

Roy really only looked at her to make sure she was alright. *Woman so out of place must be struggling,* he figured.

Curly and Joe had made sure to sit their good selves one each side of her.

Helpful as snakes in a henhouse.

Roy could hear Joe talking up how fine a shot Curly was, and making a real big thing about how he had saved them all; and how much the bounties might be on them outlaws; and how lucky the little lady was to have such good protection close by.

Most dangerous men hunt in packs.

Roy heard mention of his own poor shooting at one

point, and everyone down that end of the table stared at
him for a few moments.

Then, after checking Roy was looking, Curly said, "If
road agents ever learn to fly, that kid'll be a right danger to
'em, shootin' so high as he does."

Said it so loud the whole place stopped and looked, and
most of them laughed it up big.

Not the lady. She just pursed her lips and kept silent.
Maybe she didn't get the joke.

Maybe.

Didn't matter to Roy. He just raised his fork in the air,
nodded to Curly and smiled. Thing was, Roy never minded
strangers thinking low of him — in truth, he mostly
preferred it. He was average size, average looks, always did
his best not to get noticed. Best way to get on in the world,
way he understood it.

Most of the men here seemed harmless. But Curly in
particular, there was something about him not right. Maybe
Joe too, maybe not.

Wasn't none of Roy's business, unless they did
something to make it so. But still, he didn't like them being
so near the lady.

*One thing for birds to circle around — another thing
altogether when you're certain they're vultures.*

Thing was, Roy woulda kept an eye out for the lady,
even if she'd looked like a mangy old polecat. Some things a
man just feels responsible for. Maybe it was because of
what happened to his mother — or maybe it was from
growing up with so many women.

Whatever caused it, he was what he was — and what he was, was a protector of women.

Ain't a burden watching over this one — she's mighty pleasant to look at.

If he hadn't been keeping an eye on her, he might have missed what happened next.

A group of four men drifted in, all of them heavily bearded. Hard men, no doubt, judging by how they moved.

Danger, maybe. Roy watched them close, without seeming to watch them at all. He was practiced at that.

All four left their hats on, wore 'em low on their foreheads. They walked across to the bar, ordered whiskey. Nothin' unusual there. They all turned around and looked at the lady, of course — *well, what red-blooded man wouldn't?*

But when they turned around after ordering their drinks, the huge, big-nosed feller the others all followed had nodded — the slightest of nods, and the faintest raise of his eyebrows — at Curly. And Curly, he nodded right back at Big-Nose, in just about the same way.

Roy just sorta noted what happened, and kept an eye out thereafter. *Probably nothin',* he decided at first — the two men were most likely acquainted. Still, something about it didn't sit right.

Place was beginning to fill, and Roy saw he'd underestimated how busy it'd get. Might be opportunities to earn a few dollars here after all.

Instead of risking dessert, he left the table and wandered to the other end of the room, took up a good spot by the fire. Set himself up near one side, turned the chair so he could watch the whole room. No sense letting people behind you, not if you can help it.

He had not been sat there a minute when the lady stood up from the table. He figured she'd head straight to her room — but instead, she walked toward the fire, and sat in the chair nearest Roy.

"Miss," he said, nodding politely, and rising from his seat.

She smiled at him and said, "Not running away from me again, are you?"

What a voice. "No, Miss," he managed to say. "I just…"

He didn't *usually* run out of words, but here he was, stunned silent, just standing, undecided on what to do next.

"Yes?" She tilted her head just a touch, raised her eyebrows and waited.

Roy sat himself back down. "Doesn't matter," he said, looking past her to see that Curly was watching them intently as he ate his apple pie. "Have you seen the rooms yet, Miss?"

"No. The truth is, I'm afraid to go back there alone. *Why* did you run away when I climbed into the coach? You don't seem shy. Or afraid of things." She cast a glance toward Curly, then looked into Roy's eyes. "Despite what *some* say."

"Alright then," he said with a sigh, and he looked away a moment. "I'll tell you it straight. Every time a pretty woman steps into a stagecoach, it ruins an otherwise enjoyable journey."

She smiled — almost. Stopped herself before it spread

all the way to her face, but her eyes still smiled clear enough. Sparkled, they did. Then, while he was trapped by her eyes, she said, "So you think I'm pretty?"

He looked away again. Looked at her hands now instead. Safer than looking at her eyes. "You *know* you're pretty, Miss. And me, I ain't one for games. As you clearly plan to annoy me, I'd appreciate you bein' honest from the start. Just easier, ain't it?" He felt like he'd got back some control then, looked up again.

Her eyes widened, her head tilted some, and she let the smile spread to her mouth. Then she smoothed down her skirts and said, "Hmmm. So you think *I'm* pretty, but you *don't* like women. How wonderfully strange."

"Miss—"

"Charlotte. My name is Miss Charlotte Hawke."

Roy half-stood again, reached out his hand, took the fingers she offered, squeezed them lightly as he could, then let go of 'em like he'd been bit. Recoiled, he did, sat back in his chair, far away from her as he could get.

Different sorta tingling, them fingers of hers had caused.

He composed himself quick though, said, "Happy to meet you, Miss Charlotte. I'm Roy."

"Just Roy? No last name?"

She caught him with her eyes again then — almost felt like a contest. Roy looked away first, and it occurred to him then, this young woman was stronger'n she looked.

She laughed now, the laugh not cruel though, only pretty.

Too dang pretty.

CHAPTER 5
WOMEN AND WHISKEY

Tough and pretty ain't mutually exclusive. And she wasn't letting it go. "Well? *No* last name?"

"More than one, Miss Charlotte. But if I told you, I'd need another new one, and I'm fast runnin' out of ideas."

"Hmmm, intriguing," she said. A loud pop came from the fire, and a glowing coal jumped out onto the floor. She flinched some, made a strange little noise, but she quickly calmed herself and said, "More than one name suggests you have something to hide."

"Sounds about right," said Roy. He stood a moment, got the toe of his boot under the edge of the burning coal, sorta flicked it back into the fire, then sat back down and went on. "Miss Charlotte, can we get to business? Seems to me you came over for a reason, and I reckon I can accommodate—"

"How dare—"

"Not sayin' what you think I am, Miss," he said, raising a hand for her to stop. "Please hear me out before judging."

"Alright then." She settled back into her chair.

"Miss Charlotte Hawke, I'll be frank. You look like a fish wearin' a saddle—"

"I look like no such—"

"Keep your hair on, Miss, I only mean to say, you seem out of place here. Out of your depth maybe — although what you said about bein' afraid to go look at the rooms all alone, that speaks volumes for your good sense, so there's hope for you yet."

"Alright," she said. "Go on."

But her eyes were still all afire, and Roy couldn't nearly *stand* how the look of those eyes made him feel.

"You're worried about Curly and Joe, and maybe some others, am I right, Miss?"

"Yes," she said, her eyes darting quickly toward Curly, then back to Roy. "Yes, Roy," she added, "that's true. You seem ... different ... trustworthy, I think."

He liked the way she said his name — how it sounded from her soft voice — and it almost conflustered him a minute. *Women and whiskey,* he thought. From her mouth, it was like a caress. *Roy.* He'd never heard it sound quite that way before.

"Trustworthy? Me?" He chuckled a little. "Ain't been accused of that one before."

She giggled. A lovely sound it made too. "Yes, Roy, I think you *are* trustworthy. Despite having more than one surname, and keeping them *all* to yourself, I *do* believe I can trust you." A dark look came over her then. "I need protection, but I ... I'm sorry, Roy, I can't pay you, and I'm not the sort of woman to—"

"It's alright," he said, looking into the fire. "I don't need money, already got some. And if I need more, I'll play poker."

"Poker? You're a *gambler?*"

"Quieter'd be better, Miss. Ain't somethin' to spread all about."

She looked at him then, same way some women look at what horses have done on the street, before stepping around it. "No." It was a harsh sound, that *No.* "I should think you would *not.* I *despise* gambling, Sir. *And* gamblers."

Her look matched the tone of her voice then, and both things surprised Roy a little, but he only smiled.

"Well, Miss," he told her, "it's lucky for you we ain't friends then. Lucky too, that your hatred of my type don't affect my own willingness to help you. I'll watch over you, get you to Deadwood in one piece, with your honor intact. So, how do you plan for this to work?"

She looked only partway convinced, but clearly, she had very few choices — he saw her face change as she realized she'd just have to trust him.

"Well," she began, "they said it's two people to each room." She looked away, not sure how to proceed. "I'm to be married when I get to Deadwood, you see? I was hoping you'd ... well, there aren't any other women, so I thought ... truth is, I'm afraid to take a room alone, even *if* one is available."

"Alright," said Roy. "I'll sleep outside your room, guard the door."

Her next words tumbled on out of her, clearly relieved as she was. "Oh, thank you, Roy."

"Ain't finished," he said. "I'm worried about what your future husband will say when we get to Deadwood. Don't wish to court trouble. Folks'll talk, y'see? It's what folks do mostly, can't help 'emselves."

"I ... hadn't thought about that."

"Depends who you're marrying, I guess. Miss Charlotte, I'll be honest, it don't seem right to me that you're travelin' out there alone. Seems to me, any decent sorta man woulda met you down in Cheyenne, rode along with you on the stagecoach — or had you travel from Sidney at least, that way's safer. Perilous route for a woman, this one, all the things that could happen. As you've already seen, it's a dangerous part of the world."

She was mighty indignant, and yet she stayed patient, let him speak without interruption. Then she clasped her hands together in front of her and said, "Mister Tanner runs a hardware store in Deadwood, in partnership with a friend. He *had* planned to meet me in Cheyenne. But when I arrived, there was a note at my hotel, explaining his friend had taken ill, and he'd had to stay in Deadwood to care for him."

"Alright," said Roy. "Still..."

"He's been nothing but honest, sent me tickets for the train *and* this stagecoach, even before I left Omaha. I ... I had few choices available to me after..." Her voice trailed off, she looked down, wrung her hands together some.

"Well, that's your own business, Miss Charlotte. I feel better hearing he's a hardware man, not a miner or saloon owner or gunfighter. I'll watch over you, Miss, protect your honor. You just make sure your new husband don't misunderstand, if ever it comes to it. Because if I have to, I *will* protect myself from him, you follow?"

"Yes, Roy, I understand. And thank you."

By then, folks had mostly left the dining table and were spreading out through the saloon. There was a Faro game starting up, which most of the men headed for, including Curly and Joe — but not Big-Nose, and them other three wild-boys.

They stayed at the bar, quietly drinking their whiskey and smoking cigars.

Roy was about to suggest he and Charlotte go check out the rooms, when a nice painted lady drifted toward them and said, "I take it you two are together, but perhaps I could fetch you a drink?" Then she fluttered her lashes at Roy and added, "Unless something else takes your fancy."

Roy smiled and said, "No, Ma'am, we ain't together. I'm just travelin' with Miss Charlotte here for her protection."

"Lucky Miss Charlotte," said the scantily dressed woman, her gaze wandering down Roy's body then back to his eyes. "Well, I'm Brandy. Do let me know if you need anything. Anything at all."

Roy couldn't help noticing the look that came across Charlotte's face. Half sulky, half surly, half aloof. Look and a half, that one. She did not say a word, so he filled up the silence. "Would you care for a drink, Miss Charlotte?"

"No. I would *not*. I believe I'll retire."

"You heard the lady," said Roy, smiling warmly at Brandy. "Perhaps some other time."

"I'll look forward to it," said Brandy, drifting off toward Big-Nose and his friends.

Roy and Charlotte got up, went and asked for a room then. Proprietor showed them through himself. Roy rejected the first room they were shown before agreeing to a quieter one.

"Leave the door open," Roy said to the proprietor as he left them. Then Roy went and stood in the doorway.

"You liked her," said Charlotte. "That ... *lady*."

"Why wouldn't I? She was friendly."

"Just your type, I suppose. *Friendly*. I've come all this way, risked everything, just to *avoid* having to be *that* sort of friendly. Are you going to leave me alone now, go spend the night with her?" The words had tumbled out of Charlotte again, but they had a hard edge to them now.

It used to anger Roy when he was younger, that sort of attitude to painted cats. But he understood the world better now. Knew the difference between meanness and ignorance.

Can't blame her for not understanding, she's likely never met one before.

"No, Miss Charlotte," he said. "I'll be sleeping alone, right outside this room. Best thing any man's got to give is his word — I gave you mine, and that's it."

CHAPTER 6
GIVE IT ALL YOU GOT

Roy explained to Charlotte that he too was worried about Curly and Joe — and someone else who was here too. "Could be danger."

Besides the two beds, there was a small table with an oil lamp on it, and she sat on the chair by it now. "One of the passengers? But they all seemed so nice."

"No, Miss. Just a man here who Curly seemed to know, but they didn't speak to each other. That *can* be a bad sign. Keep all this to yourself, of course. I need to go back out there, just settle my doubts I guess. Most likely nothin', but still."

She frowned, then quickly smoothed her brow with her left hand. "You don't want me to come out there with you?"

"Best you don't." He knew she suspected he was going looking for Brandy, but he didn't have time to go through a convoluted *woman discussion.* "Miss Charlotte, I know what you're thinking, and it ain't that."

"No?"

"Miss, how can I put this? By myself, no one much looks at me. I get to see what's goin' on. But you with me? Makes me the most watched man in the room — you're too dang pretty, and that's bad."

"Bad?"

"You know what I mean. I won't be too long, maybe an hour or less. While I'm gone, keep that chair against the door handle. I'll show you how exactly — there's a knack to making it work."

She got to her feet, and he showed her just how to rig the chair, then took it off and watched as she did it herself.

Then he told her the truth of it. "A chair ain't enough to stop a determined man gettin' in. But done this way, it busts it completely to pieces, makes a hell of a noise. Slows the man down as well, gives you time to start screaming. Don't ever be shy to do so — good loud scream can make all the difference. Give it all you got if you need to."

He left then, went back to the front room. Big-Nose was off in a corner playing cards with his friends.

Seemed like they valued their privacy, so Roy stayed away. For now anyway.

He bought a beer then went to the Faro table, where Curly and Joe were. Never much liked Faro. Fool's game. Mostly led to trouble too, on account of the only way to get much advantage was to cheat.

Wherever there was Faro, there was cheating — and sometimes, innocent men got caught in the crossfire.

He went over there anyway, but only bought ten dollars in chips.

"Why, if it ain't the sky-shooter," said Curly, and Joe

laughed it up. "Less skill required here at the table. Make room for the kid, Joe."

Joe moved aside and let Roy in.

"Thanks, Joe," he said. "And you too, Mister Curly. I don't often play cards, but after you saved us today, I'm feelin' lucky. This right?"

He smiled, bet a dollar on the two-card. There weren't many cards left to be drawn, but Roy didn't bother to work out the odds — he wasn't trying to win, he just wanted information.

Dealer drew out a Three of Hearts, took just about everyone's money.

"Better luck next time," said Curly. "I seen you speakin' with that pretty lady, kid. You'd best be careful near that one, she's another man's property. What'd she want with you?"

Curly's breath sure did stink so close up, but Roy managed a smile and said, "Nothin' important." Curly looked hard into Roy's eyes then, but Roy, he just sorta shrank away from him like he was afraid and added, "Where should I bet, Mister Curly?"

"I'm bettin' on seven," Curly said, and he put down a five dollar chip.

Roy put his dollar there too, smiled a nervy, sorta scared one and said, "I ain't chasin' the lady, Mister Curly. In fact, there was a misunderstanding, from something someone else said to her."

Dealer pulled out the Seven of Clubs.

"We won," cried Roy, like as if it was some new experience.

"Stick with me, kid," Curly said, putting all his winnings on the five card this time, so Roy did exactly the same. "Misunderstandin' you say?"

"Yessir," said Roy. "I'm shy around girls, like you noticed, but I ain't no Mary. Well, after me runnin' away from her, and whatever folks said about me — either in the stagecoach or at dinner, I'm not sure which — she seemed to think that I *was* one."

Curly laughed a big hearty one at that, being already half-full of whiskey. "Well, you can't blame her for takin' that impression. You do kinda shoot like one."

"Yessir," Roy said meekly. "Guess I do. I keep meanin' to work on that, bought me a new gun and everything, but I never seem to get around to practicin' none."

Dealer put the Five of Hearts on the table, and most of the gamblers groaned.

"We won *again,* Mister Curly," cried Roy. "Why, you make this game look easy! Maybe you could teach me shooting as well. I'd pay you proper for lessons."

Curly put all his winnings on the two card, so Roy did the same, and looked at the man as admiringly as he could.

"You didn't finish explainin', kid," said Curly. "About you and the lady."

"Oh, that," Roy said, looking downcast as he could manage. Then he hushed his voice some and said, "I'm a bit ashamed is all, Mister Curly. See, she asked me to go along with her, help choose a good room to sleep in. Thought I was doin' great then. Thought my luck was finally runnin'."

"Go on."

"When she asked me to share the room with her, I just about squealed. But after the feller left us alone, she told me just *why* she chose me. Thought I was a damn Mary, like I told you before. Figured she'd be safe with me, on account of she's gonna get married when she gets to Deadwood."

Out came the King of Hearts, and the dealer took all the money, every last chip on the table.

"Dang, our luck all ran out at once," Roy said.

"Don't you dare sleep in that room, kid."

"Whatever you say, Mister Curly. Alright if I sleep outside the door?"

"Alright, kid, just make sure you don't go in there. Feller who owns that ... the feller that owns the hardware store in Deadwood would cut you up into pieces if he found out you did."

"Yessir, Mister Curly. I won't go in that room, no Sir, not even if she begged me to, knowing that. And thanks for the warning. But how's about them shootin' lessons?"

"Reckon you'll get your shootin' lessons tomorrow," Curly said. And when he said it — Roy was watching him closely — ol' Curly just couldn't help himself, he glanced across to the corner where Big-Nose was, for the slightest of moments.

Interesting.

Roy stayed out there just over an hour, stayed with Curly and Joe the whole time. Ol' Curly was so busy *not* lookin' at Big-Nose, he couldn't barely keep his eyes off him sometimes.

And at one point, just to be sure, Roy said, "Hey, them

four bearded fellers in that corner's playing poker I think. How's about we get in on their game?"

"No, kid," Curly said, shooting a quick glance at Big-Nose, then looking away even quicker.

"But I bet you're *real* good at poker, Mister Curly. And I won a whole heap playing poker two weeks back — though I stayed at the table too long, and lost more than I'd won by the end."

But Curly flat out told him, "No, kid, you listen to me. Keep away from them boys and go get some sleep. Big day ahead, and if you want shootin' lessons, you best go get yerself rested. I'm doin' the same."

He did too — both Curly and Joe went along to their rooms, and never went back past Roy in the hallway that whole night long. None of Big-Nose's boys passed by Roy down that hallway neither.

So that was just how things went — that big-nosed feller and Curly, they *didn't* go near each other, *didn't* speak to each other, *didn't* even gamble at the same table any time the whole night.

Roy knew what that meant alright.

Those wasn't *Howdy* sorta nods between the two earlier. Big-Nose's nod was a question: *All Set?*

And Curly's nod back was an answer: *Yes!*

Roy knew now for certain — the hairs dancing on back of his neck had at least five good reasons to do so.

Tomorrow there would be danger, or his name wasn't Roy Stone. And Roy Price, and Roy Pace. And lately, mostly, Roy Peabody.

CHAPTER 7
THEIR DELICATE TIMETABLES

Roy never slept well at all — dreamed he was hid in a closet, watching Curly and Big-Nose doing some sorta business together.

Damn dream woke him up every time those two dreamlike figures turned round, no warning at all, and pointed six-shooters right at him.

Woke up every time someone came past him as well. That painted cat, Brandy, went past a few times, but given the nature of her work, that wasn't hardly surprising.

What *was* surprising happened roundabout an hour before daylight. Brandy looked right into his eyes, spoke to him very quietly as she went by, but she never even slowed.

"Don't get on that stage," she whispered. "First shot's at the man on the box seat, he knows you got money."

Roy added up two and two, got himself at least four. Clear enough, Curly had used Brandy to get a message to Big-Nose during the night.

Should have thought about that.

Her own life woulda been in peril if she hadn't relayed the message. Roy sure was grateful she'd taken the risk of telling him how she had. And there was no way he'd betray her confidence.

He stayed right where he was, even pretended to stay asleep until Curly kicked him "awake" a half hour later.

"Shootin' lessons today, kid," Curly told him. *Eyes cold, but pleasure in his voice.* "Don't wanna miss out, we're leavin' in thirty minutes."

After what Brandy told him, no way Roy was getting on that stagecoach. Wouldn't be hard, he'd feign illness, and have Miss Charlotte do the same.

He knocked the special knock on the door that he'd taught her the previous night — two then four then one — and she called out, "Just a minute."

Then she came to the door, opened it a crack and looked out.

Roy looked both ways, made sure no one was near enough to hear him. "Miss Charlotte, I'm certain there's to be trouble. We need to pretend to be sick and stay here. We'll get on the next coach with available seats."

She blinked some and looked up at him, her eyes still soft and sleepy. "But I can't do that, Roy. Mister Tanner expects me. What will he think I've been up to, if he learns I stayed here with you?"

Roy knew straight off she was right. But still, he knew it was too dangerous to get on that stage. "Miss Charlotte, there's to be another robbery. Staying alive's more important than making good time — and if Mister Tanner don't like you being saved from it, he ain't no sorta—"

"But surely you're guessing, Roy!" She looked much more awake now, alert. Her voice became urgent. "Truly, how can you *know?*"

Now, Roy didn't know *why* Brandy had told him what she did — but she had put her own life in danger by doing so. He could not tell Miss Charlotte, or anyone else, of the warning.

"I guess I just know things," he said. "Dream things sometimes. Premonitions. We can't get on that stage, Miss Charlotte."

"Nonsense," she said. "I must dress now, I'll be out in a moment."

He went to cuss, stopped himself just in time.

Women, he thought, as she closed the door.

Ain't meant to cuss, on account o' their delicate ears.

Ain't meant to save 'em, on account o' their delicate timetables.

Ain't meant even to save your own self, on account o' having given your word to protect 'em.

Women!

He cussed a good one then — quiet, so her *delicate ears* wouldn't hear — but it didn't make him feel no better.

"I heard that," she called out.

"Good," he said. "You was meant to."

Feels some better, knowing she heard me. Must remember to do it again, when I'm shot up and dying from tryin' to protect her.

CHAPTER 8
DAMN DOUBLE CROSSER

R oy got up from the breakfast table before anyone
finished eating. Wrapped his flapjacks in a piece
of cloth, put it in his coat pocket, walked on out
to the stagecoach.

Joe was up on top of the coach, helping Curly
rearrange the boxes, so Curly could sit in the middle of all
the cargo.

Roy worked it out quick. *Wants the boxes round the
edges for cover, in case of stray bullets*

"I was too high up yesterday," was how Curly
explained it. "Copped a damn branch in the chops, but
this'll be better. Things I do for a hundred measly dollars."

"It's alright, Mister Curly," Roy told him, "I'll sit inside
awhile I reckon. You take my seat, welcome to it."

Curly stopped what he was doing, stood upright. Then
he spat a dark stream of tobacco juice onto the ground, right
by Roy's left foot.

"What the hell do you mean, you don't want the box

seat? Weren't no changin' yer mind yesterday." Then he altered his voice to a childish one, clearly intended to mock. "'*All the way to Deadwood,*' you said. '*Paid fair and square, gonna use it,*' you said. Well?"

"Didn't sleep so well in that hallway, Mister Curly," Roy told him, rubbing at his eyes. "Downright bad idea, that was. Might take the box seat again after lunch, but right now I need me some sleep, so I'll travel inside."

He didn't wait for Curly's reply. Climbed right on in, he did. First in, just how he liked it. Right hand seat, facing forward, next to the door.

No getting stuck in the middle — no facing back where he'd come from.

What's up ahead is what matters. Especially when you know it's likely to be at least four men with guns.

He placed his luggage between his feet, his cushion under his rump. Had his apples, his canteen of water, his jerky. Winchester between his knees, Sharps derringer in his inner coat pocket — both weapons clean and well oiled and loaded up full. Business as usual, travel wise.

Only difference, this time he *knew* there'd be trouble. Strangely, he felt reassured by the certainty of it. His neck did not even tingle.

This time, when the pretty woman climbed up inside the coach, smiled and sat down beside him, Roy did *not* run away.

He smiled at Miss Charlotte, and she smiled right back. The other passengers climbed in over the next couple of minutes, then Joe the driver called out, "Ready, Curly?"

And when Curly answered, the sound didn't come

from the box seat, but from up on top. "Loaded and ready, let's go." Right cranky he sounded as well.

"Here we go," Joe called out, "and good luck to us all."

There wasn't no trouble to begin with. It was a steep climb to Running Water Station, but only ten miles. Most action Roy noticed was *inside* the coach — that being, the other passengers still doing their best to impress the lady.

He stretched his legs there while they changed horses. Needed to make certain Big-Nose or his men weren't about to be informed of any change in plans. Roy pretended to still be half asleep, and barely answered when Curly asked him again if he wanted the box seat.

"You sure you don't want the seat, kid?" Curly asked. "No one in it now anyway. I'm learnin' to enjoy it up top, might ride there all the time from now on."

But Roy made a great show of yawning, then shrugged his shoulders and climbed back inside.

They were three-parts of the way to Hat Creek Station when the trouble began.

Began with a shot, just like last time — but unlike last time, Joe couldn't set the horses to galloping, for they were just about to enter a muddy creek, and it was all he could do to keep the frightened animals from bolting.

Charlotte threw herself down on the floor, just as Roy had told her to do at the first sign of trouble.

Roy looked out the right-side window, saw a man eighty yards off, firing a rifle. Seemed like he was firing too high, aiming up there on purpose. Shots were coming from ahead, shots from the other side too, and there was a whole lotta yelling from every direction.

For a moment, Roy considered not firing. If these men weren't shooting to kill, perhaps it would be wrong to kill *them*. Then Brandy's warning came into his mind once again, and he knew he was fighting for his own life, if no one else's.

As for Curly, he was already firing — it was his job after all, and he had to be *seen* to be doing it, even if he wasn't. Roy got that short Winchester of his out the window, aimed it and slow-squeezed the trigger, way Grampa had taught him.

No bucking and swaying of the coach to trouble him this time — that forty-four slug flew the fifty yards from the Winchester, went right through that bearded feller's chest and he fell to the ground by his tree. Dead before he hit the dirt.

"There's too many of 'em," cried Curly as the horses scrambled up the far bank, and Joe urged them on. "We gotta give up, let 'em take what they want!" But still, he continued to fire, and so did the outlaws.

On the hill up ahead then, Roy saw another feller, out in the open, firing and yelling fit to bust.

Curly fired again — and no doubt, he missed on purpose. That feller wasn't even behind cover.

Roy took aim again, waited as the stage rode itself out of a few bumps, then squeezed the trigger once he had a bead. That slug would have gone right through the man's chest like the first one — only the stage pitched again, and it upset Roy's shot a picayune. Not enough for that feller though. The bullet went into him through his left eye, went out through the back of his skull, ended up in a tree back behind him.

"Stop shootin', kid," Curly cried. "There's too damn many of 'em."

But Roy knew more than Curly had guessed, and there weren't no way he was stopping while any of them still lived.

Roy pushed past the other passengers, looked out the left window, saw another masked feller in the open, up on a rock, a six-gun in each of his hands.

That feller could almost have jumped on the top of the coach from that rock, but he clearly intended to let those two guns do the work.

Before Roy could get his Winchester aimed, that masked outlaw yelled, "You damn double-crosser, Cur—"

That was all he ever got out.

Seemed almost like Curly didn't want to hear what the outlaw intended to say — did what he was paid to instead. Curly's bullet hit that feller in the left hip, and he screamed as he spun and commenced to fall off of that rock. Sailed twelve feet to the ground, a flailing mess of legs and arms and revolvers — a free-falling wail of pain with a thud at its end.

CHAPTER 9
STUCK IN THE MUD

R oy heard the sound of a horse back behind them,
galloping away hell for leather.

"Pull 'em up, Joe," cried Curly. Then before
the stage even stopped, he half-climbed, half-jumped to the
ground, and went running back toward the base of that
rock.

Roy climbed out quick, but not quick enough.

As he stepped to the ground, he saw the bearded road
agent push himself up to sitting, push his back against the
rock he'd fallen from. Then Roy heard the man plead for
his life.

He didn't plead long — Curly had took along his
scattergun, and soon as that feller spoke, he gave him both
barrels. Blew a big damn hole through his chest and most of
his neck, and blew both of his hands all to pieces. Not
much left at all of his hands.

Didn't make Joe none too happy. "Now what'd yer go'n
do that for?" he cried as he tied his lead horses to a nearby

ponderosa pine. "We shoulda took that feller in for a good old-fashioned necktie party, as a warnin' to others of his ilk." Proper annoyed about it, he was.

Roy looked at Joe, then back at Curly, who was quickly going through the dead man's pockets.

One mystery answered, Roy thought. *Joe wasn't in on it with Curly, he's only doing his job.*

Roy half-turned toward the coach. Kept his Winchester at the ready though, and his eyes on what Curly was doing. Said, "Stay inside for now, Miss Charlotte. Danger's gone though I reckon, the one left alive won't be back. You two men who helped last time, you're needed again now."

"You should not have finished him off," Joe called out to Curly as he came past Roy.

"He went for his gun," Curly growled.

It was a baldfaced lie. Man's hands had been up in front of him, like they could protect him somehow. He had dropped both guns when he toppled off the rock. Nearest gun was four feet away, barrel stuck in the mud where it fell.

Roy headed directly up the hill to their right, to the body of the second feller he'd shot. Only one man had left the safety of the coach — Everett Ferguson was his name — and he tagged along up the hill with Roy.

"Wait 'til I'm there before you go near him," Curly called out. "Sometimes they play possum, kid."

"He's some sorta possum if he gets up and shoots us," said Everett, then he whistled through his teeth. "Been shot straight through the eye. You make that shot?"

Roy shrugged his shoulders, then commenced to go

through the dead man's pockets. There was nothing to identify him. About six dollars in small change was all. He slipped it to Everett, said, "Somethin' for your trouble. You might as well keep his rifle as well, if you want it. Might yet come in handy, this trip."

Everett eyed the outlaw's Henry but didn't touch it. He nodded his thanks, put the coins in his pocket, then kneeled beside the body, which was lying face up. The face was not only bearded, but was covered by a faded yellow bandana.

Everett looked up at Roy, raised his eyebrows and tilted his head.

His unspoken question was clear.

"Sure, let's take a look," said Roy.

Everett pulled down the bandana, and the both of them studied the face. With the exception of the neatly missing eye, it was the face of an ordinary Western white man. Mostly beard, dark brown hair, and what skin there was on display had been burned to a darkish brown from long exposure to the harsh Western sun.

"Seen him before, Everett?"

"Not that I know of. You?"

"Could be one of the men who was drinking at Rawhide Buttes last night," Roy said. "Can't be sure though."

But he *was* sure.

"Hard to tell with that beard. Maybe when we see the others."

"That last feller Curly shot," Roy said, standing up and looking down the hill. "You hear what he said? My own ears was ringin' from firin' this overloud carbine."

Roy saw then that Curly was treading lively, back toward the first feller shot. Any chance of identifying them was probably gone now — unless that one had a swacking great nose.

"No," Everett answered, "never heard no actual words. Just a whole lotta yelling noise and gunfire. Kept my head down, I'm ashamed to admit."

"Don't be ashamed of your smarts, my friend," said Roy. "You done the right thing for certain, some things ain't worth dyin' for. Let's see if we can't find their horses."

No surprise, it was Curly who got to the horses first.

By the time Roy and Everett arrived, Curly was finishing up going through all the saddlebags.

"You sure found the horses quick, Mister Curly," said Roy. "Almost like you knew just where they'd be."

Curly's eyes flared with sulfurous anger — perhaps realizing he'd been caught out. He fixed his terrible gaze on Roy and growled "What's that supposed to mean?"

Everett stood quiet as he could, like a man who wished the ground would swallow him up.

But Roy knew not to push things too far, and just how to turn it around. He looked at Curly in a most admiring fashion and said, "Just wish I knew half so much about the West as you do, Mister Curly. You *sure* shot them fellers to pieces."

Curly looked at Roy's Winchester then and said, "You did alright yourself this time, kid. Better'n I expected."

"Aw, thanks, Mister Curly," Roy said with an eager smile, and he sent his voice up a whole octave so he sounded excited. "The feller I shot, it went right through his eye, can you believe it? Straight through, clean as a whistle."

"No kidding?"

"I wouldn't kid *you,* Mister Curly, no sir. To be fair, I was aimed at his chest, but the stage hit a bump, and the gun bounced every which way, and then it sorta went off when I wasn't quite aimed right. Them bumps made me fire a few wrong'uns before that as well, and..." — Roy looked around then, as if checking no one else was listening, then went on more quietly than before. "Well, truth was, I was mighty afraid, and *did* have my eyes shut roundabout half the time. But I reckon I done pretty good, hittin' one like I did."

Now, Curly well knew it was Roy who'd killed the first *and* second of the road agents. And he almost — almost — said so.

He raised a finger as if to point it out, but saved himself from it just in time. The expression in his eyes sorta changed too. Went from lookin' at Roy some suspicious, to lookin' at him same way he had been before.

Most likely, he figured Roy just got lucky, and shot that first feller with his eyes shut — whatever he thought, his greed surely got the better of him.

"You done good, kid," he said. "If you're lucky, the one you killed'll have a bounty on him. Maybe my two as well."

Roy made his speech go faster and faster after that, and the tone of it kept going up higher and higher. "A *bounty* you say, Mister Curly? I sure could do with the money. Don't mind admitting though, I was shakin' so bad I could barely pull the trigger. But you done killed *another* two men, however do you do it so easy? I sure wish you'd give me some lessons. If I could shoot the way you do, that other one would never'a got away. Hope he don't come back, he'll be angry as bees gets at bears, us killin' all his friends. Why, I don't know *what* we'll do if—"

"Don't worry, kid, just calm down, you're makin' my head hurt. He won't come back. If he does though, I'm askin' for a pay rise."

CHAPTER 10
A GOOD CUSS

Once the bodies were loaded and the dead men's horses tied behind the stage, they got moving again. Big-Nose was the one who'd escaped, it turned out, and Roy held out no hope the three road agents would be identified.

Everett had told the others in the coach that Roy had shot one of the outlaws — "Right through the eye, shoulda seen it."

But when Roy climbed in and took his seat, and one of the men congratulated him on "such fine shooting," Roy only put a finger to his lips, shook his head, and half-pointed that finger at Miss Charlotte.

At least a woman's delicate nature is helpful in some way.

Last thing Roy wanted to do was talk about killing. Taking a life might come easy to some, but Roy was not that sort of man.

Getting through the Hat Creek Breaks was slow

going. Roy closed his eyes, concentrated on listening for anything out of the ordinary. It took a long slow half-hour to get through the rest of the breaks. Seemed like more creeks than trail for awhile there — and Roy sure appreciated the fine job the horses were doing, and the driver as well.

No one inside spoke much, their second close call perhaps having sunk in now, and scaring them more than the first. Seemed like an age before they made it to Hat Creek Station. It was almost a relief to unload the bodies — the thought of them lying there dead, right above their heads, was a gruesome one at best.

The feller who ran the swing station lived alone, and he sure did grumble about having to take care of the bodies until they could be taken back for identification.

"I'm here to look after horses," he whined. "I just ain't equipped for dead men."

Then Curly growled, "You *equipped* to become one?"

That was the end of that feller's reluctance, he got real helpful thereafter.

"Just gotta know how to communicate so as folks understand," Curly said to Joe then. Ol' Joe nodded back at him, wide-eyed and plenty helpful himself, as he helped to carry the bodies to the creek, where they would hopefully keep fresh while waiting for transport.

A few minutes later, they were back on the trail, hoping to make up time on the downhill run to Old Woman Station and May's Ranch Station, where they would stop for a quick meal.

It had suited Roy fine, everyone staying quiet. He had

killed men before today — these two took his tally to four —
but it proper sickened him to do so.

A man's life is a precious thing, not to be taken lightly.
There was only one man Roy knew for certain he would
kill without hesitation. Outside of that, he would kill a man
only to save himself — or save some innocent person who
needed protecting.

And even though it'd been him or them, he felt terrible
about killing those two men today.

Still, he understood that more killing may yet be
necessary — Roy knew without doubt that Curly had
planned for Big-Nose and the others to kill him. And while
it seemed unlikely Curly or Big-Nose would try again, Roy
knew he'd be a fool to let his guard down.

They rode mostly in silence to Old Woman Station,
where everyone but Miss Charlotte got out and stretched
their legs while the horses were changed.

Miss Charlotte hadn't looked at Roy but once since
he'd killed those two men — and he was glad of that, more
or less.

Most men got drunk after a killing — but for Roy, what
he needed was quiet time. Needed to let it sink in, the
enormity of what he'd done — and to work it this way and
that through his thoughts. He needed to be sure he'd done
the right thing. Certain he'd had no other choice.

But a mile after they got going, seemed that Roy's quiet
time was over.

"You *killed* one of those men." Her tone was sorely
accusing.

The other passengers' heads all turned away from

them. You'd have just about swore there was something of great interest outside that left window, and every one of them fellers had noticed at once.

Roy took a deep breath. Wouldn't be no gettin' out of it — women just had to talk, he'd sure learned that through the years, again and again. "Yes, Miss Charlotte, I did."

"But surely you didn't have to *kill* him ... I mean, you seemed like such a ... you seemed gentle, and decent, and—"

"You'd prefer they killed us instead, Miss? Because they probably would have. And done goodness knows what to *you* first. But if you'd have preferred that, you just let me know, and I'll leave you to travel without me."

The silence that followed was a long one — and though none of the men turned around, the air almost crackled and popped, alive as it was with their listening.

Finally she spoke — and for such quiet words, they sure had some bite. "I'm just surprised is all. I didn't think you were the type to *enjoy* killing others."

Remember, she doesn't belong here. She doesn't understand, and she's had a bad shock.

He took a deep breath before speaking.

"I did not enjoy it, Miss," he finally said. Wasn't easy to make his voice calm. "If you'll remember, I asked you not to get on this coach, so as we could avoid the suspected forthcoming violence."

"Oh, so now it's *my* fault," she cried. "You killed without hesitation. The guard called on you to stop, but no, you went right ahead and—"

"Miss Charlotte, you *will* shut your trap now and

listen," he growled at her then. He kept his voice quiet, but the menace in his own tone surprised him — he saw a resultant fear in her eyes, but he would *not* be blamed any longer. "Miss, I *told* you this would probably happen. *Told* you to wait for the next stagecoach. Even offered to pay for your fare. But as *your* timetable was more important, here we are, and those men are now dead, and that's a fact we can't change. Those men made their own choices, and that's all there—"

"I—"

"No! You *listen* now. Miss, those men are dead because we didn't wait where we were — then again, our fellow passengers *might* just be happy we *did* come. Did you even once think of *that?* Well? Dang women. Shouldn't be allowed on stagecoaches. Dang fool women, think they know everything. Dang uppity know-it-all *women!"*

"Cussing now are we? Again!"

"Yes, I *damn* well am cussing. And lucky to be alive to do so! *Damn lucky!* So I will *enjoy* a good cuss, if *you* don't mind, *Miss Fancy Eastern Lady!* Because *cussing* helps me to concentrate — and unlike you, I gotta keep my wits on things *other* than WOMEN'S ... MORAL ... CONUNDRUMS!"

No one spoke again 'til they got out at May's Ranch Station.

CHAPTER 11
BEGRIMED

Roy stepped out as soon as the horses stopped, didn't look back at Miss Charlotte. The driver and guard hadn't stepped down yet. Roy's eyes narrowed as he looked at them, and his fingers gripped his Winchester tightly.

Curly had taken to riding the box seat again, once his friends had been killed.

Roy felt wild, almost said something truthful to Curly — stopped himself just in time. What he *wanted* was to put a damn bullet through Curly's ugly face. He took a deep breath instead, but stayed alert. *His time will come.*

Joe announced it as a twenty minute eating stop, Curly went off to the outhouse without turning to look at Roy.

Roy walked a short way along the trail, stretched and squatted a few times. Waited for the others to go inside. No one spoke to him. Once he was sure they'd gone in, he turned around and came back. A man has to eat — a woman getting under his skin does not change that fact.

Best Grub Between Cheyenne And Deadwood, announced the red lettering on a white painted sign beside the door.

It better be.

Roy went in and sat down. There were strangers here — but no one of interest. Of the ten seats at the eating table, only one was vacant when he arrived — directly across from Miss Charlotte.

He sat. Didn't look at her.

There was a general hum of talk — usual in such places — but no one spoke directly to Roy, so he didn't speak either.

Neither did Miss Charlotte Hawke.

Bowls, knives and forks were already on the table, but no trace of food to be seen yet.

Bowls were blue enamelware, and as greasy as Roy had ever seen.

The cutlery was worse.

Must not know how to boil water.

An unfortunate looking man, cadaverously thin and well over six feet in height, picked up one of two large cast iron pots from the stove in the corner. He carried it over, held high up under his buzzard-like nose, his limpid gray eyes peering over the pot at his guests. When he set it down on the table, Roy saw how filthy the hideous man's bony hands were.

Two of the strangers reached for the ladle right away, but the grotesque beanstalk of a man slapped their hands away. "Wait up," he said, and his voice sounded thick with his phlegm. "There's a lady present, damn ya. Serve yerself first, pretty Miss, while I git the other pot fer the rest'a these filthy heathens."

The men grumbled, but did as they were told.

"Allow me, Miss," said one of the other men, perhaps not so much of a heathen as his friends. He picked up the ladle, dipped it into the horrible mess — it was purported to be *"BEEF N BEENZ"* — but the smell that arose when that feller disturbed it made him turn his face away in disgust. Then with a great concentration of effort, he ladled it into her bowl.

No way that's beef and beans, Roy decided. *Might best change his sign so it reads "MALODOROUS MUCK."*

Beans, perhaps possibly maybe. But beef? I shouldn't reckon so. Smells like a dying man's socks just before they rot off him.

Roy pushed back his chair, stood up, looked across at Miss Charlotte. She was leaning back some, trying not to be sick by the look of her. She looked up at Roy, then back at the "food," then at Roy again.

Roy raised his eyebrows and nodded his head, like he was suggesting she eat it. He tried to keep a straight face and failed. Then he started to laugh, and so did Miss Charlotte as well.

"This muck ain't fit for no living breathing critters I ever heard of," Roy announced then, "and anyone fool enough to eat it deserves what they get."

"How dare you, Mister," said the squalid, verminous man. "I serve the best grub between—"

"Best grub it may be," said Roy. "I just wonder where you got the grubs, and what sort they are. Maggots mostly,

I'd reckon. Let's go, Miss Charlotte, I got apples and jerky. Ain't much, but it's better'n dying. You too, Everett." Then he looked around the table and said, "You others can all take your chances, just don't die near me."

The three got up from the table and went out to the coach.

"The look on that feller's face," Everett laughed as they stepped outside. Then he slapped his thigh and cried, "Maggots!"

"I had no idea *what* to do," said Miss Charlotte. "Oh, the *smell* when the ladle disturbed it."

"I never seen hands so begrimed," said Everett. "Wonder what was *really* in that pot."

The three of them had a good chuckle, making up worse and worse suggestions regarding the possible contents of the cooking pot.

"Lizard's gizzards," Miss Charlotte said first.

"Bull's b..." Everett stopped right there and blushed a bright red, looking everywhere *but* at the one woman present.

Then, bright as ever you like, Miss Charlotte said, "Bull's *bits,* I assume you were saying." Then, after coloring a little herself, she added, "Whatever *that* means."

Roy was surprised, the way she'd gone along with Everett's somewhat risqué jest. *Maybe not quite so sheltered a life as I thought.*

"Snake's eyes, I reckon for sure," Roy suggested.

Miss Charlotte laughed and said, "Swamp slime?"

"It surely was the right color," Roy said.

Everett held up one finger and cried, "Skunk snot."

Then all three screwed up their faces, and Miss Charlotte said, "I do believe that's the winner. In fact, I think perhaps *all* of those things were inside that horrible pot. Now where are those lovely apples you promised us? My appetite's suddenly returned."

"Musta been the mention of skunk snot," said Everett, and the three of them laughed fit to bust.

Then the three new friends smiled happily, munched away on their apples, and before long, it was time to get going again.

The other passengers came out and they all climbed back in the coach. Turned out that they'd all refused to eat the swill in the pot, and partaken of cold beans instead.

"Tasteless," one man said, "but at least we'll survive it."

A mile or two down the road, and most of the passengers dropped off to sleep, the way stagecoach passengers tend to, right after lunch. Even Everett *seemed* to be sleeping — although Roy suspected he was faking, so as Roy and Miss Charlotte could talk.

He's a clever feller, that Everett, thought Roy. Most men would not have picked it up, the thing that hung in the air there between them — but to an astute sort of man, it was a clear enough thing. Roy and Miss Charlotte had something they had to discuss.

CHAPTER 12
"IF YOU WERE MY…"

"Roy," Charlotte said very quietly, once it seemed like the others were sleeping. They were sat close together, and her mouth was quite near to his ear. And when she said his name *that* soft, it was somehow even better — *which is worse* — than it had been before.

"Yes, Miss?" He almost whispered, but kept looking straight ahead, not at her.

"I'm sorry for what I said. I know you tried to avoid the violence. I should have listened to you. Thank you, is what I'm trying to say."

He turned his face toward hers. She was mighty close. Closer than he'd ever been to a woman, except for ... well, they were too close. The lashes of her eyes, and her breath, and her lips, all too close.

He blinked hard, mumbled something like, "Mm-hmm," and looked away quick.

She's to be married, you damn fool.

There was thoughts, and there was wants, and there was feelings, and none of that mattered at all. Not really. Not even if she felt it too.

And as much as the wild part of Roy tried to tell him she *did* maybe feel it too — and that he could still maybe do something about it — his practical side drowned it out, and he turned his face away, closed his eyes like he wanted to sleep.

But she didn't shut up.

Thing about Charlotte, she *was* feeling something for Roy. And while she *had* sent a letter agreeing to marry Mister Tanner, she knew that if Roy would ask her, she'd marry him instead.

They could get out of this coach at the very next station, go back where they came from, go somewhere else, make a life. It was a wild thought, she knew — but somehow it *felt* right.

"Roy," she whispered, so close to his ear it felt somehow deliciously wicked, but she wasn't ashamed. "Why aren't you married yet?"

He turned away from her, looked out the window, as if he'd seen something important. Then he turned back toward her and said, "I ain't fool enough for that, Miss. Me and women ain't suited, is all."

"Ha," she said — not a whisper, but a sharp little sound that stabbed at the air. "I saw how you looked at ... *Branndeeee.*" Way she said Brandy was cruel, disrespectful — and *jealous.* "Clearly, Roy *Whatever-Your-Name-Is* ... you and *some* women are *perfectly* suited."

"Now, Miss Charlotte, that's hardly fair—"

"Hardly *fair* is it? Yes, I see what you mean. Women are only of use for one thing! And if some of us don't wish to give you that thing, why, we're of no use at all!"

"Miss, please, that ain't it at all."

"Isn't it? You've no wish to marry, but you'd not hesitate to spend the night with the likes of … *her!*"

Roy shrugged his shoulders. "Miss Charlotte, I don't know how you've lived, and ain't judging you. But if you're to get by in Deadwood, you may need to relax your attitudes some. You've obviously got some problem with whores—"

"*Whores?* I never called anyone … I mean, I certainly wasn't judging—"

"'Course you were. Folks generally look down on people they don't understand. Miss Charlotte, painted doves are just people like anyone else — some are bad, some are good. Most are just trying to survive. You think any one of 'em ever sat down as a child and thought, *Reckon I'd like to become a whore when I'm all growed up, that ought be real fun.*"

She wrung her two hands together some, smoothed down her skirts, looked straight ahead. "Well, no, when you put it like that — I mean, I never really thought about it."

"Well, ain't my job to educate you, only protect you. But I'll tell you this, free. Won't be many women in Deadwood, and most of what's there'll be painted. Not sayin' to trust every one of 'em, that'd be downright foolish. But *some … some …* are the very best people you ever could meet — and you never know when you might need an ally, in such a place."

There was no sound he could hear then but the trundling of wheels. For a minute he thought she wouldn't answer.

Then soft and small came her whisper — again, precious close to his ear.

"Are *you* my ally, Roy?"

She was impossibly beautiful in the soft light inside the coach, a strange mix of strength and vulnerability, and Roy wished ... well, he just wished. More wishing he done, more hollowed out he became.

Wishing ain't no use to anyone.

"I'm your ally for now, Miss," he said, all matter-of-fact. "But once we're in Deadwood, it's best you don't speak to me again. Husbands being how they are, is my point. I mean, if you were *my* ... well, you know."

Didn't matter how much he wished it — she was to be married, and besides, he had a man to kill.

"Best we don't know each other no more, Miss, once we get to Deadwood."

CHAPTER 13
ROBBER'S ROOST

A t Robbers Roost Station, they were warned that road agents *and* Injuns had been active on the trail up ahead.

Even Curly looked rattled, but he only growled something about "doing the job," before casting a glance at Roy.

"You'll protect us, Mister Curly," said Roy. "And I'll help if I can." It wasn't easy to act eager and friendly toward the man, but Roy wished to make certain he didn't get himself noticed any more than he already had. It would be easier in Deadwood, the less people knew of him.

Turned out they had company along the next stretch, up through the mountains to Custer City. The previous day's stage had been robbed a couple of miles down the road, and had broke an axle trying to outrun the road agents. No one got shot, but one of the road agents had held a gun to the head of a ten-year-old girl, pulled back the hammer and laughed at her terrified parents.

"Weren't goin'a travel alone after that," said the likable old driver. "Not when I knowed Joe was comin' along the next day. Seffty in numbers orright. Some a'these new road agents jess don't cotton the basic rules a'the game. Dang mod'n world, ain't hardly no right-behavin' folk in it."

Roy noticed that Curly didn't much like the man guarding the other stage, and the feeling was returned about double — somehow that made Roy happy, and helped him relax.

They wasted no time at Robbers Roost. To make it to Custer City by dark, they could not afford to delay.

To begin with, Roy could see why road agents and Indians mostly chose this area for holdups. The deep heavy mud and wide creeks allowed little chance for a stagecoach to escape — and there was no shortage of huge rocks to hide behind for cover.

And yet, today they went unmolested. Got all the way to the S & G Ranch without seeing another human being, let alone a hostile one.

Had to average out sooner or later, Roy decided.

Once they started to climb, he watched the scenery go by outside of his window. Seeing the world — *really* seeing it — was one reason Roy loved to travel, and what he saw here was, to his eye and mind, a place so crushingly beautiful he felt he must surely be dreaming. The rolling hills and the forests, the rugged cliffs and buttes, the winding streams that snaked through it all, glistening purple and lovely — and it seemed a great pity to Roy then, that so many men were coming this way, only to dig it all up.

Gold and silver had just never seemed that useful to Roy. Seemed to him that *growing things* was a proper use of the land, and somehow in harmony with how most of the world really worked. Tearing the land all to pieces, and destroying the water supply — way it seemed always to end up from mining — surely could not be allowed to go on much longer.

Seemed like that was just common sense.

The day rolled on by, the horses and drivers doing their work, and not much conversation took place inside of that coach. Second long day of such a trip, folks are always worn down and tired.

But it wasn't only that — there seemed a sort of a distance now between Roy and Charlotte. But that was the right thing, he knew, so he made no effort to fix it.

Best thing any man's got to give is his word — and another man gave her HIS word, promised her he would marry her. And she gave her word back to him.

Roy was *not* the sort of man to mess with all that, no matter what fool feelings he'd started having.

I'll forget all about her in a week anyway, he told himself. Though he wasn't sure he believed it.

Before they knew it, it was late afternoon, and the drivers both blew on their bugles — the other driver actually blew a tune of sorts — to warn those at Twelve Mile Ranch to have their horses ready.

Weren't no delay neither — both teams of horses were ready and waiting, and Roy and Charlotte barely had time to stretch their legs before they were back in the coach for the final twelve miles of the day.

As they got going, Roy looked at Everett, who was sitting across from him now. "Looking forward to a good sleep in Custer. Ever been there?"

"Been there?" Everett answered. "I live there. Me and my brother got a pig farm out on the edge of town. Doesn't earn a man much respect, raising pigs — but we failed miserable searchin' for gold, and pigs pays a real good livin' up here. Folks got to eat, no matter what."

"Good for you," said Roy. "Farming anything's downright useful. One day, maybe I'll do some sorta farming. You or your brother married, Everett?"

"Reckon I'm not no more, and he never was. I just dropped Kate off in Cheyenne. Likes the big city she does, and she's got sisters there. Can't blame her for leavin' I guess, it's hard for a woman up here."

Roy glanced at Charlotte, saw she was listening, then he said, "Surely you coulda let her travel to Cheyenne herself? Especially as she was leaving you anyway."

"No, sir," said Everett abruptly. "Wouldn't let a woman travel alone on the stage, not even if I disliked her. Wouldn't be right."

"What if you'd been ill?" said Charlotte then. "Or had other things of importance to attend to?"

"Miss Charlotte," said Everett, "I won't say nothin' general about it, on account of your own situation. I only say what's right for me. And no one ever can say I spoke a word about you, or whoever sent for you, and that's all I'll say on the matter."

"Alright," she said. "But if you were as busy as Mister—"

"Miss, me'n my brother's been busier'n a one-armed Indian in a arrow-shootin' contest. But some things, a man makes the time for. When I told him I was going, Hank never even questioned it, though it doubled his workload, and he'll be in a right sorry state by now to be sure — but it had to be done, and we'll just catch up on things once I'm back, you see?"

Truth was, Charlotte was already tired of making excuses for Mister Tanner. He should *not* have left her to travel alone, not on such a dangerous route. And *why* had he not had her travel from Sidney, it being supposedly safer? It was raising doubts in her mind alright. But what else could she do other than keep going, already being halfway there, with nothing to go back to?

"I hope the beds are comfortable where we're staying in Custer," she said, by way of changing the subject.

"Good luck with that," said Everett. "Haven't yet heard one good word about the hotel."

Roy didn't like the sound of that at all. "Perhaps we could stay somewhere else? I got money enough for two rooms, and after last night, I'll be needing a proper night's sleep."

"There's only the one hotel with rentable rooms now, Roy. They tore the other one down and moved it to Deadwood. There's two big saloons with lots of rooms as well — but no one there does much sleeping, if you get what I mean."

"Bordellos," said Charlotte.

"Yes, Miss, though they ain't hardly fancy enough to deserve such a high-falutin' word. Well, one is sorta fancy, to make up for the poorness of the other. But I'm sure you wouldn't like to stay in either of 'em, Miss Charlotte. Although I reckon Roy here..." His voice trailed off, he glanced quickly at Roy, then turned back toward Charlotte and said, "No. Neither of you would like either place. Hotel'd be best for you both, I'd reckon. It's only one night after all, then you'll be in Deadwood with Mister ... what was the name again, Miss?"

"Tanner. He's a partner in a hardware store there."

"Hmmm, Tanner," said Everett. "Must be new. Only Tanner I know of up there's a hostler. Still, it's a fast-growin' place, Deadwood is, and I can't barely keep track of myself, let alone the folks there. Well, I wish you good luck, Miss Charlotte. I hope you'll be happier than my own wife was. Hope she'll be happy now too, in a place where she's suited. How about you, Roy? Plan to do some mining in Deadwood?"

Roy had been looking out the window again, admiring the wild country they were trundling through. "No, just searching for a ... just looking around is all."

"Well," said Everett, "if you don't much enjoy Deadwood — and a lot of folks don't — you're welcome to come stay with me and Hank awhile. Maybe help us catch up on the work some. Pay you proper, of course."

"Thanks for the offer, Everett," said Roy, "but I don't know much about pigs."

"Well, the offer's there if you want. Or just come by for some grub — we don't put *real* grubs in like some folk."

And the three of them had a good laugh together again, and that's how they came into Custer.

If only they'd known the turn things was just about to take — they surely would not have been laughing it up how they were.

Custer City was bigger than Roy had expected. He'd heard it was more or less deserted once Deadwood got going — and compared to Deadwood, it was small. While the population of Deadwood now numbered in the thousands, Custer was yet home to some hundreds, by what he could see.

"Might even get a decent feed here," said Roy as he opened the door to step down into the street.

"Don't eat at the hotel," Everett warned him. "Eating house there across the road serves up proper food. If you come over soon, you'll meet my brother Hank. We eat there every chance we get. Can't see our buckboard around yet, but he knows I'm comin' today."

Roy stepped out and stretched, almost got knocked down as an old-timer staggered across the street, drunk. He steadied the man, stopped him from falling into a pile of horse dung.

"You sheen a gray horsh, shunny," said the old man as

he swayed. There was a gray horse tied to the hitching post outside the restaurant — more bones than horse it was, had to be thirty years old. Roy pointed the old-timer at it, set him moving in that direction, and watched as he weaved his way there.

Somehow he made it the whole way. Then the old man leaned against the gray, and the gray leaned against the old man, and Roy couldn't help wondering if perhaps one or both of 'em had died, so still they became then.

Everett had stepped out of the coach by now, and had offered his hand to help Charlotte climb down to the street.

"That's Silver Sam, the town drunk," said Everett. "Real clever feller when he's sober."

"When's he sober?" asked Roy.

"Ain't never seen him sober yet," said Everett. "But I heard tell he's clever when he is. Was a Injun fighter in his youth so they reckon. But he don't talk none about it."

By then Joe had opened the left side door and announced, "Me and Curly'll bring all your bags in a minute. But y'all best get inside quick if you wants a bed to yourself. There's seven in the other coach plus the driver'n guard, and they sometimes runs outta beds in such doubled up circumstance."

Roy shook Everett's hand and said, "We'd best get inside quick, but we'll come eat with you directly ... that's if Miss Charlotte would like to, of course."

"I would like that," she said. "Thank you both very much."

Then Everett had Curly throw his bag down — seemed

almost like he threw it in the mud patch on purpose, but it wasn't no use complaining.

Roy and Charlotte watched Everett cross the street and go into the restaurant, then they stepped up onto the boardwalk and walked toward the open door of the hotel.

That was when two hard-looking men stepped into their path, and the older, taller one — six foot he was, long and lean, maybe thirty — took off his hat and said, "Are you Miss Charlotte Hawke?"

"Why, yes," she said. "Yes I am."

"Miss, my name's Fleet Darrow, and I've come to collect you. Mister Tanner sent me." He reached out to take hold of her arm, but she was too quick.

She cowered away from him, bumped into Roy and said, "But surely—"

Roy stepped forward, putting himself between the men and Miss Charlotte. "Where exactly *is* Mister Tanner?"

Fleet Darrow looked down at Roy — first at his face, then the over-short Winchester, then at his face again, and said, "Small man, small rifle ... what else is small, little feller?"

His orange-haired companion sure thought it was funny. "Small everything, I reckon."

"I asked you a question," said Roy.

"I reckon the answer ain't none o' your business, little man," Darrow answered, his voice fraught with menace. "Me and my gumpish friend here was sent to collect the lady, and that's what we're goin' to—"

Smile left Fleet Darrow's face when Roy levered one into the chamber. Then Roy spoke real slow, real clear. "I said: Where ... Is ... Mister ... Tanner? With all due respect, you could be anyone at all — and the lady's going into this hotel, and then on to Deadwood, unless Tanner shows up to collect her himself."

Darrow's mouth twisted some, but it turned into a smile. "I like a brave man," he said, "and prefer not to kill them when possible. And you got sand, feller, so I'll give you the benefit of doubt — for the moment. Who are you?"

Roy saw that each of these men wore a pair of fancy six-shooters, their tooled leather holsters hung low in the style of Texas gunfighters — but all their guns were tied down, so Roy wasn't worried.

Not with his Winchester in his hands, ready to fire.

He looked from one man to the other and said, "Miss Charlotte hired me to protect her — and I'll do that job 'til the moment she tells me not to. So I'll ask you boys one last time now. Where ... Is ... Tanner?"

That was when Curly jumped down from the coach, slapped the dust from his clothes and said, "Kid, don't go mixin' with these fellers, they'll have you for breakfast."

Darrow's hands were hovering nearby his hammer straps, but Roy held his Winchester in both hands, every sense heightened, ready for whatever would come.

"**M**ister Curly," Roy said slow and clear, "this ain't none of your—"

"No, listen, kid, calm down now," said Curly. "And you, Fleet, you should know better than to rile a young feller for sport. He's a good kid, you leave him alone, and let me sort this out."

"Sure, Curly," said Darrow. "I was just havin' some fun. No offense, kid."

Didn't ease Roy's mind one bit, Curly getting involved. But at least Fleet Darrow was now holding his hands out in front of him, and smirking like it had all been a joke.

"Kid, listen," said Curly now. "Leroy Tanner ain't no fool, and the girl was never so unprotected as she mighta seemed. He paid me proper to keep an eye on her during the trip, that's why I took an interest when you spoke with her at Rawhide Buttes. Tanner told me he might meet up with her in Custer, as he had to come see the bank manager."

"The bank manager," said Roy. Charlotte still stood behind him. Seemed he could actually *feel* her uncertainty hanging in the air there between them.

"Told me he might open another new hardware," said Curly, "right here in Custer. That's if the bank will give him the finance to get it all started."

Roy wasn't nohow convinced. "Then where is he?"

Curly said, "Most likely the bank, right boys?"

Darrow and Orange-Hair both nodded their agreement, although Darrow just couldn't help himself, and said, "Not that it's the little man's business."

"Don't matter nohow," said Curly. "Mister Tanner gave me strict orders to deliver the little lady to the Sheriff's Office. Told me he'd pick her up from down there once he's free, and the Sheriff would watch over her 'til then."

"The Sheriff's Office?" Roy said. Still wasn't too sure of the story. Didn't ring right somehow.

"That's what he told me," said Curly. "That where he told you to take her, boys?"

"Sure is," said Darrow, with that smirk again. He seemed to be enjoying himself.

"See, Kid? Just like I told you — all sound on the goose."

Roy spoke over his shoulder, never taking his eyes off the men. "Miss Charlotte? It's up to you."

Her voice was uncertain, but clear. "Will you come along too, Roy? To see the Sheriff?"

"Sure, Miss Charlotte, we'll all go see what he says."

Curly told Joe he'd be back in a minute to help him, and the old driver was tetchy as a teased snake about it.

They could all hear him grumbling until they went out of earshot.

Sheriff's Office was about sixty yards up the street, and Roy made it a point that he and Miss Charlotte walked behind the other men 'til they arrived.

"You sure are an untrusting feller," said Darrow. "And after us being so welcoming too."

But Curly said, "Leave him alone, Fleet, he's a good enough kid, and we had two good scares on the trail. We was just about buzzard food I reckon, so it ain't no wonder suspicions has tickled his bones."

"Stage got robbed, huh? They get much?"

"Not this time, Fleet. The kid here helped out real good. Might even have bounty money comin'."

Darrow's head jerked sharp toward Curly. "How many killed?"

"Three each time, Fleet."

Darrow glanced at the orange-haired feller, then looked around at Roy for a moment, then back toward Curly. "Anyone special?"

"Didn't notice nothin' special about 'em," Curly said. "Might be hard to identify. But no one important, by my reckoning."

By then they were coming to the Sheriff's Office. Roy watched everyone close as he could, but he couldn't look in every direction at once.

"If it ain't Curly Brown," said the Sheriff, standing up behind his desk, and casting his gaze quickly over each of their faces. "Good to see you. Trouble with the stage run, was there?"

"Two attempted robberies, Sheriff. They seem to think the stage easier pickings while it's traveling northward. Story can wait though, I gotta get back, go help Joe."

"What's up then, Curly?" He sat back down, kept his eyes only on Curly.

"Fact is, Leroy Tanner's gettin' married. He asked that you be entrusted with the care of his little woman here, 'til he finishes up his business at the bank. He don't trust us other rough types with her, I guess."

Darrow and Orange-Hair laughed at the joke, while the Sheriff's eyes darted from Curly's to Charlotte's to Roy's, and back then to Curly's.

There was nothing strange in how the man acted — and he *was* the County Sheriff, after all. Still, Roy didn't like this one bit.

"Congratulations, Miss," said the Sheriff. "I hadn't heard. But then, your future husband's business is none whatsoever of mine. And of course you can stay here with me. Anything for Mister Tanner."

"Thank you," said Charlotte. "He's ... well respected then?"

"Oh, yes," said the Sheriff. "Mister Tanner's well known. Got his finger in all sorts of ... well, it ain't my business, as I said, and you'll see for yourself soon enough."

Roy started to speak, but Curly spoke over the top of him. "Well, I know you're busy, Sheriff, we all best get going then, leave you to it."

"I got questions first," said Roy, and the Sheriff glanced at him, nervous-like, then looked back to Curly, then Darrow.

But Miss Charlotte was already speaking. "It's alright, Roy, I'm happy to wait with the Sheriff. Thank you so much for watching over me — I'll be just fine from here on. Perhaps I'll see you in Deadwood — introduce you to my new husband."

She seemed a little wistful, but content.

And that was it, there was nothing much else Roy could do. He took off his hat, nodded to her and said, "Goodbye, Miss, it was nice to have met you." Then he turned away from her, walked out into the street, and down toward the hotel.

But as he strode along, the hairs on the back of Roy's neck danced a terrible dance — and he knew only one thing for certain.

He wasn't leaving this town 'til he'd met Leroy Tanner.

CHAPTER 16
WRATHY

Roy was already wrathy when he walked into the hotel — but when he walked out two minutes later, he was madder'n an old wet hen.

Couldn't even bribe his way to a room.

The clerk looked at Roy over his spectacles and said, "It is not a question of money, Sir, but simple chronology. If you had entered the hotel at first moment, you'd be safely ensconced in your room now. As you did not, it was rented to another. Will there be anything else, Sir?"

"Must be somewhere I can stay," Roy said, trying to keep his temper. "A barn'll do."

"I'm sorry, Sir, there's nowhere at all." Then he cast furtive looks left and right, crooked his finger at Roy and leaned forward to speak to him quietly. "There *are* two saloons, Sir. Both have their beds filled with ladies, if you understand me."

"And?"

"The *Strike It Lucky* is the least expensive for such

services. A woman might be had for the whole night for as little as fifty dollars. A woman and a *bed*, Sir. It's the best you'll do, I'm afraid."

Roy thanked him, picked up his bag and stepped out into the night. There was a storm brewing it seemed — no moon, no stars, and it sure had turned cold for summer. The *Strike It Lucky* could wait, right now Roy had to eat.

He crossed the street to the restaurant. Had to step over old Silver Sam to get to the door, as he'd fallen asleep on the boardwalk. Looked like the old gray horse was asleep too — unlikely it was dead, for it was standing yet.

Still, looked like it couldn't be long.

Roy looked down at the old man again. He was wearing a coat, and had his arms wrapped around himself for warmth — but still, if it got much colder before he woke he could freeze. There was a rolled blanket on the horse, among other things. Roy took the blanket, unfurled it, spread it over the old man, who looked up momentarily, half-smiled, half-nodded his thanks.

Roy turned and crossed the boardwalk then. Stepped inside, was immediately struck by the warmth. Not just the warmth of the air, but the mood of the place. It felt unexpectedly friendly, after all that had happened his initial half hour in Custer.

"Roy, over here," called Everett from the right rear corner of the room.

Roy made his way over to Everett, who introduced him to his brother, Hank. Roy nodded, set down his bag, carefully leaned his Winchester against the wall behind him, before finally shaking Hank's hand.

He had a good, trustworthy sort of handshake, and Roy decided right off that Hank, too, was very likely a man to ride the river with.

"You didn't tell me you and Hank was identical twins," said Roy as he sat down.

"You never asked," said Everett. "But we ain't identical. Any fool can see I'm much handsomer."

"Yessir," laughed Hank, "you're a right Belvedere, ain't you, Brother!" Then he turned to Roy and said, "I reckon he's got himself a magic mirror. Seems actually to believe we look different. All I know is, we got pigs at home more handsome than the both of us put together."

Everett nodded at Roy's bag and said, "You missed out on a room."

"Dang clerk wouldn't be bribed neither," said Roy.

"Oh, he's a stickler for rules," Hank said. "If he spent as much time washing sheets as he does explainin' rules, that place might not be so bad to sleep in. You got the best of the deal anyway, there's a spare bed at our place, and it's clean."

"Oh, I couldn't—"

"Be insulted if you don't," said Hank.

"He's even uglier when he's insulted," said Everett.

"So it's settled," said Hank, and Roy thanked them both very much as a pink-faced young waitress arrived.

Roy ordered a steak with roasted potatoes and a double helping of green beans. Then when the girl left, he told the twins what had happened with Miss Charlotte, all the way up to where he'd left her in the care of the Sheriff.

They both listened to the whole story without saying so

much as one word — though Roy noticed identical expressions of alarm on both faces whenever he mentioned Fleet Darrow. But even then, they didn't butt in.

Then when the explaining was done, Everett said, "Roy, this is all a bad business. Darrow's been here two months, killed three men already."

"Four," said Hank. "Killed some new feller while you was down in Cheyenne. As for Sheriff Hosea Grimes..."

It was like Hank forgot how to speak then. He and Everett just sorta looked at each other awhile. Durndest thing it was — seemed almost like they had a quick conversation, though not even one word was spoken. It was only eyes and eyebrows that moved, and maybe heads tilting a little, and Hank rubbed his chin once — but it seemed they came to consensus fifteen seconds in.

It was Everett who spoke, but quietly — and not 'til he'd checked there was no one close enough by to hear him. "Roy. You ever heard of a man called Joe Brand?"

"No." He shook his head, and the hairs on back of his neck tried to tell him something important.

Roy wondered if maybe Everett didn't have misbehaving hairs on the back of his own neck, for he looked mighty fearful now, his eyes darting about every which way while he worked up the courage to speak again.

"Darrow works for Joe Brand. Rumor has it, the Sheriff does too."

"Go on."

"Ain't much else to know," said Everett, "except for Brand's been here ... oh, maybe six, seven months ... and he owns the Golden Nugget Saloon. We stay outta there, mostly."

"I frequent the place on occasion," said Hank, "single man as I am, and having such needs as us single men do. The Nugget has a ... better quality, I'd word it ... of painted dove, comparative to our other saloon. I prefer the Nugget, more prosperous times — five dollars a poke there though, not two like the *Strike It Lucky*."

Hank's ears colored as the waitress put Roy's meal and two serves of apple crumble on the table, one each in front of the twins. She smiled warmly at Roy before she left, but being out of sorts as he was, he barely noticed her. He was busy adding things up about Charlotte and Tanner and Brand and Darrow and Grimes — and he didn't much like the answer of what it all added up to.

Once the waitress was gone out of earshot Roy looked from Everett to Hank and said, "How's about we go to the Nugget tonight? Sounds like a place full of treasure. And I got as many five dollars's as you shaky-legged plunderers can drag yourselves upstairs to spend."

A half hour later they walked into Joe Brand's Golden Nugget Saloon, the twins wearing identical smiles of anticipation.

CHAPTER 17
THE GOLDEN NUGGET

When they walked through the doors into that big bright saloon, a mustachioed feller was playing a right lively tune on a fancy piano — and though it was early, the place was already half full of men spending their money. There was faro and poker, and even roulette.

There was more entertainment than that — four girls in tights and pink frills on a stage at one end, kicking their legs up so high to the music, every man in the place kept at least one eye pointing their way.

Roy always did feel at home in a quality whorehouse — the one he'd grown up in was a fine one. Or at least it became so after Big Jim Starr went on the run.

So, ordinarily, the sight of the four pretty pink-clad girls dancing, would have done Roy plenty of good. But in this case, the hairs on the back of Roy's neck danced faster and better than those scanty-clad girls ever could have.

The West was a wild place, beginning to end. No

mistake, it was dangerous. A dozen men trying to kill you in all different ways on a Thursday — then on a Friday, a dozen new ones would add 'emselves to the list. Ordinary Eastern men had a devil of a time keeping up with so much deadliness, and tended to expire most horribly. Quickly as well. But Roy had done all his growing up in a whorehouse, and there he had learned a few useful things, maybe more.

Despite his comparative youth, he was used to having some amount of certainty.

For instance, he *knew* he could always win at poker, unless there was a top notch cheat at the table — and even then, Roy always *knew* if such a man was in attendance, by the time he'd played a few hands. First thing he'd do when he sat down, draw out any sharps and tricksters. Sometimes that wasn't easy, but he'd learned from the best — had it down for a certainty.

Another certainty he had, he was never coming back to anyplace he visited again. The West was a mighty big place, but as long as he didn't double back, he was certain he'd find Big Jim Starr somewhere, sooner or later.

From here he'd go on and search Deadwood, Rapid City and Lead — and if Big Jim wasn't none of them places, Montana was next on his list.

But this dang place — and this *woman* — had put Roy somehow off kilter. Even his usual *certainties* seemed only like *maybes,* so when he looked around that room, saw so many opportunities to win some money at cards, he knew what he needed to do.

Do what you're best at, Roy, get your mind back on

*track. This Tanner thing will all fall into place, once you get
your own wits back in order.*

He followed his new friends to the bar, but when Hank
offered to buy him a whiskey, Roy asked for a beer instead.
Neither Hank nor Everett were much interested in
gambling, but they sure enjoyed watching the dancers.

"Even though she only just left me," said Everett, "I've
gone a good long while without." He looked a little guilty,
like as if he still felt a loyalty to his wife. But that look of
guilt melted away, when a pretty young woman who
worked there came up and said, "Well, look at you,
Handsome. Buy a girl a drink?"

Seemed like Everett and that calico queen couldn't
drink their drinks quick enough — wasn't four minutes later
they hurried away up the stairs, her leading him by his
hand while he smiled a wide one. He'd barely even noticed
when Roy slipped a half eagle coin into his spare hand.

"Happiest I've seen him in months," said Hank, raising
his glass in a kind of salute, then drinking it down in one go.
"Sad thing to see, the breaking down of a marriage.
Specially when it weren't either party at fault, but only a
wrongness to their match from the start. City girl she was,
born and bred. Can't blame her for bein' what she is."

They sat quietly looking around them a minute, then
Roy said, "Darrow's not here, and neither's the Sheriff.
Don't suppose Joe Brand's in the room?"

"No," Hank replied, "he usually don't come down 'til
later. You wanna get drunk?"

"Never was one much for drinking," said Roy, "but I
reckon I might play some poker."

Right then, Hank turned to his left — he'd been scanning the room the whole time — and saw a tall, somewhat hefty girl with a sweet little face and an overlarge chest, and his eyes sure lit up a treat.

"Uh, yes, Roy, that's a ... yes, you go play some poker I reckon."

Roy could barely keep the laughter from his voice. "And you, Hank? What do you have a mind for right now?"

"I reckon I just seen my future, and I'm anxious to greet it headlong. That's to say, before some'un else beats me to it."

"Enjoy yourself, Hank," said Roy, slipping him a half eagle. "I'll see you later."

With both brothers gone for the moment, Roy once again felt like himself. He was used to being alone, liked the way he could blend in to a place such as this. He looked into a mirror a few moments, took a sort of pleasure in knowing he was different than what people thought when they saw him.

The wispy beard he wore changed his appearance some, but its thin and patchy look only caused him to look even younger — more naive, was one way to put it.

He thought back on the way he'd *used* to wish he was taller, more solid, better looking — but he was happy to look how he did now. There was much to be said for his averageness of height, the ordinariness of his looks, and the way his everyday clothes hid most signs of his wiry strength.

Even his short Winchester — though it had been carefully chosen for fitness of purpose — brought him down a peg in most men's eyes. It was not on display here though, for this was the type of saloon where all guns must be given over to the care of the barkeep. Such places were a *little* less dangerous, but only a fool would believe it wasn't chock full of derringers.

Roy sipped his beer slowly, pretended to be watching the dancers — but really, his eyes were all for the poker games, and anything that could affect them.

He looked around at the placement of mirrors, saw nothing untoward from where he was — still, he would not trust to that, but check again once he sat at a table. A seemingly benign room could become a cheater's paradise from a drop of whiskey spilled on a table — such a drop, proper placed, as good as a mirror to the right man.

To his surprise Roy saw someone he recognized, a gambler he'd once butted heads against in Reno, Nevada. Dan Turner, his name had been out there in Reno a year ago — chances were, it'd be changed by now. The table hadn't been big enough for the both of them there, and it wouldn't be so here either. They respectfully acknowledged each other's presence — in each case, the slight lift of an eyebrow — and Roy waited for a chair to become vacant at the *other* poker table.

Didn't take long, and a somewhat grubby miner type pushed his chair back, shook his head in disgust, said, "Ah'm out while I still got fi' dollars to buy me a fine upstairs pleasurin'."

Roy got moving quick. By the time the miner vacated the chair, Roy was pretending to walk past it, on his way to the stage and the dancers, as if to take a closer look.

"Here's a winner, if ever I saw one," said the gambler across from the vacancy. He was dressed flashy compared to most others, wore a string tie and kid gloves and a well-trimmed mustache. "I just bet poker's your game, kid," the man said.

Roy was good at acting surprised. "Who, me?" He fiddled with the buttons of his shirt, looked away quick at the dancers, then back at the man again.

"Sure, clever youngster like you," said String-Tie. "Sit down and play, why don't you? Meant to be, way that chair got unfilled right before you walked by. No, your mother didn't raise no fools, not if we judge her by you."

It hurt Roy, *any* mention of his mother, but he fought it down quick. "I do enjoy the challenge of poker, but I ain't got much money to spare. And besides, you boys look the type to get serious." He made as if to leave.

"No, kid, it's just a friendly game," said String-Tie. "Dollar ante, dollar bet, but certainly no upper limit — that'd be an insult to luck. This is a table you can start small, maybe win big. Come on, sit down, try your luck."

"Mister, you sure got the talk — nearly wish there was two of me now, so the both of us could play."

"Good lad, sit down, sit down."

"Alright then," said Roy, "just a hand or two, 'til my friends come back down from upstairs."

Roy settled into the seat, looked wide-eyed and innocent at each man in turn, and rubbed his left boot for luck.

For a man so keen on dragging Roy into the game, String-Tie was one disastrously dreadful exponent of the noble game of poker.

He was so bad, Roy was suspicious. And the other two weren't any better — miners the both of them, roaringly drunk, to the point where one sometimes had to be woken to pick up his cards. It took all of Roy's considerable skill *not* to win every hand.

He won the first two, managed somehow to lose the next couple, then won the two after that. At least it was easy to lose when he dealt.

By the time Everett and Hank came back downstairs, Roy had won well over three-hundred dollars, and was in the process of putting some of it back in the pockets of his fellow players — best way to leave with a profit was a "run of bad luck," Roy had learned. Made your opponents less disposed toward violence, putting something back in each of their pockets.

But just as Roy was ready to leave, Curly showed up at the table.

"Looks like you hit a lucky streak, Kid," he said.

""Sure did for awhile, Mister Curly," he replied. "But these fellers been gettin' me back for awhile now. My head's gone soft from no sleep, is my best guess to why."

Curly laughed and said, "Yeah, you youngsters need sleep alright. Reckon I'll take your place, if that's alright with your friends here."

"I was just leaving myself," said String-Tie, and he got to his feet, scooping up what little he had left. "I'm off to Deadwood in the morning on the stage, you see. Thanks very much for the game, friends."

One of the miners grumbled about everyone leaving, and Curly said, "Sit back down, Kid, play a few hands before you drag your carcass to bed."

One of the miners — the slightly less drunk of the pair — looked some suspicious. "You two friends or what?"

Curly sure looked amused. "Me and this kid friends? Ha! Just met on the stage from Cheyenne. But just so we all know not to worry, let's have a fresh deck." Then he turned and called, "Barkeep! Fresh deck," and caught it one handed when the barman threw it across the room with a well practiced arm.

"Mister Curly's been teaching me all sorts of things about the West," Roy said to the miners. He noticed Everett and Hank then, looking happy enough at the bar.

"Reckon it's time I taught you all about poker," said Curly, as he wedged his big behind into the seat across the table from Roy.

Roy unwrapped the deck right over the table, making sure everyone saw him do it. Didn't let on what he noticed about the deck either. Thing about marked decks, they were generally of a poor quality — the card stock itself, not the printing — but only professionals noticed that, for the most part.

"Poker's like shooting, Kid," Curly said. "Just takes skill and practice, but some men think luck's as good. Dead, broke, or both, those men at the end."

Roy handled the cards a little clumsy, kept his eyes on them the whole time he shuffled. But he knew what he was doing — he'd used this exact deck many times, not only in public, but hour upon hour in hotel rooms, alone.

Before dealing them out he looked up though, right into Curly's eyes, and said, "Don't suppose you know if Mister Tanner collected Miss Charlotte from the Sheriff's Office yet?"

Curly lied right through his teeth then. "Sure, Kid. They already left town in Tanner's buggy. Be halfway to Rapid City by now."

"Thought he was from Deadwood?"

"Got interests all around, so I heard. Our business concluded when he paid me for keeping an eye on his property. Told me to thank *you* as well — didn't offer no payment though. Maybe you'll run into him in Deadwood."

"Maybe I will, Mister Curly," said Roy. "I sure can't wait to see Deadwood." Then he dealt out the cards.

Roy well knew the darkness this night made traveling the area too dangerous. Curly was a well practiced liar, but Roy had no doubt Miss Charlotte was still here in Custer.

He watched Curly reading the cards — he could read them, but not quickly, and that would play into Roy's hands, when the time came. He allowed Curly to win the first hand with two pair.

The miner to Roy's left was so drunk now he barely could deal — he could not have read the cards even if he knew how. Roy watched Curly while they played that hand. He wore a look of smugness whenever he or Roy mentioned Miss Charlotte.

Curly won that hand with three nines, and the next hand as well, with a straight.

That fourth hand, Roy raised Curly, mentioned the way luck couldn't keep running, and threw away an even hundred dollars — even knowing his own three tens were no match for the flush Curly held.

"Wow, five dang Diamonds," said Roy. "That's four outta four, Mister Curly. You *do* play cards just as good as you shoot."

"I do my best, Kid," Curly said. Seemed mightily pleased with himself.

"Though maybe your skills comes and goes some," said Roy, while studying Curly's expression. "I mean, it took you quite a few shots to shoot only two men, that last robbery. Yet three from three shots, the first time."

Sure wiped the smile off that mud-fence-ugly face.

Woke the miners up too, and they shifted some in their seats.

Curly threw back a large shot of whiskey then growled, "Just deal, Kid,"

"Sure, Mister Curly," Roy said, but continued to

shuffle. "Didn't mean no offense, just sayin', sometimes luck's a fortune."

"Luck don't matter nothin' to skill, Kid." He glared at Roy a moment, but they both watched the cards as he dealt them.

It's a funny old thing, the way strong dislike can change the way a man's "luck" runs. The strength of Roy's dislike was measurably growing — and Curly's "luck" shrinking commensurate with it. Roy had dealt a little quicker this time, just enough to make sure Curly missed the chance to read a card here or there.

Thing was though, Curly was just like most men who get on a winning streak — he'd gotten reckless. And the three aces he had made him more so, and he opened with a bet of a hundred.

"That's a bluff there if ever I seen one, Mister Curly," said Roy after looking at his own cards. "I don't doubt you got skill — I just don't believe even *you* can win five hands of poker at a stretch. Laws of luck don't nohow support it. Fact is, either me or one of these others wins this hand for certain."

Seemed the miners agreed with Roy, and both stayed in for the moment. Now, whether Roy dealt the next cards off the top of the deck or the bottom, no man could ever rightly say. Or if he could say, it might be a bad idea to do so.

Curly grunted, looked at his two new cards, and somehow — by luck, by providence, by skill, or maybe all three — he found himself looking at a full house. Aces and Nines it was. But he was an experienced man, and could scowl with the best of 'em, no matter how fortunate the cards.

He scowled a good one at Roy and said, "You done made it personal, Kid, all that gab about *luck* — reckon it's time you was taught a real good lesson."

CHAPTER 19
"STRIKE ME DOWN FOR A DEVIL"

C urly wanted to teach Roy a lesson alright — but for now, he couldn't use his most favored method.

Violence would have to wait. Still, Curly also enjoyed teaching lessons that filled up his pockets — and he bet accordingly.

He tried to look nervous, shrugged his big shoulders — then smiled what he hoped would look like a bluffer's one and announced, "Boys, I'm all-in." Counted out the money before him and pushed it to the center — it took his bet to just on five-hundred.

Too rich for the blood of the miners, they both cursed and dropped out. But Roy only narrowed his eyes, held his cards behind his two hands in the manner of some raw beginner. He peeked at his cards, looked over the top of 'em at Curly, peeked at 'em again. Then he put 'em face down on the table. Lifted up a corner once more, put it back down. Screwed up his face some and rubbed at his temples with one hand, while leaving the other on his cards to keep them all safe from harm.

"Mister Curly," he said then with a forced sorta laugh, "I do believe you're a bluffer."

"Sure am, Kid," said Curly. "That's why you should stay in. Come on now, the luck's with you, remember?"

Roy set his eyes to darting about some uncertain. He would never usually do what he was doing now, always preferring quiet victories, small stakes — and as little attention as possible.

But the man across the table had planned on killing him, and if he'd succeeded, Roy would not have been here to play — more important, he would not have lived to extract his vengeance on the murderer Big Jim Starr.

No. Curly pays, here and now, no matter who sees what I am.

"You *are* bluffing, Mister Curly," he said. "You have to be, no one's that good, and this is the best hand I'm ever likely to get. Honest it is. So that'll be over a thousand in the pot, right?" Then Roy took some extra money from his pocket and commenced to count it all out.

A small crowd had gathered by now — the word *thousand* always seemed to draw them — and that crowd included Fleet Darrow. The smirking gunfighter leaned down and whispered something to Curly, who smiled, then looked again at Roy.

"How much you got on you, Kid?"

"That ain't how it's played, Mister Curly. I read up on the rules in the Hoyle's, and that sure ain't in 'em."

"Not tryin' to cheat you, Kid. Just makin' things

straight. Lettin' you know, you can raise again — if you got the sand. My friend Fleet here says he'll back my play for however much you got. Know what else he says?"

Roy glanced fearfully up at Fleet Darrow, and said, "W-what?"

"He says you're all mouth, Kid."

"Mister Darrow's probably right," said Roy. "I just hope..."

"You hope what, Kid?"

"I just hope he ain't seen both our cards."

Them words caused more than a murmur, and everyone behind Roy — Hank and Everett included — scattered quick. Roy glanced quickly at the newly cleared space either side of him. No one wanted to be nowhere nearby when Fleet Darrow got riled.

But no violence erupted from Darrow — though the laughter that exploded from his throat was as crisp and loud as a bullet. "You ain't gettin' out of it that easy, Kid," he said then. "Bet all you want, play that hand you're so careful protecting, and don't dance around it if you wanna call me a cheat. *Do* you say I'm a cheat, Kid?"

"No sir, Mister Darrow. And to make it proper clear, I say I reckon you're honest." Roy shortened his breath up, playacted for all he was worth. Took his kerchief from his top pocket, wiped it over his brow. "I'm just a bit flustered is all, Mister Darrow. Could I take a minute to think before I decide?"

"Highly irregular," said Darrow. "But sure, I'm enjoyin' the show." He lit up a cigar, blew thick smoke out over the table, and Roy coughed on it a little.

"Come on, Kid," said Curly. "More you pay for the lesson, the better you'll learn it. And besides, you *know* I'm just bluffin', I remember you sayin' so."

"That's a contradictory, bamboozeful statement, Mister Curly. But I think I see what you mean, which is that you already taught me the lesson, and I should maybe just let you keep what's already in the pot, or just ask to see, or ... aw, Mister Curly, just what *would* you advise, in my situation, to help, by way of a lesson?"

"Well, strike me down for a devil, I seen it *all* now," said Fleet Darrow. "Go on, Curly, advise your young friend what to do, I'm all-fired agog in my anticipation."

The assembled crowd laughed it up, Darrow clearly enjoying it.

Everett stepped forward, put a hand on Roy's shoulder, looked down and said, "Not the finest idea, Roy, askin' your opponent for advice. Maybe you should just—"

"Shut up, friend," said Fleet Darrow coldly. Everett shrank back from his menacing gaze, and shut his trap like he'd been warned to.

"Mister Curly's taught me plenty these two days," Roy murmured as if to himself, but loud enough so Curly and Darrow could hear it. "My own dang Pa never taught me nothin' but manners, manners, damn manners. But Mister Curly, he's a..." He let his voice trail off, sat there looking ashamed.

"Kid," Curly said with a smile. "I reckon you keep back fifty dollars, and bet everything else you got. That's the damn truth. A man has to back his beliefs. What with you believin' I'm bluffin' and all, and luck not allowin' me five damn hands in a row. And besides, you got such a good hand, be a right shame to waste it."

"I reckon maybe two-hundred more then," Roy said with not much conviction, "as I'll need a room in Deadwood, and—"

"Oh, Kid, I thought you had sand."

"Well, I guess I could go to ... make it *three-hundred* more then, that'll leave me enough to—"

"You've disappointed me, Kid," said Curly, with a slow, disgusted shake of his head.

"Five-hundred more then," cried Roy, impulsive-like, and the crowd all gasped as one. "That's a thousand *each* in the pot, and damn you to hell, Mister Curly, if you're still disappointed."

"You please me now, Kid," Curly said, drumming his fingers on the table. Darrow put in five-hundred, and Roy turned out his pockets, put his money up too. They all saw what he had left, which was only six dollars and change.

Curly smiled a wide one, reached to turn over his cards — but Fleet Darrow, cool as ever you like, said, "Wait up a minute."

Roy, his hand still on his cards, gasped, "What is it, *please,* Mister Darrow? I can't take no more, let's just show 'em and have it all done."

But Darrow said, "Kid, I forgot to tell you. Sheriff Grimes says you got two-hundred comin', the bounty on that feller you shot. His name was Floyd Wilkins."

Roy wasn't the only one who gasped, but he sure was the only one looked like he might just pass out. But his playacting didn't stop him noticing the angry look Curly shot at Darrow when he said *'Floyd Wilkins.'*

"Oh, Lordy," said Roy.

"It's a SIGN," said Fleet Darrow, big-voiced like one o' them Preachers that gets all caught up in the moment. "When your luck's in it's in, Kid." Then he ashed his cigar on the shoulder of a gawker who'd stepped too close to him.

That gawker sure stepped back quick — didn't even brush off the ash 'til he'd stepped back out of Darrow's sight.

"It *was* a lucky shot I guess," said Roy. "And I did survive *two* stagecoach robberies."

"Tell you what, I'll put in that two-hundred for you," Darrow said, "and the Sheriff can pay *me* the bounty when it comes in. If you're *game* to take your bet to twelve-hundred, that is. You're game, ain't you, Kid? It's the *story,* that's what's important! See, even if you lose, it's a story to tell your grandchildren — how the turn of a card cost you twelve-hundred dollars, in Custer Damn City, same day you killed your first man."

"Why not!" cried Roy triumphantly. "Ain't like I'll ever get paid a bounty again. And this *is* the best hand I ever had."

Darrow threw down another four-hundred, took a good pull on his cigar, blew a large smoke ring out over the table, then a smaller one straight through the large one.

"Wow, ain't that somethin' that smoke," said Roy then. "I'll sure put *that* in the story when I tell it, Mister Darrow."

"Moment of truth, Kid," Curly said. He turned over his

cards, held 'em in place with his right hand, spread 'em out one by one with his left, so all present could watch things unfold. Nine ... Nine ... Ace ... Ace ...

He kept that last one hid underneath a long moment, as all present held in a breath — then he showed it, a beautiful Nine, and the gathered crowd gasped and applauded.

"Oh," said Roy, his face a dark cloud. "All I got's two pair..." — and he turned the cards over, looked Curly in the eyes as he spread them — "two pair of tens."

Roy never knew a man Curly's size could throw a punch so quick from a seated position.

CHAPTER 20
A GAMBLE OF SORTS

An hour or two later, Roy was feeling a dang site worse for wear, as he and the twins discussed all that had happened back at the Golden Nugget Saloon.

"It's not the way I'd have chose to meet Joe Brand," Everett said, as he dabbed ointment on the cut in Roy's chin.

"What the *dickens!*" Roy half-squealed. "That hurts worse than the punch Curly done it with!"

"It's a special mix we use on the pigs," said Hank with a laugh. "Don't you put none on me, Ev."

They were back home at the pig farm, and all three looked sorry sights, for there had been a whole lot of trampling, as well as fists flying, not to mention bottles and glasses and chairs, and a table or two.

Least harmed among these three was Hank — he had only a little bark off of him, but the other two looked like they'd fought off a couple of bears.

When Curly had throwed that first punch, it caught Roy a painful surprise. He still hated Curly for planning to kill him earlier, but he sure had to respect the man's abilities. Roy was a pretty skilled fighter, had learned to box as a child, and loved the art of it. Enjoyed the brutality too, the manfulness of it. He'd also learned all sorts of throws and evasion techniques since, from a very small Chinaman who even Roy could not manage to hit.

But that punch of Curly's arrived before it began, or so it seemed at the time. Toppled Roy backward it did, but still in his chair — then he'd gotten some trampled in the ruckus that followed. Well, plenty trampled, more accurate.

Thing was, more'n two-thousand dollars on the table was too much temptation for some folk — even in Joe Brand's establishment, and with Fleet Darrow standing right there.

Bigger the hellabaloo, the more chance of getting hold of some cash in all the may-hay that follows. Men threw punches, hit others with whatever came to their hands, there was kicking and trampling and headlocks, but luckily no knives got involved — wonder of it all was that only the one shot was fired.

That gunshot sure froze 'em in place though.

Half because *what* it was, and half because *who*.

It was Joe Brand who'd fired it.

Up there at the top of the stairs he seemed altogether too big, his great bald head with the light shining off it, and his voice ringing out through the silence, striking fear through strong men. "Next man moves ... dies."

Voice like a spade digging into wet gravel.

Back of Roy's neck tingled so bad, he thought for a moment he'd broke it, so damn wrong it felt. He sure had no interest in moving, and neither did anyone else. He'd been on his way to getting up, but was frozen in place now. Stayed still as the dead, on his knees, just watching the play.

"Sheriff Hosea *Damn* Grimes," Brand had called down the corridor then, "put your iron back in your britches and get out here now."

Roy couldn't tell if it was himself shaking, or the whole damn world shaking, him still.

The Sheriff came then to the top of the stairs, a'hopping and stumbling into his britches, but not a body dared laugh. Sheriff stood himself up beside Joe Brand, though perhaps a little behind him. He unthinkingly touched his left hand to his badge, looked down at the raggedy standstill assemblage below, and turned toward Brand without speaking.

"Gun, *Sheriff* Grimes," Brand growled. He was a huge man alright, heavy set, gone a little too fat from good living, but incredibly strong, no mistaking. Not a hair on his head, but for the great bushy eyebrows that looked like gray wire — and that huge doughy face, it was all nose and jowls, like some strange wild beast in a circus.

"Sorry, Mister Brand," said Grimes, as he fumbled a plain-looking revolver out of its holster, and pointed it vaguely at those in the room down below.

"Sheriff, kill any man that moves or speaks 'less I say so," said Joe Brand, waving his own gun about in his gloved right hand. "Now. Fleet Darrow. Perhaps you could tell me which'a these damn whoremongers caused this ruckus in my fine establishment?"

Darrow was the only man in the room who right then looked merry and joyful. He took a short pull on his cigar, then blew out the smoke as he looked first at Curly, then down across the table at Roy on his knees, then at one or two shrinking others close by. Then he cocked his head as he looked up at Brand, and without a hint of hurry he said, "Misunderstanding, I'd put the thing down to for now, Boss."

"Misunderstanding? Broken glass, busted chairs, me disturbed from my thoughts. Mister Darrow. Which of these men has to pay? Or would that be you?"

Roy grudgingly admired Darrow then — for while even Curly looked fearful, Fleet Darrow seemed merely amused.

"Best sorted in-house, Boss," he said, and most of the men in the room breathed a sigh of relief. Relief changed quick for some when he added, "Though I'd suggest you have the Sheriff shoot the head off any man who don't replace whatever he … *accidental-like* … grabbed off this table in all the confusion." Then he smiled that languid smile of his, and quizzically raised his left eyebrow.

"Do you know how much was on the table, Mister Darrow?"

"I do."

"Well, all you damnable whoremongers heard the man. All them who … *accidental-like* … helped scoop up the money off that table … *for its own damn protection, I'm guessing* ... may move forward now, put it back where it belongs."

There was some men moved quick, and others whose eyes darted round some before they moved forward — but there was no man fool enough to stay where he was, if he'd scooped up a share of that money.

Roy's kneeling was a discomfort, and he thought of getting to his feet while people was moving. Decided to stay where he was though, in case them that moved yet got punished.

"Count it," growled Joe Brand.

Darrow counted the money. "All here and then some," he said. "Some generous soul gave twenty extra, perhaps thinking it a collection plate."

A weasel-faced miner close by to him patted his pockets, before raising a finger into the air — then thought better of it, and hung down his head.

Joe Brand shook his head slowly. "I'm all for high spirits, you men all know that by now — but if this ever happens again, I *will* come out shooting. Bring the money and all parties involved to my office, Fleet. The rest of you, get back to spending — drinks half price for the next fifteen minutes!"

The stampede for the bar in that moment — an hour ago it was now — was where Roy had got most of his injuries.

He pointed them out now for Everett to put on the ointment, while Hank went and poured some more coffee.

"So, what *did* Brand say upstairs?" said Everett.

"Bet his office is fancy," said Hank.

"Well, I guess it was sorta fancy," said Roy.

Everett was itching for details. "But what *happened?*"

"Well, we went upstairs and into his office, then that damn Curly started to speak, and Brand just up and belted him one, right across the chops. Curly cowered away from him too, didn't so much as look at him again. Like a poor damn bear on a chain, he looked. I just about felt sorry for him."

"You musta thought *you* was for it," said Everett, putting the lid back on the ointment jar, and handing Roy his shirt to put on.

"Didn't know what to think," said Roy, then he pulled on the shirt. "Been happier places for sure. First thing, Brand narrowed them damn beady eyes of his, studied my face real close, asked if we'd met someplace before."

Everett's eyes went wild and wide, and he said, "Well, had you?"

"Told him the truth — that I'd never met no one called Brand in my life, or at least never knew it if I did. And that I'd surely remember a man of his size and strength."

"I sure would too," Everett said.

"Then the Sheriff told Brand I'd come in on Curly's stage. Told him my name as well — that struck me strange, seeing as how Grimes never asked me my damn name when I delivered Miss Charlotte to him earlier. But I didn't let on nothin' about it."

"What then?" said Hank, passing Roy a cup of coffee in a beaten-up blue enamel mug.

"Thanks," Roy said. He lowered his face to the cup and he blew across the top of it and smiled at the steam before taking a small sip from its edge. Coffee was a lot better than he expected. "Brand asked if I was the one killed Floyd Wilkins — Darrow jumped in right away and said that I was. But that Sheriff, he sorta coughed then and shook his head funny, and they all kinda looked at each other, and Brand changed the subject right quick."

"I heard tell of Wilkins," said Hank. "They say him and some buddies gunned a rich man down in Cheyenne, and there was two-hundred bounty on each of 'em. Know what else they say?"

"Just tell it, Hank," Everett said, slapping his brother on the shoulder. "I hate when you draw it all out."

"Quit it, Ev," Hank replied, hitting him back. "They say Big-Nose Brown was one of 'em."

"Uh oh," said Everett. "That ain't good."

Roy was still in the dark. "Why?"

"Big-Nose Brown's Curly's brother."

"All makes sense," said Roy, looking up from his still-steaming coffee.

"But if one of the road agents was Curly's brother..." said Everett, thoughtfully rubbing his chin.

"You got it," said Roy. "Curly was in on the whole thing. Not the first robbery, only the second. His shots were all missing on purpose."

Everett looked at Roy then, a bit funny and sideways. "Good thing you made that one lucky shot, Roy."

"Two lucky shots," Roy replied. "Curly only killed the third one to stop him shouting his name."

"We're in deep trouble," said Hank, banging down his own cup, and spilling a little coffee on the table.

"Maybe not," Roy answered. "Long as we never let on we know who's who, they've no reason to kill us. That explains why Curly looked hard at Darrow, when Darrow mentioned Floyd Wilkins at the gambling table. Darrow only done it to get me to gamble the extra two-hundred, and no doubt thought it all a good joke."

"He's cold, that Darrow," said Everett.

"He's the worst kinda trouble," said Hank.

"But he's flippant," said Roy.

"He's a *what-nnt?*" said Everett, with a violent shake of his head, like as if he had water in his ears and it might get it out.

"Frivolous, sort of. Doesn't respect anyone," Roy explained. "Everyone has a weakness, and that's Darrow's. He doesn't believe anyone can touch him — thinks the whole world's a joke, only there for his own entertainment. As quick and as deadly as he is, he *does* have a weakness."

"Good luck with that," said Hank. "One thing to know a man's weakness, 'nother thing to exploit it. What else happened in there?"

"Not much else." Roy finished his coffee, put the cup down on the table, nodded appreciatively at Hank then went on. "Darrow explained exactly what happened, the truth to the absolute letter. He's got honor, I'll give him that. Poor Curly sat there like a dog that expected to be kicked — and once or twice, Brand looked down at him like he just might. Then Brand ordered Darrow to count out a thousand and hand it to me."

Everett whistled through his teeth, shook his head and

said, "Gave you most of your stake back, but not what you'd won."

"Lucky to get even that," said Hank.

"More to it," Roy said. "But just while I think of it — does Joe Brand always wear them kid gloves?

The twins looked at each other, uncertain-like, and had another of their silent conversations, same way as when they first mentioned Joe Brand, back at the restaurant — it was all eyes and eyebrows and head-tilts and chin-rubs, no words. And again, it was Everett who finally spoke. "Neither one of us ever noticed, not even tonight. Don't see how it matters none either."

"Maybe it don't," said Roy, and went back to the story. "So I took that thousand in my right hand, and held out my left for the rest. 'I won that hand fair and square, after these fellers goaded me higher,' was all that I said."

Everett's teeth were sure getting a workout from how he kept whistling through them. "Dammit, Roy," he said then, "did you *want* them to kill you?"

"Guess it was a gamble of sorts, but I had my reasons."

Hank looked over Roy's face, as if searching for something particular. "They hit you for sayin' it, at least?"

"Brand looked like he might for a moment. Then he laughed like nobody's business. Asked Darrow if it was true — if I'd won the hand fair and square. Darrow gave him it straight — even added in how him and Curly dragged my stake from five-hundred to twelve. Thought it a lark and a merriment, Fleet Darrow did. Said it was worth every penny to see Curly's face."

"That Darrow," said Everett with a shake of his head.

"Strange one alright," said Roy. "So then Brand told me he was keeping back six-hundred for damages, but Darrow'd bring the other thousand to me in the morning — hand it to me once I'm on the stage."

"That's some lucky streak you're on, Roy," said Hank.

"Told me to get out of his sight then, and never tell no one either way if he gave me the money. Said to skulk on out with my head down, so folks downstairs'd reckon he kept it."

"Sure fooled me," said Hank.

"Not me," said Everett. "I've been learnin', Roy does most things by contraries. So when he looked beaten down, I figured he had some of the money."

"Let's hope no one else figures me out. I've yet got work to do here, regarding Miss Charlotte."

CHAPTER 21
HOOVES AND HOT BREATH

The distance to Deadwood being short, the stage
wasn't scheduled to leave until ten, and that
suited Roy pretty well.

More people about the better, way he figured things.

The cut in his chin was more or less closed up and
healing — that pig ointment sure was the business. His ribs
still hurt from where he'd got trampled, and his left eye had
a swelling beneath it, but he felt pretty good, for the most
part. Coulda been worse anyways.

Couldn't quite have said the same for Curly, but Roy
didn't yet know that.

Roy left the twins to do their chores and headed toward
town at first light on one of their horses. He was a plain
little gelding, a bay who didn't get rode near as much as
he'd like to, and it didn't take long before Roy felt a great
kinship with him. Woulda felt good to be on any horse
again, but this one seemed somehow special — Roy liked
the neat compactness of him, his plainness, and the smell of

him too. Most of all he liked the way that little gelding wanted to do more than whatever was asked of him.

The way that little bay worked with him, responding to even his gentlest actions, it seemed almost like that horse was reading Roy's thoughts.

Shoulda asked what your name was, my friend.

Roy and that horse spent a good few hours together, just munching on apples and thinking, just off the trail that led out of town toward Deadwood — didn't *just* lead to Deadwood, of course, but to everyplace north, pretty much.

Horse got uppity around about eight, started to hanker for some action, made more noise than Roy was happy with at that time — so he mounted back up, took that horse north along the trail a ways, 'til he found a good safe stretch to let that horse really run. Turned him back toward Custer City, held him tight a few seconds like it was the start of a race, then he shouted, "Let's go."

Horse sure did know what GO meant, and the both of them reveled in that next sixty seconds, flat out with their ears all pinned back, thunder of hooves and hot breath, the pair of them slicing the air, a kindredness no man could have with another, horse and rider together, wild hearts beating joyful as they flew under bright morning sun.

That's what I needed, Roy thought — or maybe it was the horse who had thought it, and Roy heard the thought with his mind, the pair being now connected.

Horse and rider having blown out the cobwebs, both were content to watch the world quietly go by about them. Roy watched that trail some more, from off behind a good stand of trees, just two minutes ride from the town.

"This is the spot," he'd decided soon as he saw it.

He'd had two reasons for going out there so early: one to choose the right spot for later; the other to make sure Miss Charlotte wasn't spirited away without him knowing.

Everett and Hank had a friend who owned the mercantile next to the restaurant — across the street from the hotel — and they arranged to meet Roy there at half after nine. They'd explained to him how to sneak in there the back way without being seen by the regular townsfolk.

Everett was on edge, worried for Roy's health when he hadn't arrived quite on time. But then he heard a horse out the back, looked out and saw Roy dismounting.

He opened the door and waved him inside. "See what you needed to, Roy?"

"She ain't left town," Roy answered, "but I still need to watch."

"Hank's keeping watch from upstairs," Everett told him. Then he led Roy up there, with a brief introduction to the mercantile owner on their way.

"No sign of her from here," said Hank.

"Good," Roy replied, rubbing his hands together and taking up a good vantage point by the window. "Found the perfect spot for my plan. Thanks for the loan of the horse, he's something special."

"*That* horse?" said Hank, and he looked at Roy strange, before asking, "So what *is* this plan?"

But Roy only raised up his eyebrows, smiled a hint of a smile, and commenced to look out the window.

Hank was mighty curious, and began to question Roy on his plan again. But Everett told his brother to leave off with his questions, and just allow Roy some space to work out his thoughts. "Besides, Hank, he's so dang contrary, even if he does answer, it won't likely mean nothin' sensible to a pair of pig farmers like us. His head works on some different latitude, I reckon. Way cats works different to dogs."

Roy smiled to himself and wondered if there weren't some small truth in what Everett had said. His Ma used to say he was catlike — most especially when the back of his neck would tingle a warning. She reckoned cats had extra senses, and he'd be wise to pay attention to such things as they did.

The three of them watched from upstairs there as Joe brought the stage around on his own. There was no actual stage station here, and the livery was two-hundred yards away. No boardwalk down that way neither. So they'd bring the stage to the hotel, rather than have people carry their luggage down there through the mud.

Five minutes later, Curly came out the front doors of Joe Brand's Golden Nugget Saloon. His face was set hard against his pain as he limped along the boardwalk. Stopped halfway, sorta hid in a doorway — leaned on his rifle like it was a walking cane then.

His face weren't no uglier than it had been before, but judging by his tentative movements, Curly had been sorely beaten since last Roy had seen him.

Whatever Curly said to Joe when he got there, it surely weren't complimentary. Ol' Joe threw his hands in the air and commenced to walk away in frustration, but after three or four steps he stopped dead in his tracks — hung his head then came right on back. With no small amount of struggle he helped Curly climb up to the box seat, then handed his rifle up to him.

"I'd just forget that other thousand, Roy," said Everett, looking out from where he was hid behind the mercantile's curtains. "If you get on that coach, Curly'll do for you somewhere between here and Deadwood, ain't no doubt and no gamble."

"He sure can't stay here though," Hank argued from beside him. "And Curly Brown himself's the proof of it. If Joe Brand does such as that to his friends, think how Roy'll end up if he stays."

"Oh, I'm staying," said Roy. "But first, I'm collecting my thousand."

The twins just looked at each other. Might as well have looked in a mirror, for their identical features told the same tale of helpless exasperation. They shook their heads at each other, and together, did not say a word, for they knew it a waste of their breath to talk sense to Roy now.

CHAPTER 22
"SHARP MOVE, KID"

Roy watched and waited, waited and watched. Men wandered out from the hotel, others came up along the boardwalk. The string-tie gambler from the night before climbed on in, and before long the stage was almost full up. One seat left, by Roy's count.

As for Curly, he sat on the box seat, cradled his rifle, kept a lookout for Roy.

Roy took out his pocket watch and checked it. *Two minutes to ten.* He put the watch back in his pocket and looked along the street. Finally came Darrow, striding alone up the boardwalk, folks stepping out of his way soon as they perceived him. Some darted into shops, others crossed the street. Not a one of them failed to react.

Roy told his new friends, "Stay here, I'll be twenty minutes."

Winchester in hand, he walked down the stairs, stepped out the Mercantile's front door and crossed over the street — watched by Darrow, by Curly, and by Joe, who stood holding the right-side coach door open for him.

"Saved your favored seat for you, Mister Peabody," said Joe.

Sounded strange to Roy in that moment, the foolishness of the name he had chosen for this trip. *Peabody. Just think if the wind changed, and a man got stuck with it for eternity. Sure don't want it on my grave marker.*

Thing was though, ol' Joe had spoken the name with respect. By now he'd have heard of what happened the previous night — and though some would believe Roy a fool, Joe at least seemed to admire his courage for being here.

"Thanks, Joe," Roy answered. "Best seat there is, 'cept the one next to you. Like to take that one again, some other trip."

Curly didn't say a word, but Roy guessed the man's hands were warming the stock of his rifle. Roy was glad he'd cleaned and oiled the Winchester.

Darrow had stopped to watch a few moments, but was moving again now. Seeing him, Joe skedaddled quick, climbed up onto the box beside Curly, all ready to go.

Fleet Darrow stepped down from the boardwalk, screwed his nose up as he detoured round some fresh horse dung, stopped a yard in front of Roy and smiled. "You got sand, Kid," he said. Then, loud enough to make sure Curly heard it, he added, "Just so you know, Kid — our mutual friend has been warned not to teach you no more lessons. Even got given a taste of what that'd earn him."

There was laughter in his voice when he said it — yet no hint of malice.

"Thanks for the assurance, Mister Darrow," said Roy, and he held out his hand for the money.

"In the coach first, Kid," Darrow said quietly. "Keep your hand low so nobody sees."

Roy looked inside the coach, saw no nasty surprises awaiting. He climbed in, then opened his hand and looked out at Fleet Darrow.

"See you again, Kid," said Darrow. He pressed the cash into Roy's hand, then closed the door.

"Bet on it," said Roy with a respectful nod, and put the cash in his coat pocket without looking at it.

Joe released the brake and the stage pitched and swayed as he set the horses in motion. Roy stuck his head out the window, looked back behind him. Fleet Darrow was already walking away, a path opening up before him as he went.

Joe guided the stage north-west out of town, and two minutes later Custer City was gone from their sight. This was the place Roy had chosen, early this morning. They slowed as the trail went downhill to cross a small stream, and Roy opened the door.

The man facing Roy growled, "Close the door you damn fool, we'll get wet when we—"

"You can close it yourself," answered Roy. And holding the short Winchester in both hands, he jumped out onto the trail, ran a step or two with the momentum, then came to a stop with the Winchester pointed at the stage.

That feller snapped his head back inside without

closing the door, then raised a good lively ruckus, just like Roy expected. Cried out, "He's got a damn gun pointed at us." Then Joe craned his neck to look back and see what had happened.

Roy waved him on, and Joe kept the team moving all the way through the creek, then up the hill a ways on the other side, before stopping just after the trail took a turn to the left.

By then, Roy had taken cover behind a fair size tree to the left of the trail, twenty yards or so back from the creek.

He reckoned Curly would maybe have a go at him anyway, despite what Fleet Darrow had said. Curly was a prideful sorta feller. He hadn't took kindly to being bested at cards — and the beating he'd since received hadn't sweetened his mood.

If Curly *did* have a hankering for trouble, Roy had at least made sure he went into it on his own terms — that being, from behind cover, with the short Winchester already aimed and ready, at around Roy's favorite range.

At sixty-five, seventy yards, most men figured the baby Winchester to be out of range. That had worked in Roy's favor before, and he hadn't forgot it.

From Roy's position he couldn't see Joe, but he *could* see Curly. That mud-fence-ugly man had turned around quick, ignoring his pain — the prospect of imminent death helps a man forget most of his troubles, renders him able to do whatever he must.

It must have hurt something fierce to get in position, but Curly was now standing on the box seat. He was three-parts hid by the coach and the boxes of cargo on top of it —

and he had his rifle already pointed, back in Roy's general direction, though he hadn't yet spotted him.

"I'll be heading back to town now, Joe," Roy called good and loud. "Changed my mind about going to Deadwood. Seems a mite dangerous, given the company."

It wasn't Joe who answered, of course.

"Sharp move, Kid," Curly called. "Deadwood'd have you for breakfast, you'd not last a day."

Roy stayed where he was behind cover. "That a lesson, Mister Curly? I heard your license for teachin' got revoked."

"Just friendly advice, Kid. You plannin' on stayin' in Custer?"

He'd said it like he hoped the answer'd be *Yes*.

"I aim to stay, Mister Curly. You comin' back now to play?"

"Not me, Kid. Custer City's got a fine bone orchard, and it's been filling up quick — I'll visit you there in two days when the stage comes back through."

"You sound pretty sure about that, Mister Curly." Roy had never said truer words, the man sounded certain.

"If you got any sense, Kid, you won't go nowhere near Joe Brand. But then, you already know that."

"What about Mister Tanner? Should I go visit *him*? He's still here in Custer, ain't he, Mister Curly?"

Seemed like there was no sound at all then, no sound but the water in the stream, for a good long ten-second at least. Then out of that eerie quiet Curly shouted. "Trail to Hell's paved with good intentions. It was almost nice knowin' you, Kid. Tell Old Scratch to stoke up the fires, I'll see you'n him down below soon."

Roy watched and listened awhile as the stage trundled off toward Deadwood — he could still hear Curly laughing after all other noise of the horses and wheels of the stagecoach were lost to the wind and the distance.

CHAPTER 23
THE DIRT

Maybe it was Curly's laughter; maybe it was his words; maybe it was the ten long seconds of ominous silence before them — maybe it was all three.

Roy needed to think on things more.

He decided to take five more minutes, before walking back into town. He sat on a fallen tree, leaned his Winchester against it.

Some things were certain, some weren't. He stood, picked up a stick, drew a line in the dirt with it. Good straight line, up and down.

To the left of the line at the top, he wrote the letter *C*.

C for *Certainties*.

Then to the right of the line, he wrote the letter *M*.

M for *Maybes*.

He scratched a line crossways under those letters, so now his two lines made a cross — two columns in the damp ground, a place for his thoughts to get clearer.

One certainty was, he'd have to watch out for Curly, when he came back two days from now — but Roy living that long seemed now like a *Maybe,* so he put the C for Curly in the *Maybes* column, as *maybe* it wasn't an issue.

Miss Charlotte, he put under *Certainties.* He had no doubt at all she was still in Custer City — no doubt things were not as they had seemed to her when she arrived.

MC—CC he wrote.

As for the mysterious Mister Leroy Tanner, Roy was strongly of the opinion that no such person existed — still, it was possible, so he put this probable ghost in the column called *Maybes.*

Scratched *MLT* into the dirt there.

The deadly threat of Joe Brand — and therefore Fleet Darrow — was in *Certainties* of course. Sheriff Hosea Grimes too, as he clearly did Joe Brand's bidding.

Brand owning the Sheriff how he did, made the three of them even *more* dangerous.

JB, FD, SHG, he scratched in the dirt. Then he ran the stick over them letters again, etched 'em all in good and deep.

Biggest *Maybe* of all, was to do with identity.

Who Joe Brand was, was a question nowhere near settled. Still in the '*Maybes*' column, that one.

He scratched *JB* in the dirt there under the *Maybes* — which meant *JB* was now on both sides — then he ran a line up from the *JB* to the *MLT,* and made each end into an arrow. Almost certainly, Leroy Tanner was really Joe Brand. Chances seemed high, that Miss Charlotte had no idea what she'd let herself in for.

*Dang women shouldn't be allowed in stagecoaches —
leastways not without husbands. Should be a rule.*

Roy closed his eyes, let himself drift back in his
memories. Back where he didn't like going — back where
he mostly only went in bad dreams. He went back, he went
forward, he went backward and forward again. He tried to
imagine how time would have changed things, the passage
of years on a man — a particular man, a man called Big Jim
Starr.

Roy had cultivated fixed ideas on the subject of how
the years might have changed the man's looks — and he
now realized, fixed ideas could well be mistaken. His
thoughts drifted again, went to guns and to blood pooled on
floors and to blowed apart fingers. His thoughts went to
voices like spades in wet gravel, he heard things and felt
things, was too small then too big, saw guns with pearl
handles, saw gloves and felt how his neck tingled, not just
last night, or back when he was seven, but also — also,
right now.

He felt good healthy fear, and he opened his eyes with
a start, but no one was there. The Winchester was in his
hands before his eyes had time to focus.

Roy studied the damp dirt in front of him — the lines
and letters and scratches he'd made of his thoughts.

He stared at the *JB* he'd scratched in the dirt for Joe
Brand.

Then below it, so light the stick barely made an
impression, he scratched three more shapes into the dirt —
B J S.

He turned the thing over in his mind. Tasted the

possibility of it. He'd been tasting it twelve hours now, and the taste of it didn't seem right — but it wasn't wrong either.

Maybe, he thought again. *Maybe.*

Always figured I'd know for a certainty, the very moment I saw him.

He drew a circle, enclosed *JB* with *B J S.* Looked at it, maybe a minute, maybe an hour.

Didn't help.

There were too many *maybes,* and too many *certainties* too.

He closed his eyes, thought of Miss Charlotte Hawke. No matter what else, he had to see her right.

Someone had to protect her.

He kicked at the dirt then with the toe of his boots, kicked all other letters away, until all that remained was *MC,* and a whole lot of loose dirt all round it.

Finally, Roy drew a circle round the letters *MC* — but he'd done so in haste. And when he looked at it, the circle looked more like a heart.

He just about spat his next words. *"Dang fool women,"* he said, as he turned away from the evidence of his damn thoughts. *"Shouldn't be allowed to ride in stagecoaches at all."*

Then, one foot in front of the other, he commenced the walk back to town.

CHAPTER 24
WRITTEN IN STONE

Took only five minutes, the walk. Didn't help none. He was still kicking the dirt some when he walked down the back lane that led to the mercantile. Even the sight of that fine little gelding failed to cheer him as much it probably should have.

Everett was waiting there for him, nervously smoking. "We was worried, Roy. Didn't hear no shots, but you been gone more'n an hour."

"Curly'll be back in two days. Reckons Joe Brand'll plant me in the boneyard by then. Where's Hank?"

"He stayed upstairs by the window, in case there was something to see." Everett's eyes darted about, he took a final puff, threw what was left of his quirley on the ground, stamped it out and said, "Roy. I been thinkin' some on it, and I reckon Curly told you the truth. Brand'll have Darrow kill you when he sees you're still here, and the Sheriff'll ratify it somehow. He just don't *allow* men to go against his wishes — and he treated you fair with the money, told you not to come back."

"It *was* my money," Roy said. "Ain't like it was a gift."

"He won't like it, Roy, you know that even better'n I do."

"Well," Roy said with a laugh, "I guess I'd best get it over with then. I'm goin' down to see him right now, so he knows where we stand."

"No, Roy."

Roy made two nervous fists as he spoke, curled and uncurled them, danced some too, on his toes. "Everett. You know how you had no choice about delivering your wife to Cheyenne? Well, I ain't got no damn choice neither."

"Miss Charlotte?"

"Yes. But not only her. There's something I have to find out. Something maybe only Joe Brand can tell me."

"Oh, Roy. I thought you was sharper than that. You're acting like some fool kid who thinks he's a gunfighter. Them kids get shot up, soon as they run into a Brand, or a Darrow, or even a damn Sheriff Grimes."

"You got me wrong, Everett." Roy checked that no one was watching, untucked his shirt, then untied the money belt he wore underneath it.

"Please, Roy," said Everett. "I'll give you this little bay horse you like. Look at him there, ready and waiting. You can ride outta town, maybe head to Rapid City, Brand'll never know you came back. Maybe go to Sidney from there. You made some money, had an adventure, got gifted a nice little horse — ain't all that enough?"

Roy handed the money belt to his friend. "If I die, you're to buy Miss Charlotte's freedom with this money."

"What in blazes are you—?"

Roy gripped his friend's shoulder as he spoke. "Only offer three-thousand at first — he'll go back on his word once he has it, but don't argue with him or get angry. Let him push up the price, he might let her go by the time you get up to seven."

"Roy, you lost your damn mind or what?"

"I'm trusting you, Everett," Roy said, looking into the eyes of his friend. "Don't go past seven-thousand. Don't sass him, only talk to him in public, don't go in his office. If he don't let her go once he's taken the seven, it'll mean he *is* who I think he is — so if it comes to that, you go to Deadwood and hire a top man to kill him. Whatever it takes. There's twelve-thousand dollars in there."

"What the—?"

"Keep whatever's left over, but make sure Miss Charlotte goes free, whatever it takes."

"Roy. This all don't seem..." Everett ran out of words then. Could see Roy wasn't loco, didn't know what to do, what to say.

"You'll do it for me, Everett?"

"Sure, Roy."

"Don't waste much on my burial. And don't put *Peabody* on my grave marker, that ain't and never was my name. Don't put no last name at all. Just Roy'll do. Just write *Roy, 22, done his best.* But make sure the marker's of stone."

"Written in stone, that's forever."

Roy nodded and said, "Stone," enjoying his own private joke. Then he turned and walked away from his friend, perhaps for the very last time.

CHAPTER 25
FEATHERS

"Roy, wait, I'll come with you," Everett called after him.

But Roy told him to stay, said he had to do this alone. Said it was all maybe nothing. That he'd likely be back in twenty minutes.

And he took off his hat, ran his fingers through his hair, smiled at Everett, turned away. Put his hat back on his head and strode off toward Joe Brand's Golden Nugget Saloon.

It was still before midday, a Saturday, plenty of people about as Roy walked down the boardwalk. He held the Winchester in one hand, and he felt as wild and free as he had when he'd galloped the horse on the trail that morning.

If he died, he would not die alone.

Out front of the Golden Nugget, tied to a hitching post, was Silver Sam's bony old gray. Roy ran a hand over his neck a few times, smiled and said, "Looks like you and your owner might both yet outlive me, old boy."

Then he turned, took three steps forward, pushed the batwing doors aside and walked in.

First thing, from his right, the voice of Fleet Darrow, amused as ever was. "That was quick, Kid." Then louder, he called out, "Hey, Boss, you owe me a thousand."

Roy had spun quick to face him, but there was no danger. Not yet.

Darrow was seated at a corner table, front right corner of the room, back to the side wall, all alone and eating a steak. "Come sit awhile, Kid, while we wait. You hungry?"

Roy stayed where he was, glanced about the big room, almost empty. Barman polishing glasses; Silver Sam at the bar looking tidier than he had last night; four men playing poker off to the left of the room — a painted cat stood behind the youngest of the four, running her fingers through his hair before cackling loudly. She was pretty 'til she'd opened her mouth.

"Kid," Darrow said, then he sighed. "I told you, come sit awhile. Boss'll be down in a minute, and we'll all have a talk."

Roy walked over to Darrow. No one complained about him keeping the Winchester with him.

"Mister Darrow," he said politely, but didn't sit down yet.

Darrow sighed again, slowly put down his knife and fork, put his hands out away from his sides, and slowly, he stood.

"See, Kid? Put it down, you're not under threat. If you were..."

He had no need to finish the statement. Roy took the

seat against the front wall, leaned the little Winchester against it beside him. Aside from the seat Fleet Darrow was in, this was the best in the room.

Darrow picked up a whole egg, forked it into his mouth, chewed it a little and swallowed. He picked up a napkin, wiped a small yellow trickle of egg from the corner of his mouth, pointed the napkin at Roy and asked, "You have trouble with our mutual friend, Kid?"

"No, Mister Darrow."

"Good," was all the gunman said.

"Why does Mister Brand owe you a thousand?"

"He reckoned you too clever to come back. But when I said 'See you again,' you told me to bet on it. I always was one to follow a tip when I get one. Thanks a lot, Kid. I just hope the *boss* don't resent it."

"Me too, Mister Darrow. Me too. Ain't you gonna ask why I'm back?"

"Now why would I do that? Not like it's any great mystery."

Roy's head spun some then. *Did* they know? Too many things went through his head then. *What? Which things could they know?*

And right then came that voice, like a spade digging into wet gravel. "This what you come back for, Kid?"

And there at the top of the stairs was a sight unexpected — standing in front of Joe Brand, in red and in white and in purple, in feathers, in silk, and in lace, dressed up like the highest class whore any man ever saw, was Miss Charlotte Hawke.

CHAPTER 26
BEAUTIFUL LIES

Roy was barely aware of Joe Brand in that terrible moment. If they'd had any notion to kill him, Darrow coulda done it seven times over, and Roy would never have noticed. The man could have whistled a tune as he walked to the bar; could have reached down behind it and picked up a shotgun and loaded it; could have turned back around and blew Roy all full of dark holes.

Roy was looking at Miss Charlotte — but Miss Charlotte wasn't looking at Roy. Indeed, she was actively *not* looking at him.

Then Joe Brand's gravel voice broke into the moment. "Well, say hello to your friend." He was behind her — had hold of her somehow, Roy knew.

If he went for the Winchester, he'd be dead before he touched it. He knew the upset showed on his face. He was a child again — half helpless, and half filled with vengeance. The heartbreak was written on him clear, and he sorely knew it.

"Hello, Roy," she said then, her voice so broken and small it barely carried down to where he sat. "I thought you were going on to Deadwood."

"Hello, Miss Charlotte," he said. "Changed my mind."

"I'm sorry, Roy."

By then, he was starting to think clearly again. "It's alright," he said. "I knew."

She burst into tears, as he knew she would — but it had to be done.

"Get along to your room, Girl," growled Joe Brand, and he slapped her a crisp one on the back of her bare thigh, the sound like a whip to Roy's ears. And Miss Charlotte darted away, was gone from his sight.

"You must be right angry with her, Kid," Brand said with a laugh, as he made his way down the stairs. "Damn whores make fools of us all, 'til we learn how to treat 'em."

Roy gathered his thoughts, and he realized they still had it wrong. There was hope yet for Miss Charlotte, and hope yet for himself.

Darrow spoke from beside him, and for once, his voice was not mocking. "Forget it, Kid, they all lie, she never meant it personal against you."

As Joe Brand passed the bar, the barman handed him a bottle of whiskey and three glasses. Then as Brand was approaching he said, "Took you in good, didn't she, kid? Wouldn't be the first time a whore lied about her occupation. Tell me, when did you work out what she was?"

Fleet Darrow loved a gamble, couldn't help himself

interrupting. "It was when she spoke false at the Sheriff's Office," he said. "Two-hundred says the kid knew it then."

"I'll take your two-hundred," said Brand. "Kid still didn't know when he left here last night. He worked it out this morning when he saw I'd had Curly'd beaten." He put the glasses down, then the bottle.

He's wearing the gloves again.

Situation could have been worse. The certainties and maybes were changing each moment, but Roy knew he had something to work with.

His mother's words came to him now — *'Fear's good and natural, it'll save you again and again, long as you pay attention, and never stop thinking.'*

Roy thought quick, and he also thought clear. He needed to buy a little time. Looked as broken and sad as he could. "Can I have a drink?"

Darrow poured one for each of them. "Let's drink to *them* — to all the *nymphs du prairie,* and their wonderful, beautiful lies," he said.

He and Brand raised their glasses in a toast, and held them up a few moments before drinking — though Darrow held his spare hand over his heart, while Brand put his over his pocketbook — but Roy only raised his the briefest of moments, swallowed it down, then said, "Could I have another?"

"Soon as you give us the answer, you can drink the whole damn bottle," Brand answered. He was clearly enjoying Roy's suffering.

"I ain't maybe so clever as some," said Roy. "But I'd sure

like to know, Mister Darrow, how you knew to say Mister Tanner sent you, when we got off the stage."

Darrow's eyes darted from Roy to Joe Brand then back again. It was a stumble of sorts, but he sure come up from it quick. "She told us by letter, of course, Kid. Mister Brand's associate back East had warned her of starry-eyed kids making marriage proposals — so she had the idea to tell she was already betrothed. Wrote Mister Brand to pick her up from the stage, and say Mister Tanner had sent him, in case of young fools."

"Dammit," Roy exclaimed, "I *was* a damn fool. A little. I mean, I never asked her to ... well, you know."

Brand, pouring the drinks, said, "So when was it, Kid? When did you know for sure she was a whore?"

And Roy said, "Figured it out when the stage left town just this morning. Ground was still wet, got me thinkin'. Remembered it stormed and rained most of the night, so Mister Damn Invisible Tanner couldn't have driven her nowhere, it being too dark for travel. Thought back on how keen she was to stay with the Sheriff — barely offered so much as goodbye, once we was down there. Thought about that some more, and knew then it was all made up stories she'd told from the start. One damn game after another, just playing with my heart all for practice, or maybe for fun. Though maybe she liked me some too, and hoped not to hurt me."

Fleet Darrow laughed and said, "You still owe me eight-hundred, Boss."

"Don't take it personal, Kid," said Joe Brand. "If you

knew the first thing about women, it's that they're all whores at heart."

"Not Miss Charlotte! There's *more* to Miss Charlotte than that!"

"Oh, Kid," said Fleet Darrow, "you're a riot. We should keep the kid around for entertainment, Boss. How's about you give him a job?"

"I don't want no job," said Roy. "I want my dang lucky streak back. I want ... I mean I thought ... I mean, it ain't right, this whole thing. Miss Charlotte's too *good* to be whoring."

That set both Brand *and* Darrow to loud guffawing. They slapped their thighs and laughed it up big, and it gave Roy a few seconds to study Joe Brand's face without arousing suspicion.

He had always figured Big Jim Starr would change his appearance as well as his name. But he had been a great bear of a man, with not just a dark beard, but hair growing full from every part of his head.

This man had no hair at all. And yet ... *and yet...*

It had been fifteen years. Big Jim had been thirty-five then, he knew that for a fact. Could such a flocculent feller go so bald so quick? He sure was big enough to be Starr — and mean enough too. Ugly of heart and of word.

Sudden-like, Roy had stared for too long.

"What the hell you lookin' at, Kid?" Joe Brand's dark eyes bored into Roy, and for a long second, he feared the man knew exactly what he'd been thinking.

"Sorry, Mister Brand," Roy somehow managed to say. "I was lookin' straight through you, I guess, and my Pa would sure whip me for doin' so. Least he would if he was here."

"That a fact, Kid?"

Roy warmed to his task — he needed to set them to thinking he had no clue what the truth about Miss Charlotte was.

"Yessir, Mister Brand, sir. He's a mean one for manners, my Pa. Truth is, my head weren't even here, let alone starin' or studyin' sensible. I was caught up in thinkin' of Miss Charlotte, and about what *you* said. Reckon you're maybe right, and I *am* a mite angry, her takin' me for a fool."

"Don't take it too personal, Kid," said Joe Brand. "She might well'a took me in too, back when I was your age. All them fancy manners, them big innocent eyes, and that soft way she has of speaking. *'Words soft as skin,'* that's what my man back East told me. One reason he offered her the job, and top money with it. But she knows just what she's here for, Kid, make no mistake about that."

CHAPTER 27
A PAIN IN THE NETHERS

Roy's head was a little light, unaccustomed to strong drink as he was, and having had two in succession. But he made out he was worse off than that, played on it good. He cried, "How much?" Then he banged his glass down on the table, let his eyes run all wild, like he'd come to a new way of thinking, and no one could stop him.

Joe Brand laughed and said, "How much indeed? She's untouched goods yet, Kid. That's why I paid so much for her. She'll draw quite a premium, first time."

"Not that, Mister Brand. I mean, how much would you sell her for? Your interest? I know you racked up expenses, and she can earn you five dollars on top of five dollars, and night after night a few years. But when I thought she wasn't a whore, I just about..."

Roy went quiet then, looked at Joe Brand then Fleet Darrow, then away from them both. Done the best he could to look ashamed and embarrassed.

"Just about what, Kid?" said Fleet Darrow. "Come on, let us hear it, this is some prime entertainment."

"Leave the kid alone, Darrow," said Brand, but he sure didn't mean it. "I'd have you say it anyway, Kid. I need to be clear on what you mean, to make a decision. Best for us both that you put every fact on the table."

"I ... aw, Mister Brand, Mister Darrow, this ain't hardly fair and you know it. I thought I could love her, you see, and I ain't ashamed to admit I was fooled, she's a real good liar like you said."

"They all are," said Darrow, and he poured himself another drink. "Still, they're not to be blamed, way men treat 'em."

"But she's young yet," said Roy, "and Mister Brand, if it's true what you said—"

"Which part?"

"About her bein' as yet untouched."

"It's guaranteed — I had my most experienced whore do a check. She wouldn't be game to lie to me — it'd be worth her life."

"Well, I know it sounds foolish. But I reckon Miss Charlotte might yet make a wife, Mister Brand, and I got money to pay you for all your expenses, and a real good profit."

Brand looked into Roy's eyes. "How much you got, Kid?"

But Darrow shook his head, laughed it up and said, "Shoulda had this discussion at night, all lit up on the stage. Coulda charged folks ten dollars to watch it, and cheap at the price."

"Shut up, Fleet," said Brand. "Forget him, Kid, how much you got?"

"I got two-thousand, you know that." He studied Brand's face, pushed himself to look like he believed the man might say yes.

Joe Brand laughed then, laughed in his face. "Fleet's right," he said. "You *are* hilarious, Kid. But I'll tell you what. Make me a strong offer, you might get first run at the whore."

"But ... please, Mister Brand."

"I bid five-hundred," Fleet Darrow said. Then he turned toward Roy and added, "Sorry, Kid, but I ain't had a beginner since I was fourteen, and this one's adorable pretty."

Roy looked at Fleet Darrow like he might cry. Wasn't hard. He didn't speak for the moment, he was trying to think. He looked up at Joe Brand.

Seemed to Roy that Brand had organized his doughy features into a most evil shape. Way his little eyes almost disappeared, and his mouth almost drooled as it twisted the ugly words up from the depths of his badness. "You'd pay more than five-hundred, the both of you. But you give me an idea, Fleet. Reckon we'll have ourselves an auction, give the winner first run at the prize."

"Now that's some inspired thinkin', Boss," said Darrow. "This is why I like workin' for you, I just love a good entertainment. How's about tonight, on the stage?"

"*No!*" cried Roy, clearly panicked — wasn't *all* acting neither. "I ... what if I ain't got enough money? What if someone outbids me?"

"Kid's got his heart set on bein' her first, Boss. You gotta admire his sweetness. Should be some fun auction alright."

"Give me a week, Mister Brand," said Roy, sounding suitably desperate. "I been on a lucky streak, I just bet I can win some more money by then, playin' poker."

He was trying to buy time. And maybe he *was* on a lucky streak after all — for Joe Brand's massive mouth opened wide as he burst into laughter, and changed the whole game.

"Share the joke, Boss?"

"Kid gave me a top-notch idea. You ever been married, Fleet?"

"Knew a lotta miserable fellers who were, but not me. My own Grandpappy taught me all I ever needed to know. Set me down and explained me that marriage was a fine, enjoyable thing — first week or two of it. After that, a damn persistent pain in the nethers."

"I was married one time," called out one of the miners. "And your Grandpappy had it to rights. One *damn* fine week I had of it — follered close up by five long years a'misery, true as I'm a top-notch drunk'n a gambler, feckless'n bootless'n broke more off'n than not."

"See, that's just it exactly," said Joe Brand, slapping Darrow on the shoulder. "Kid's a damn genius, is what he is.

"How so, Mister Brand?" asked Roy. "You sayin' you *would* sell Miss Charlotte to me? If I get some more money?"

"You'd need an awful lot for that, Kid. And I just couldn't do it. Be a terrible thing, good kid like you, throwin' your whole life away on a whore. But that idea, about the *week*. There's a seed in that there idea, and it's all germinated inside me, and soon to bear fruit."

"Shoulda done this at night on the stage," said Fleet Darrow again. "Even better'n four pink-dressed whores kickin' legs up to music — though them four's hard to beat, if you take 'em all upstairs right after, get the room with the big bed."

Roy looked at him then, eyes wide open, like as if he'd never heard of such a thing. Darrow laughed right at him, of course, even wiggled his eyebrows.

Then Joe Brand looked from one to the other, said, "Here it is, boys, for the truth. We send word to Deadwood, let 'em all know that the prettiest, softest, most chaste and virginal whore ever was, is right here in Custer City, half-dressed and ready to be auctioned."

Darrow whistled in admiration, while Roy looked suitably crestfallen, then Brand went on.

"Here's the clever part," Brand said. "Instead of just one poke — or even an entire night — we allow the winning bidder a room here. That man and his ... his *One Good Week Bride,* there you go, that's what we'll call her. See how it's genius, boys? They gets a room here for a week, which is, as previous stated, the one top-notch part of a marriage — then he's free of the rotten damn whore the rest of his life."

"Forget the damn auction, Boss, I'll give you a thousand right now, go directly upstairs."

"Twelve-hundred," said Roy.

"Twelve-fifty," Silver Sam called from the bar, clear as

ever a word had been spoken. Barman got such a shock he dropped a damn glass on the floor, and the whole place went silent, as everyone there turned and stared. Then old Silver Sam shrugged and said, "Man gets old still feels his oats, time to time."

"I'd pay five-hundred to watch you die trying, Old Man," said Fleet Darrow. "Reckon one glimpse of her naked'd kill you, my friend."

"Ah, but what a fine way to go," said Silver Sam wistfully. And his rheumy eyes looked up above him then, appearing to follow *something* the others couldn't see — *angels perhaps,* Roy decided.

Then Fleet Darrow busted the silence, as his voice rang out clear, "Fifteen-hundred."

But before Roy — or anyone else — could speak, Joe Brand said, "Tell you what, all you boys. I ain't greedy, we'll leave all the Deadwood crew out of it. Why should they get in on our fun? We'll run an auction tonight when the Nugget is busy — twenty-five-hundred reserve. If I don't get twenty-five-hundred, I'll happily enjoy her myself."

CHAPTER 28
NEWS TRAVELS FAST

Everett and Hank wore identical expressions of relief when they saw Roy still alive. They had watched, plenty worried, from their vantage point down the street — could barely believe it was him when he stepped out the Golden Nugget's doors and into the sunshine.

"Longest hour a'my life," said Everett, when Roy met up with them inside the mercantile. Everett wasted no time untucking his shirt to relieve himself of his burden. "Here, take your damn money belt back, it weighed on me somethin' terrible."

Clearly, he hadn't told his brother about it, for Hank wore a look of great puzzlement when he said, "Heavy? Couldn't weigh but three or four pounds, less you filled it with coin."

"Wasn't that sort of weight that was doing the weighing," Everett told him. "You're just lucky I spared you the details, what the belt meant. Well, what happened, Roy?"

"News ain't great, but it could be worse. I'll tell it as we go — you boys must have a whole lotta work needs doing, and helping you some might assist me to think."

Roy rode the little bay gelding beside their buckboard, told them most of what happened as they went, and the rest while they ate a good meal of bacon and eggs.

"Can't believe that lovely little girl took up cat-work," Everett said when Roy finished.

Roy looked at him, taken aback, and realized he'd left out some key parts of the story — the part where Miss Charlotte had been tricked, being the part most important. But he didn't have time to say anything before Hank spoke up.

"Whores is just like other women, Ev. Deep down I mean — and don't go degradin' that statement, and makin' out I meant somethin' dirtful."

"I know what you meant," said Everett, "and I wasn't about to accuse you. I even agree with you, mostly. But dammit, Hank, if you met this *particular* girl, you'd be better able to grasp all my meaning. Doesn't ring true somehow. Is there something else to it, Roy?"

"Could be," Roy said. He popped an oversized chunk of prime bacon into his mouth, and commenced to chew a whole lotta chewing. Better than having to answer in detail — he wanted to consider the whole thing more carefully, and only tell his new friends what he had to. Half to help keep them safe; half to keep them out of his way; and half to keep them from letting something slip to Joe Brand if he asked them.

Least of that side they know the better. At least for the moment.

All Hank and Everett knew really, was that there was to be an auction, and Roy planned on winning it.

Even if he hadn't told them, they'd have heard soon enough. News traveled quick in Custer City, and Joe Brand was making double sure he'd get a big crowd tonight for the auction.

Roy and the twins couldn't barely get any work done, way folks kept stopping by to spread news of it.

It wasn't ideal. Roy would have preferred that the auction didn't happen just yet. But at least it kept the Deadwood folk out of it, and Curly wouldn't be here to complicate things. And Roy knew one thing for a certainty — Joe Brand knew the value of a girl being untouched, so Miss Charlotte was safe for the moment.

Long as she does nothing stupid, anyways.

Problem was, there was no other lawman around here with any sort of jurisdiction. Grimes was the County Sheriff, and there wasn't no way to trump him aside from a bullet. If Roy could somehow get a United States Marshal involved, there was maybe a chance of getting Miss Charlotte out unharmed.

But that wasn't going to happen, nohow and no way. Custer City was a long way from meaningful law. The *existence* of telegraph wires was one thing — the fact that the Telegraph Office was part of the Sheriff's Office made it another thing altogether.

Might as well just invite 'em to shoot me, as try to send a telegraph message. I'd be dead before sunrise.

So much for wishes, hopes and maybes.

All he had to count on for sure was the auction — and Roy was a man for practicalities; for thinking on his feet; for allowing plans time to unfold. As long as he won the auction, he might buy himself a week in which to do something.

And there yet exists the possibility of that ally.

He helped the twins a few hours, wrote two letters, had an afternoon nap to build some energy, cleared his head best he could.

He fired the four slugs from the derringer, cleaned and oiled it, took utmost care reloading it fresh.

Then just before dark, the three of them headed into town and ate at the restaurant.

The town was abuzz, for sure and for certain, and many things still undecided — most especially Miss Charlotte's future — but Roy was a man well prepared, and he'd give it his best.

CHAPTER 29
THE PRIZE

The Golden Nugget Saloon was full near to bursting by the time Roy walked in with the twins. Further along the street, the Nugget's only opposition — the Strike It Lucky Saloon — was more or less empty, for the very first Saturday night in its two-year history.

Roy had known Joe Brand would not start without him. Indeed, he knew Brand's whole plan, for he'd been there when the man worked it out.

Brand had advertised an eight o'clock start time — but he knew such an auction would draw a huge crowd, and a huge crowd meant extra profit. He would drag it out several hours, keep the men drinking and gambling and spending, make it an event to remember — keep it going, one way or another, for most of the night.

One reason Roy took his time getting there was to allow all others to have more time drinking. His plan was to gamble, of course — to win all he could at the tables, make sure he had the money to outbid all others.

He figured the bidding may even surpass what Joe Brand expected — but five-thousand would surely be enough. That amount seemed plumb crazy, for it was a *thousand* times the usual price of five dollars.

But Miss Charlotte was special, she was — and money worked different in mining camps, that was a fact. When every day is a gamble, and fortunes are suddenly made on the scrape of a shovel or the swish of a gold pan, men tend to throw money around like it's water. And somehow they understand too, that each day might well be their last — so they spend up big when they have it, and damn the next day.

Roy wore the money belt — just in case — but he only left five-thousand in it, hid the rest at the pig farm. Showed Everett where, of course. Told him if anything went wrong, to do as he'd asked him to earlier. "Just the last bit."

Everett had seemed balled-up, bamboozled and buffaloed then. He had previously thought it all settled, regarding Miss Charlotte becoming a painted cat from her own choosing — and therefore not requiring saving.

But Everett, too, was a man for practicalities and getting on with things, so he'd only said, "Money's for the bounty to have someone kill Brand, right?"

And Roy had said, "Yes. There's a note I wrote too, that explains it. Explains just what to do, every step. But don't read it 'til after I'm dead, that's proper important."

It was almost nine when they walked in, and the four

pink-dressed ladies kicked their legs up higher than ever, in time with the music.

The place was all such a place should be — smoky and happy and musical and gay. The only thing flowing faster than whiskey was all the dang money at the tables.

Roy hadn't been inside five minutes when a seat became vacant at a poker table and he slid on into it. The deck wasn't marked, and any spills on the table were quickly cleaned up by the staff.

Seemed like Joe Brand had determined the place should seem straight as a gun-barrel — *seem* being the word that most mattered. It was unlikely the Roulette and Faro would be any straighter than the left hind leg of an old yellow dog with the rheumatizz.

Roy took only two hands to settle in, to make as sure as he could that no one was cheating — though he always at least half-expected it.

It was clear by all conversation that the nature of tonight's auction had all the men's spirits up. It was something different — unique, in its way — and to men who toil day after day, digging and scratching in rock and water and mud, the promise of something pure had sparked their attentions.

Miss Charlotte's the prize, and there's men here determined on winning.

Roy was surprised by the stakes at the table he sat at. On a normal night, the word "hundred" would draw a small crowd to watch. *Every* hand here was going that high.

Second hand he played, he won over four-hundred dollars, with only a pair of Queens. Didn't even seem possible. Made him wonder what Deadwood itself would be like on a good night.

By the time the four pink-clad ladies left the stage, Roy was already winning two-thousand, and Fleet Darrow joined the table.

"Kid," he said. "I see your lucky streak's back."

"Mister Darrow," Roy replied with a nod as he shuffled the cards. "Thought it was my lucky night. But you sitting down makes me wonder if my piece of pudding's over. No offense meant."

"None taken, Kid. Just figured you to be my main opposition for the auction. If I can limit the size of your bank ... worth a try."

Roy looked into Darrow's eyes as he dealt. "Truth is, Mister Darrow, I was hoping you might let me win."

Fleet Darrow's eyes narrowed just a little, then he started, slowly, to smile. The other two men had picked up their cards, but not Roy or Darrow, not yet. Then Darrow chuckled, slapped the table, picked up his cards and said, "You're somethin' alright, Kid. For a moment I thought you was serious. Don't go gettin' killed, Kid, you're too much good fun."

Roy smiled and said, "Thanks, Mister Darrow. Don't you go gettin' killed neither."

CHAPTER 30
AN UNBROKEN FILLY

Turned out Darrow was more-or-less no good at cards. Indeed, he didn't hardly bet, but just kept a close eye on Roy, way he'd been sent to.

Roy won a few, lost a few. Couldn't let Fleet Darrow catch on to how good he was, as it might become important later on. He still added to his bank overall, but he did so in such a way he just looked like a kid on a lucky streak, rather than a gambler who knew all about what he was doing.

He made certain to make one or two fool mistakes, even lost a thousand dollar pot he should have won, then swore at himself like he'd really lost his composure.

Secret to poker wasn't what most thought it was.

Secret to poker was *acting,* Roy had learned a long time ago. And while some acting's done with the body, the best, most convincing part of it is done with the eyes.

An old voice creaked its way to Roy's mind now. *"Long as a man can read eyes, he yet stands a chance of survival, no matter the stakes."*

Roy balled up his fists in mock frustration, as he watched the man to his left scoop the thousand toward him with his big gnarly hands — even the most successful miner loves the feeling of a good win at poker. Miners are gamblers at heart — that's the simple of it.

Roy could feel Darrow's eyes on him as he sat now, balling his fists ever tighter. Then he blinked maybe four or five times, and screwed shut his eyes. "I give up, Mister Darrow," he said then. "I can't take this no more, it's eatin' away at me, all the not knowing and such."

"Come on, Kid," said Darrow, "we'll go have a drink, come back and play when your nerves are more steady."

Soon as they left the table to walk to the bar, Fleet Darrow stopped, pointed to the top of the stairs, and said, "Watch, Kid, this'll be a fine entertainment."

It was Joe Brand up there, his baldness disguised by a big fancy top hat, his massive body covered by a European suit, the coat of it having tails almost to the floor. He took out a pearl-handled revolver, fired it into a beam above his head.

A half-moment later, Roy understood where the words *dead quiet* first came from.

Worse than midnight in a boneyard it was, and he felt dizzy with anticipation.

It's going to happen.

"LADIES ... AND ... WHOREMONGERS," Joe Brand cried at the top of his great graveled voice, and the hairs on the back of Roy's neck danced a polka, but in double-time, and he thought he might nearly be sick.

"Tonight," Brand went on, "for your worldly pleasure,

the Golden Nugget presents, the auction for the One ...
Good ... Week ... BRIDE."

He fired the gun again with his right hand, held out
his left as Miss Charlotte shuffled into view — *timid and
fearful* — from the hallway that side. The Sheriff was a
half-step behind her, holding her left hand, as she reached
out for Joe Brand's left hand with her right. And of
course, she was dressed in the outfit Roy had seen her in
earlier.

Shocked him some now, in a way it hadn't before, the
sight of her bare legs on display, for every leering man in
the place to lust after.

She smiled — or rather, showed her teeth and tried not
to cry — then she jumped a little in fright, as a brass band
quartet came from Brand's other side, playing a lively tune
fit for the Fourth of July.

Must have been two-hundred men in that room — and
by the sound of it, a hundred-and-ninety-eight of them
broke into a ruckus of whistles and cheers and catcalls.
Only two men stayed silent was Roy and Fleet Darrow, it
seemed like.

Even the painted doves were all cheering, and it hurt
Roy's heart as he watched Miss Charlotte break a little
right then. Helpless, that's how she seemed, as her eyes
sought the heavens.

Then Joe Brand and Sheriff Hosea Grimes commenced
to lead her down the stairs, each of them holding one of her
delicate hands. They stopped four steps down though, and
then Brand released her. He half turned toward her, used
one hand to indicate the assembled rabble should be quiet,

and the other to point out the prize that awaited the winner of tonight's auction.

They hushed right away, as commanded.

"Is she not the most perfect beauty all you men ever saw?"

They roared their approval — and again, Joe Brand put a hand up to quieten them.

"This is the prize — and such a one as will haunt the dreams of each man who misses out. Let me tell you right now, she ain't gonna be cheap, but she's gonna be worth every penny."

"A hundred," someone called.

"A thousand!"

"*Quiet,*" Joe Brand called then. "Quiet." Then he took off that tall foolish hat and held it before him, his face dark and grave.

And as serious as an Undertaker, he said, "Ladies and whoremongers. No man — or woman for that matter — will be refused the right to bid on this magnificent specimen of young womanhood. She is ... *UNTOUCHED* ... guaranteed. Eighteen years she's waited for this moment. From a fine family, descended from French Royalty, that there's the truth of it. And possessed of a softness of voice, a softness of skin and of heart, that makes her so *precious* ... so *unique* ... so *desirable* ... that I may yet change my mind, and outbid you all!"

A few men, perhaps drunker than the rest, let their feelings on that be known, and commenced to hiss, and to boo — but Brand didn't take it so harsh as he usually would have. He threw his hands up before him, said, "Just making sure you were listening, boys. I'll take myself out of the running — had myself an unbroken filly two years back in Cheyenne, and I'd reckon it greedy of me to take this one too. And I tell you, promise you true, for those who ain't had the experience — though the one in Cheyenne didn't no way compare to the beauty of the woman before you — there ain't no pleasure comes close in the whole damn wide world."

The crowd sure were worked up by now, but Brand wasn't done. He stood nearby to Miss Charlotte, held his two gloved hands in front of his eyes, and looked at them in wonder, as if they'd caught him in a trance.

"Imagine, these hands of mine, if these hands was yours. Why, surely you'd not keep them gloved, when so near such a woman."

Then he waved the hands around some, like each was a magic Persian carpet, then set the hands moving all about Miss Charlotte's body — following her curves, as it were, but never quite touching, and wearing a look of great wonder on his gruesome, grisly face.

"Oh, if these hands were your hands," he said. "And for a whole week, to touch where you choose — and not only with hands, but anything else you can think of!"

Roy became aware then that Fleet Darrow was watching him closely. "It ain't right," Roy said to him. "It just ain't, no matter that she agreed to come here and work. It's degrading, Mister Darrow, it is."

"I don't much like it neither," said Darrow, then he shrugged his shoulders and slapped Roy a good one on the back. "Entertaining though, I guess, for those debauched and dissolute."

"Alright, whoremongers," Brand shouted then. "This now was only a look, a chance for you all to see the quality of tonight's merchandise. Who knows how long it'll be 'til such an opportunity next presents itself? Likely never, I'd reckon — life is short, friends, as you know, and we'll all be in Hell soon. So get back to them tables, win up big as you can, the auction's on in an hour." Then he looked about the room and said, "There can be only one winner — but remember, it's for the whole *WEEK*. A whole *week* of *owning* this perfect young woman — a whole *week* where she won't say no, no matter the extent of your disgusting depravity! *Drinks half price, next fifteen minutes!*"

CHAPTER 31

"FUN, AIN'T IT?"

I t was a gambler's damn paradise, and Roy couldn't even enjoy it. Problem was, Miss Charlotte was a rare treasure, and such an opportunity as was here being offered, might never come up again — not a legal one anyways. So he'd guessed all along that the bidding would go pretty high.

But he had *not* reckoned on Joe Brand's showmanship, on the man's great ability to whip a crowd into a fervor. He considered sending Everett back to the pig farm to collect the rest of his money — but then, if things went awry, that money would be needed later.

No, he decided, *I'm a gambler, and this whole situation was made for me. If I can't even do this, how will I ever muster the nerve to kill Big Jim Starr?*

Naturally, most men figured their best chance to be Faro, Dice or Roulette. But Roy knew all that was plain foolish — the chances of any of those games being played straight were about non-existent. Especially on such a big night.

No, poker was the true opportunity, as always. There were several games going, and Roy wasted no time finding one. He figured he had two hours — Joe Brand would put off the auction as long as he could. Keep the men gambling he would, keep the money flowing in.

Roy had walked in tonight with five-thousand, and had added two more so far. Fleet Darrow was off at the Faro, keeping an eye on things, which left Roy pretty much free to keep steadily winning. Within a half hour, three new men had come and gone from his table, and Roy had won another two-thousand.

Then that gambler he'd butted heads with in Reno — *Dan Turner,* he'd gone by there — sat down across the table from Roy.

What the dickens is going on here?

The gambler was possessed of a sharpness not often seen — an intelligence of the eye would be one way to put it. A handsome man still, even though he must be pushing fifty. He had grown a long drooping mustache since Reno, and his graying hair was long too, in the style of Wild Bill Hickock. "Evening, boys," he said with a slight nod to each of them.

The other two players only grunted, but Roy said, "Busy night, Mister, how goes the battle?"

"Won some, lost some," the man said. "Name's Daniel Rowntree."

Roy answered, "Roy Peabody," and *Rowntree* smiled

ever so slightly, then picked up the deck and examined it a moment or two.

"Ain't a damn social club," growled the man to Roy's right. "Poker's the game, not conversatin'. Shoot, Luke, or give up the gun."

"I've always thought that a dangerous expression," the gambler replied, and commenced then to shuffle the cards. *"Shoot, Luke ... or give up the gun."* He'd said it slowly and clearly, enunciating each syllable as if it was a taste to be savored — and he looked at Roy the whole time. "Its meaning is apt to be misconstrued, and a thinking man might do well to consider each possible interpretation."

The man who'd originally said it glared at Rowntree a moment. "You here to teach lessons or gamble, Mister?"

"Perhaps a little of each," Rowntree answered, continuing to shuffle. "Indeed, one often melds with the other, don't you find, in a fortunate cohabitation?"

"You talk funny, Mister, and I don't cotton to it — or to you." The whiskey-slugging miner was of that type whose anger grows by the glassful.

This fool miner ain't got no idea of the danger he's in.

But Rowntree stayed calm as a lamb. "Apologies, dear Sir," he said. "Meaningless patter on my part. I do it only to soothe my own fractured nerves." Then he started to deal, which seemed to placate the feller some.

Thing is, there's gamblers and *gamblers* — and like any other profession, those few who excel can do things that ordinary folk only dream of.

Dan Turner — or rather, Daniel Rowntree, as he was

now known — was assuredly one of that type. It was two years since Reno, and Roy was already pretty good then. He had made things difficult for the more experienced man, but Roy wasn't yet good enough to beat him, not at that time.

Still, Roy had been an inconvenience — for Rowntree was not a flashy type either. He too preferred to win slow and steady, not take too much from any one man, not get noticed no more than he needed to.

When Roy had sat at the man's table in Reno, he'd had to sorely extend himself — he and Roy both — and before long, the pair had got noticed, and drawn quite a crowd.

Roy had no idea why the man had come to his table now — they had dined together after their battle in Reno, and made an agreement to stay out of each other's way ever after.

Still, this was no ordinary night. Perhaps 'Daniel Rowntree' had designs on Miss Charlotte, and knew Roy was the man he must beat.

Still, them words were right strange. He wasn't so cryptic in Reno, wasn't like that at all. Said what he meant, meant what he said. Why so different?

When Rowntree dealt that first hand, Roy found himself looking at a King and four Aces.

He looked at the cards, put 'em face down on the table, kept his hand over the top of 'em. Looked across at Rowntree, who looked back at him plenty amused.

Roy used his eyes to send some thoughts at the man. *You tryin' to get us both killed? Or just me?*

Rowntree sent some thoughts right on back. *Fun, ain't it?*

Roy only bet ten dollars like the feller to his right did, and got rid of two of his cards, an Ace and the King. When Rowntree dealt the extras, he'd given Roy two more Kings.

What are you up to?

When the bet came around, Roy knew it'd seem funny if he didn't raise, and worse if anyone looked at his cards if he folded. Looking at discarded cards was bad form, but sometimes men did it when drunk, and there'd sure be questions to answer if it happened here.

And these fellers are drunker'n skunks at a once-a-year skunk dance.

Feller to Roy's right dropped out, Roy raised forty, then the last feller raised again, went all-in, every damn cent he had.

Rowntree and Roy matched the bet. The three still in looked around the table, staring each other down, almost as if there was going to be a gun battle. Serious business, a good hand of poker — so no one showed their cards right away.

Even that angrified feller didn't disrespect the moment by trying to hurry them up.

After a few long tense moments, Roy broke the silence. "Full house, boys." He threw his cards down on the table and spread them for viewing.

"Can't believe it," said Rowntree. "I had two Jacks and discarded one to go for the Straight — then I got two more Jacks." He put the hand down and showed it. Nine, Ten, Jack, Jack, Jack.

"Damn fool," said the drunk angry miner.

"You coulda had four," said Roy.

Rowntree looked into Roy so hard his dang eyes just about burned. And as he kept up the staring, Daniel Rowntree's next words came out careful, meticulous even. "From now on, in a tight situation, I'll shoot for the Jack every time."

"The Jack?"

"Decision's made, I won't change it," said Rowntree.

The feller to Roy's left had stayed quiet, enjoying his victory — of course, he'd gone all-in for a reason. "Four sevens," he now slurred triumphantly, and scooped twelve-hundred dollars toward him.

"Too good, Mister," said Roy. But he didn't look at the miner, for he was trying still to read Rowntree's eyes. "I'd have just about bet my life on the hand I had, too."

"Man shouldn't bet his life 'til he has to," said Rowntree. "Sometimes ... Mister Peabody ... things are not what they seem. Still. You never can tell where a stroke of good fortune might come from — or an unexpected ally."

The other two at the table were so drunk they weren't hardly listening — one putting his money in neat piles, the other taking slugs of whiskey and bemoaning his run of bad luck.

Roy looked closely at Rowntree, said, "Be nice if something showed up when you needed it most."

"Bet on it," Rowntree said, almost under his breath. "Well, boys," he added more loudly, "when I deal a man four Sevens, I say to myself, 'What time is it?' And I answer, 'Is it time to shoot, Luke, or give up the gun?' And I think about which choice serves me best, that particular moment." Then he got up from his seat.

Roy looked at him quizzically and said, "So you're choosing to give up the gun?"

"This time I am," Rowntree answered with a smile. "Man has to choose his battles. You have yourselves a good evening, boys." Then, once again staring into Roy, he added, "But next time ... yes, maybe next time ... we'll play for it all."

Roy played a couple more hands, it making no sense to let that fool miner keep the money he and Rowntree had just gifted him.

Took three hands for Roy to take his half back, then he left the game. Went out the front doors, stood on the boardwalk and looked at the street. Good place to think, he decided — and he had plenty to think *about*.

All them strange things Daniel Rowntree had said. Clearly, the man had *told* Roy that he was an ally — but all that talk about shooting for the Jack? Not to mention, 'shoot, Luke, or give up the gun,' and all its possible meanings?

Then there was the cards he had dealt. Now that was outrageously strange — four Aces, four Sevens — and almost, yet not quite, four Jacks.

What does it all mean?

Whole thing made Roy's head spin, and he needed to

clear it. At least he was sure he had enough to win the auction, and that was the main thing for now.

One thing at a time.

Then he heard cheering inside, knew it was time, and went in.

Joe Brand and Sheriff Grimes led Miss Charlotte down the stairs once again. This time, Brand didn't talk as much when they stopped off halfway down the stairs.

More warnings than anything, it was. Made it clear that no trouble would be tolerated, no matter the result of the auction — but also, he explained that extra special treatment would go to the underbidders, in respect of what new painted doves were coming in soon, and he hinted at what might be allowed that usually wasn't.

"But don't wait for that, bid for this one," he shouted. "This pure untouched beginner, an Angelica the like of which ain't never been seen in a den of iniquity before — your wife for one perfect week, and nothing off limits at all."

The cheer just about raised the roof, and it was all Roy could do not to punch a particularly obnoxious man next to him, for the things he was saying about Miss Charlotte, and what he had planned for her.

Then, well protected by Fleet Darrow and the rest of Brand's hired muscle, Brand and Grimes led Miss Charlotte through the crowd, and up the stairs onto the stage.

She looked infinitely beautiful, of course, to every man and woman in attendance — but to Roy, even more so than that,

Miss Charlotte looked *helpless*. He had once seen a young deer standing next to its dead mother, not knowing what to do. The eyes of that poor baby creature, Roy had never forgotten — and the memory of it came to him now, as he looked upon Miss Charlotte, saw her dreadful blank helplessness.

She stood with her hands clasped in front, as if trying to somehow hide her bare legs from view — she folded herself in somehow, as if making herself shorter would hide her from all of these men. Then Joe Brand turned toward her, leaned in and spoke into her ear — and the poor girl's eyes widened in fear.

She tried to smile, lifted her head, held it high.

Brand spoke again, and she put her hands on her hips, faced the room squarely. Clearly, he had trained her to do it — such training would not have been kind, and Roy, his rage clean and hard, wanted right then to kill him.

But there would be no killing, not now, only an auction.

Brand took off his top hat, held it aloft and in his great gravel voice, he called, "Who'll start me off with a thousand?"

"Twelve-hundred," cried a very drunk miner, throwing one hand in the air as he sprawled on the bar.

Brand laughed and said, "Truly a man of quality and discernment."

"Fifteen-hundred," called Silver Sam, and the whole room broke into laughter. "Don't see how it's funny," he said when the laughter subsided, and they started right up again.

"Two-thousand," said Sheriff Grimes himself, making a point of letting his gaze run all over her body.

"Two-five," Silver Sam cried.

"Three," called Fleet Darrow.

"Four," came a familiar voice — and Roy wheeled about to see the long hair and drooping mustache of Daniel Rowntree.

Roy stared at him, and under his breath said, "Some ally."

Rowntree was smiling, open-mouthed, and his lips never moved as he quietly said, "Reasons, Roy."

"Five-thousand dollars," Fleet Darrow called then, and the crowd gasped almost as one.

"Come on," called Brand, "let's stop insulting the girl, shall we, and get to the serious bidding."

"Fifty-five-hundred," Silver Sam called.

And Fleet Darrow laughed and said, "There ain't no refunds, Old Man, when you don't get to use the goods for the purpose they're auctioned."

Broke the whole place up it did, and even Joe Brand so enjoyed it he waited a half-minute before putting a stop to the howls of laughter.

"Think you're so damn funny," said Silver Sam. "Won't be funny when you lose the auction though, will it? I got some yet in reserve." And he nodded with certainty and threw back a shot of good whiskey.

Brand saw that Darrow was merely amused, so he let things go on as they were, and even added to the merriment. "I'm inclined," Brand said, sounding thoughtful, "to accept Silver Sam's bid right now." He waited for the jeers and complaints to die down before adding, "After all, even if the sight of her nekkid don't kill him, his ancient equipment sure won't get the job done, and her bein' untouched I can auction her again, and thereby earn from her twice!"

Old Silver Sam attempted to climb up on top of the bar then, and had to be restrained from it. Seemed like his plan was to drop his britches and prove he still had what it took.

Then Fleet Darrow said, "You win the auction and prove it up here on the stage, Sam — and I'll give you back half your stake."

For a man who'd killed four men in this town since he came here, Fleet Darrow sure seemed mighty popular. There was a whole lotta hootin' and hollerin' alright — although one feller made the mistake of patting Darrow on the back, and the whole place went quiet as Darrow spun toward him and made like he'd gone for his gun.

Kept it shucked in the end — but when Darrow yelled, "BANG," that feller just about died on the spot, and reckoned ever after he'd got a weak heart from that moment.

"Six-thousand dollars," Darrow finally said. Then he turned toward where Roy was standing.

"Six-five," Roy said.

"Six-six," cried Silver Sam, and Fleet Darrow saluted him.

"Seven," said Rowntree.

"Dammit," cried Silver Sam. "Bottle o' the good stuff then, Barkeep!"

"Give it him free," called Fleet Darrow, "on account of entertainment provided."

Then Silver Sam gave a deep bow, and everyone cheered.

"Bid's seven-thousand, from Rowntree just by the front doors," Joe Brand called from the stage. "Going once..."

Miss Charlotte looked at Roy, and she looked more like that baby deer than the deer had itself.

"Going twice..."

"Seven-two," Roy called.

"Seven-three," Rowntree said right away.

"Seven-five," Roy called louder.

Rowntree patted his pockets, put a finger in the air as if remembering something, smiled and said, "Seven-six."

"Seven-thousand, seven-hundred, and seventy-seven dollars," Roy called — and then there was such complete silence, you'd have heard a woman frown at her husband at the other end of town.

"Going once," called Joe Brand, and still no one breathed. "Going twice ... and three times ... *SOLD* to young Roy Peabody."

As a crush of slack-jawed loafers encircled Roy — some to shake him by the hand, others only to touch him for luck — Daniel Rowntree leaned forward and whispered into his ear. "Sevens, good, shows you been paying attention. Now go shake his hand, and don't bet your life 'til you have to."

Roy stood there dumbfounded a moment, while Rowntree shook his hand. Then out loud, Rowntree said, "Better go get your Queen, young feller. Enjoy the week."

If ever a man had mixed feelings, it was Roy in that moment, as he made his way forward to claim his prize. He was relieved, of course, to have won — to have saved Miss Charlotte from whatever fate she'd have suffered at some other man's hands. But this wasn't over yet, not by a long shot.

And as he made his way forward, Roy wanted to kill every leering fool that shook his hand and said, "Give her one for me," by way of congratulations for winning the auction.

The whole thing just about made him sick.

He was vaguely aware of Fleet Darrow close by, the man saying, "Nice touch, all the sevens, Kid. Prime entertainment."

Then Roy found himself up on the stage, standing at Miss Charlotte's side, looking out at hundreds of fools — and a very few friends.

"Hold her hand, Kid," said Joe Brand from behind them.

"What?"

Then Sheriff Hosea Grimes placed Miss Charlotte's hand into Roy's, and the touch of her brought him back to what was real, important.

Then Grimes walked off to one side, and Joe Brand — who was standing behind and between them — placed his left hand on Miss Charlotte's shoulder, and his right hand on Roy's.

"It's alright, Miss Charlotte," Roy said, and she gripped tight his hand. Maybe she felt reassured, and maybe she didn't. Didn't look no less like that deer though, as she forced a smile.

"We are gathered here," Joe Brand called then, his gravel voice grating even more than before, "to join this young couple in *ONE* ... *GOOD* ... *WEEK OF MARRIAGE!*"

The crowd enjoyed it, of course, and Brand hammed it up, nearly worse than the very worst actor Roy ever saw.

"Do you, Miss Charlotte Hawke, promise to pleasure this man every which way ... no matter how drunk he gets ... no matter how depraved his wishes ... and enjoy it, beginning to end?" The crowd hushed for her answer, but she didn't speak right away.

Brand's mouth turned into that of some vile beast, and

he squeezed her shoulder a little as he growled, "Well, do you?"

"Yes," she said meekly, and again, the crowd roared their approval, banged on glasses and bottles and tables and walls, and suggested all sorts of things they'd have done to the girl if they'd won her.

"Do you, Roy Peabody, promise to do your duty by us all? To give this beginner all that's comin' to her? To break her in good for the rest of us? And to set her up for a lifetime of pleasuring men the way she was born to?"

Roy said nothing a moment, just looked out at the animalistic crowd gathered before them, and he knew his eyes must surely be blazing in anger — then he felt Miss Charlotte's hand squeeze his own even harder, and she whispered, "Say it, Roy."

He didn't just say it — he cried it, he yelled it, he spat it. And it burned as it roared from the depths of his throat, *"YES I DO!"*

Joe Brand, wild in his power and pleasure, growled at the top of his voice then, "By the power of owning this place, and this woman, and this Godforsaken damn town ... I now pronounce this fine couple ... *Whoremonger and WHORE!"*

CHAPTER 34
FAT IN THE FIRE

Roy knew he'd lost his control, knew he had to do better. He breathed slowly, deliberately, calmed his thoughts as he and Miss Charlotte walked through the crowd then upstairs. They were following Joe Brand, Sheriff Grimes and Fleet Darrow — for the money had yet to be paid.

They reached the top of the stairs and the others turned right, headed down the corridor toward Joe Brand's office. Roy turned a moment, looked down across the huge room below to where Daniel Rowntree still stood. The man had not moved since the auction. He looked up at Roy now, lifted a hand in the air for the briefest of moments — then moved it, as if to shake some invisible hand.

Roy heard Rowntree's words again now, clear as if he was speaking them into his ear. *'Go shake his hand, and don't bet your life 'til you have to.'*

Roy didn't have time to respond, even if he had wanted

to — for Rowntree's back was all there now was to be seen, as he left the Saloon by way of the swinging front doors.

Roy's mind went back to work, watching and looking and noting things down in his head. At best, he had bought himself a week to save Miss Charlotte. A plan of the building may help — but he knew he'd best not draw it on paper, it would have to remain in his head

It was a huge building alright.

You could turn left or right at the top of the stairs — the corridors ran right along the rear of the building, and if it were daylight, you could have seen the rear yard and the stables from windows every ten feet or so. You'd have had to go left at the top of the stairs to get to most of the cat rooms — but there were also two cat rooms to the right. Numbered Eight and Seven, they were.

By the sound of things, both were in use.

From there on, the rooms were all locked and quiet. But even those had numbers on the doors.

Roy assumed Brand's three protectors lived in these, plus perhaps the establishment's Madame. He was mostly correct — three rooms belonged to the men, but soon Roy would see that the other was Miss Charlotte's prison. It was the one right across from the bathroom — at least the place had indoor necessaries, built off the back of the hallway, one down each corridor. And not just with tubs, for each had a quincy as well.

They all walked past Rooms Six and Five, then Brand stopped, took a key from his pocket, unlocked and opened Room Four. "Get in," he growled at Miss Charlotte.

She glanced quickly at Roy, then did just as she had been told. Brand locked the door, put the key in his pocket and laughed.

"Isn't that key for me, Mister Brand?" said Roy, holding his hand out, palm up.

"Not 'til you paid in full it ain't," said Brand, then he started to walk on further down the corridor.

He had to stop though, for Roy said he needed to pee.

"Quincy's in there," Joe Brand growled, "and don't waste no time at it."

Window in there looked like it could open just fine, though Roy didn't risk trying it. The damn thing had bars on it anyway — no escaping out that way.

He was back out right quick, and they all walked along past Room Three — *That'll be Darrow's room for certain* — then past Room Two.

Brand's bedroom.

Any fool could have guessed which were Brand's private rooms — their doors stuck out like the stones on an old yellow dog. Every *other* door in the building was plain as the day — thin boards, strong enough for normal use, hung straight on good leather hinges. Strong enough so no one could burst in too easy. Doors that got the job done.

But Doors One and Two looked like they belonged on a bank vault. Heavy planks, reinforced at the edges with metal, and hinges of metal as well, somewhat oversized— and not only keyed locks, but heavy metal clasps that could be padlocked inside *and* out.

"Well, Kid, you did it," Brand said once they were all in

his office. He took off the tall hat and put it down on the desk, then without even looking at the man, said, "Make yourself useful and pour us all a damn drink, Grimes."

Fleet Darrow closed the heavy door behind them, said, "You must almost have been out of cash, Kid."

"Just about, Mister Darrow," said Roy, sitting in the chair he was offered, right across the desk from Brand himself. "Just glad my luck held tonight at the tables. Some surprised though. Figured on it costing less than half where it ended up."

"No accounting for the extent of male depravity," said Darrow. "My own included, if I'm honest. At that price though, I'll happily await my turn, and good luck to the victor."

"Silver Sam was a surprise," said Sheriff Grimes, sitting down next to Roy after pouring the drinks and handing them out. "Never knew he had that sorta money."

"Maybe he don't," said Fleet Darrow, "Though I doubt he'd risk bidding in that case. Still, old men can do crazy things at times. Might just have been playing to the crowd."

"That damn Rowntree sure weren't playin'," said Joe Brand. "I been watchin' him these weeks. Comes in a few nights, always wins, but never too much at once. Goes to Deadwood and Rapid City too — heard tell he does the same there. Found out his weakness tonight though."

"Did he lose tonight?" said Roy.

"No, not that," said Brand, mysterious-like.

"But you said—"

"Weakness don't always cause a loss, Kid," said Brand, placing his left hand over his right where it rested on the table in front of him. "Heard tell you played against Rowntree tonight, Kid. Heard tell he gave it up quick. You and your lucky streak too much for him?"

Roy could feel them all watching him closely. "No, Mister Brand, not at all. Reckon I'm gettin' pretty good, but strange enough, neither of us won. He only played the one hand then excused himself. Right superstitious, that Rowntree. Bet up big on a good hand, but lost a thousand-dollar pot to a feller with four-of-a-kind."

"You don't say?" said Brand.

"I *do* say," said Roy. "Rowntree deals this feller four sevens, then acts all off his chump and walks away after he loses. Puzzled me plaguily it did at the time. Then when he stood right behind me and bid for Miss Charlotte, it threw me right bad, I can tell you. Wonder now if the man only played that one hand to put fat in my fire. Feller rattles me some, is the truth of it."

Fleet Darrow looked back at Brand then and asked, "But what about Rowntree's weakness, Boss? Matter of interest is all, me being a brown study for human nature, among other complex entertainments."

"You always overthink things, Fleet — that's *your* weakness, and why you missed his. Rowntree's weakness is obvious — it's a pretty beginner, that's all. He works from the shadows for the most part, but the chance of winning the auction drew him out of his hidey-hole. Reckon we'll find ourselves another girl, maybe have a new auction soon."

Seemed to Roy they'd forgotten he was there, just

about. So he did the smart thing, shut his mouth up and pricked up his ears.

Grimes rubbed at his chin and spoke up then. "Can't you just take this Rowntree's money at the tables? Same way you get everyone else's?"

"Never touches the Faro or Dice," Brand said. "Never so much as looks at the wheel. Hard to get an edge on professionals at Poker, that's why they always play it."

"There's ways," said Grimes.

"Ways, is there?" Brand scoffed. "Man like Rowntree'd pick a marked deck in a second."

Roy realized then they were drawing him out, and it'd be a giveaway if he didn't speak up then. "Marked deck? Mister Brand, marked decks ain't for real. I played enough poker to know that! They's an old ladies' tale, I reckon. Any fool'd pick a marked deck right off, and then there'd be shootin' and death. Man'd be a fool even to try such a thing."

"Kid knows his stuff," said Fleet Darrow, barely concealing his merriment. "Maybe the Kid could work the poker tables, Boss. Couldn't just be a lucky streak, he sure was too good for Curly."

"Curly's a damn fool," said Brand. "Can barely read his own name, let alone a deck of marked cards. Should have had them boys beat him worse, causing such a ruckus as he did. But that Rowntree, he's *good*. Better'n he ever lets on. He'd be *just* the sorta feller to work the Poker for me here — and maybe the right girl would lure him in."

"Speaking of pretty girls, Mister Brand," Roy said

politely, "would you mind if we got down to business? I'm just itchin' to go see Miss Charlotte."

The other three men all laughed, and both Darrow and Grimes slapped Roy on the back too, good-natured.

"Sure thing, Kid," said Joe Brand. "Get it out and start countin' — and don't forget the extra seventy-seven."

CHAPTER 35
SHOOK

Roy counted it out, every last dollar of it. Seven piles of a thousand. Seven piles of a hundred. A pile with seventy in it. All that was notes. Then he placed down a pair of three-dollar coins, one on top of the other, and fished through his pockets where he found a shiny silver dollar. He liked to keep the old silver ones for special occasions, and this sure was a nice one.

Lucky.

Roy held the shiny coin up in front of him. "Flip you for the lot?" he said. Then he hastily placed that final coin down on the others. "Just joshin', Mister Brand," he added quickly, and offered his hand to Brand to shake on the deal.

Brand only nodded and stayed right where he was — *not a man for shaking hands.* Roy scratched his cheek with that hand then picked up his glass with it, drank the few drops that were left, put it down on the desk.

"Might get along to bed now," Roy said then, with the right amount of wonderment and joy in his voice. "Maybe in the morning we can breakfast together at the restaurant. Reckon Miss Charlotte would like that."

"Kid," Joe Brand said gruffly. "The whore don't leave the premises, you hear? I'm strict on that, and if it happens, I'll shoot you without hesitation."

"I ... but ... sorry, Mister Brand, I guess I forgot..."

"It's alright, Kid. You can have your meals brought across from the restaurant like we do. Best the whore stays in her room though. Not fair to other men, seein' her before she's available. Could lead to trouble, and we don't want that. Might bring her down the last day though — auction off who gets to go second, that'll bring a extra price than normal I reckon. Fleet'll bid on it, I'm sure."

"I'll decide on that at the time," said Darrow. "Reckon I'll wait 'til I see her condition at the back end of a week. The Kid bein' young, dumb, and not long begun, I reckon he might just about wear her down to a frazzle in gettin' his money's worth."

Roy stood, and so did the others, and they all walked out of the office. Brand locked the door behind him, then the four men walked along to Miss Charlotte's room, where Brand finally handed Roy the key.

Roy slipped the key into the lock — then he suddenly turned around, and, excited as a kid before Christmas, grabbed Joe Brand's gloved right hand in both of his own, and vigorously shook it as he said, "Thanks so much, Mister Brand, thanks again."

The handshake was over and done before Joe Brand knew it was coming.

By then Roy had already turned away, was shaking

Fleet Darrow's hand too, thanking him just as excitedly, and wearing the smile of an overexcited child about to open his present.

"Thank you too," Roy said to the Sheriff, and patted him friendly on the shoulder. Then he half-turned to unlock the door, stepped through it backward, rubbed his own hands together with glee, and closed that door in their faces, still smiling like a kid who just got given a puppy.

I'm a dead man, Roy thought, standing breathless in Miss Charlotte's room, staring at the closed door.

He took a step to the side, reached inside his coat for his derringer — and without taking it out of his coat, he aimed at the door, waited for it to burst open.

It didn't happen.

Didn't happen.

Didn't.

Not yet, anyway.

With his left hand, he placed the key in the lock. Turned it, and *still* nothing happened.

He had done it.

He had squeezed Joe Brand's hand.

With the delicate touch of a man who made his living from cards, Roy *knew* what was there and what wasn't.

Cotton wadding, five cents worth.

No pinkie finger inside that glove.

Joe Brand IS Big Jim Starr.

CHAPTER 36

"SEVEN-THOUSAND REASONS..."

Miss Charlotte sat primly on the edge of the bed, the blanket draped over her legs. Her usually wonderful voice was thin and afraid. "Roy?"

He turned toward her, raised the forefinger of his left hand up to his lips to quiet her — let her see what he was doing, as he eased the derringer out of his coat with his right.

He waited. Put his head against the wall, just next to the door. Listened.

Roy was a *real* good listener, it was something he practiced.

The three men were walking away now. All three men were laughing. Two kept moving — but one of them stopped.

He looked at Miss Charlotte; pointed at the wall so she knew there was somebody there; put his finger to his lips again.

Then he stepped — very quietly — across the room toward her before speaking. He wasn't overly loud, but loud enough.

"You look so pretty, Miss Charlotte. Ain't you glad it was me won the auction?"

"I'm not what he said I am, Roy."

"Don't go givin' me that, Miss," he said loud and forceful-like. "No more lies between us, alright? That story of yours is done and dusted, it's time now for actions."

Roy put the derringer in his coat pocket, made two fists and pretended to throw little punches, pointed toward the poor confused girl, then himself.

"How dare you!" she said.

"Oh, I'm gonna enjoy this, Miss Charlotte," he said. He pointed at the wall and cupped his ear, before doing the punching actions again with his fists. Then he took two loud steps toward her.

"Stay away from me," she cried, and he rapidly nodded his head, waved his hand in a circle to tell her to keep up her yelling, then got his fists going again.

She looked rightly flummoxed a moment, then a look of understanding washed over her. Finally she'd twigged to his game, and joined in with the playacting. "Get off me," she cried. "Get off me, you beast."

Roy jumped onto the bed beside her, a playful smile on his face. And louder now, as he jumped up and down some, he said, "Stay still you damn fool, and be nice."

"Get off me," she cried. "Roy, please!"

"*OWWW,*" he cried then, good and loud. "Well that just ain't nice, Miss Charlotte, I reckon I'll learn you some manners. You can shuck off your clothes with my help or without, but off they's all gonna be."

"They will not," she squealed. "Unhand me!"

Roy slapped his left palm with his right, and it made a fine ringing noise, which he followed close up with an "Owww." Then he stamped a boot on the floor and said, "So. You want it rough, do you? Well, I got over seven-thousand reasons to force you if I have to, Miss — but I'd rather you give it up willingly. So you got five minutes to think while I get settled in. But if you ain't changed your mind then, there'll *sure* be some degree of forcing. You can *bet* on that, Charlotte Hawke, you damn stupid *whore!*"

Her mouth fell open in shock when he said it, and he mouthed the word, *"Sorry,"* to her.

He put his finger to his lips again, and they both went quiet a few seconds. Still no sound from out in the corridor.

"Aww, Miss Charlotte," he said then more kindly, "you don't need to cry. There, there, it's alright. I can wait awhile for it, I guess, we got the whole week. You just sit some and catch your breath now."

Roy got down and put his ear to the floor, heard the footfalls outside. Whoever had come back to listen was finally satisfied.

At long last, they were alone.

He didn't speak to her yet, but instead, checked the room out for spy holes. Quite often, whorehouses had them, and it was important he found it, if indeed one existed.

She watched him from where she still sat on the edge of

the bed, while he looked behind the painting, under the rug, behind the desk and the small chiffonier.

Room was wallpapered in a paisley pattern, so it took a good while to check the parts of it that seemed like an eye.

If they'd been in Deadwood, such a room might have had nothing much more than paper for walls. But when Custer was first settled last year it had grown quickly — hundreds of houses were built, then abandoned by men moving to Deadwood, where a bigger gold strike had occurred. Such a hurried evacuation had left an abundance of materials behind, and it had been there for the taking when Joe Brand arrived — the result being, walls of logs or good solid boards to divide all the rooms.

The window was nailed shut, of course. He would never get it open without tools, and even if he had them, it would make too much of a ruckus.

As bedrooms went, it was a mighty fine prison.

Roy had Miss Charlotte get off the bed so he could move it and check for any spy holes — but in the end, he decided there wasn't none at all.

He pushed the bed back in place then they sat side by side, almost touching. Spoke quiet as a pair of mice stuck inside a cat's kitchen.

Roy whispered into her ear. "Did he hurt you, Miss Charlotte?"

"He hit me once," she said quietly. "But not too hard. Said he'd ... he'd ... I'm not what he said I am, Roy."

"I know that, Miss. I know a lot more than you think I do."

"Oh, Roy," she said, turning her face toward his.

"Thank you for ... all your ... help." Her eyes were soft as a doe's, and Roy couldn't barely stand to look into them.

Their situation was dangerous and deadly, yet his greatest urge now was to kiss her, and his clear thinking drifted away, lost in desire. She was so close he almost could taste her, the way her breath mingled with his, their lips only inches apart. Her gaze went from his eyes to his mouth, her ragged breath drawing him to her, each breath now almost a pant, so soft yet so loud to his ears — and there in that moment, Roy almost lost all his control.

But sudden-like, he remembered the *real* reason he was here — and instead of kissing her, he spoke. "Miss Charlotte, do you trust me?"

"Yes, Roy," she said, looking up into his eyes. Then she closed her eyes, let her lips part...

And Roy said, "Good. Let's think up a plan." And he jumped up off the bed, started pacing the room — and Miss Charlotte, who could barely believe it, just looked at him, dumbstruck.

CHAPTER 37
A HITCH IN HIS GIDDY-UP

Didn't take long to work out, there wasn't no way to escape. Since that moment he'd almost kissed her, Roy had been careful not to get too close — careful too, not to touch her.

She was vulnerable and afraid, and it just wouldn't be right take advantage of that.

Her own clothes had been taken from her — even the hat with the bird on it — and all she had now was the painted cat outfit she'd worn for the auction. To begin with, she'd kept a blanket over her legs — but it had been an hour now since Roy got there, the night was hot and the window nailed shut, so the blanket had now been discarded.

He tried not to look — for the most part.

Hadn't been easy.

She was sitting on the one chair now, which sat in front of a small desk in front of the window. She'd turned the chair quarter-way round so it faced the bed. As for Roy, he lay back on the mattress, fully clothed except for his hat and his boots, and he had his eyes firmly shut.

"Don't worry, Miss Charlotte," he told her. "I'm difficuled by it right now, but—

"Difficuled? What sort of a word is difficuled?"

"It's the sort of word accurate describes how heaping our troubles — but don't worry, Miss, we got ourselves a whole week yet to nut something out."

"And then what?"

"And then nothin'," he said, as if surprised by her lack of faith in him. "We'll be gone before then, somewhere else, and you'll just have to trust me on that."

He lay there with his eyes shut, and he ran it all through his mind. It wasn't easy to think straight, not now he knew what he knew. Problem was, the rescue of Miss Charlotte Hawke was not just a big nut to crack, it was a hitch in his giddy-up the damn size of Texas.

Roy had lived all these years with one aim — to find and kill Big Jim Starr. First part of that, for all of this time, had seemed like the hard part. But now the *finding* was done, the *killing* was a whole lot more difficult than he ever expected.

Because of her.

Thing was, Roy always knew he might bite the ground himself, in the process of killing Big Jim. Half expected it, somehow, and he'd made his peace with that.

And here he was, firmly entrenched in a room in the man's own saloon. Sure, Roy didn't have his Winchester — and it seemed high unlikely he'd be able to get it snuck in.

But he had his little Sharps derringer, and had shot it at targets many thousands of times through the years.

Despite the tiny twenty-twos it used, Roy was deadly with it up to twelve feet. Even that from inside his coat, for the thousands of shots had been nohow random, but always taken in the spirit of training, training to take a just revenge. And now, Big Jim Starr — *no, Joe Brand, I must think of him as, lest I slip up with my words* — was well in Roy's sights.

He *knew* he could walk downstairs now, walk up to Brand smiling, put at least two slugs through his chest before even Fleet Darrow could react.

But Darrow — and others — *would* react. Roy would be dead too, and then, what would happen to Miss Charlotte?

It was a stumper of biblical proportions.

He wondered what Grampa would advise him. The man Roy called Grampa wasn't really his blood relative at all — but he *would* have become his legal relative, if Big Jim Starr hadn't killed Roy's mother and Reese Scott.

"*Grampa*" was Reese Scott's own father.

Roy laughed a little as a memory of the man's words came into his mind.

"What's funny, Roy?" asked Miss Charlotte, her voice calm and soft again now.

Never ceased to surprise him when he heard that voice float on out of her. *Soft as the fur on a kitten that lives on a cloud.*

"Roy?"

"Minikin," he told her. "Funny word is all."

"What were you thinking of?"

It occurred to Roy then that she had a right to know.

Not so much what he was thinking, but the truth of the size of their problem. But it wouldn't do to just blurt it out — he'd best work up to it slowly.

"My Grampa calls me by it sometimes," he said. "Minikin. Only him, no one else. First time I ever heard it was when he gifted me this baby gun. I was seven years old then, so I guess it was just about right-sized, now I look back on it."

"Oh, that's just *awful,*" she said.

"That I was so slow to grow?"

"That he gave a young child a *gun* — what an awful, terrible thing for someone to do."

Roy turned his head quick then and opened his eyes — her face looked as sad as she'd sounded.

"No, Miss," he told her. "It was just the *right* thing to do, and somehow that wise old man knew it."

"How so, Roy? Tell me. Please?" She got up from the chair, came and sat on the bed and looked down at him. Charlotte Hawke had a kindness about her that was different than any he'd known. Not that the women who'd raised him weren't kind, most especially Maisie — but Miss Charlotte Hawke was softer, more innocent was all.

"I want to tell you. I do. But I got secrets, Miss Charlotte. Secrets I can't never tell. Not unless..."

CHAPTER 38
STORIES

Roy was afraid to look at her, afraid he might not find the courage he needed, for it was no easy thing to be true to a woman — and to keep some things from her as well. But then she reached down and touched his cheek with the back of her fingers. Ran it along there she did, as he looked up into her eyes.

"Roy. We both have secrets. I'm not a fool, Roy. I know I must seem one to you—"

"No, Miss," he said.

"But I *was* one, we both know, to come here. To be fooled in this way. It's alright, Roy, we both know it's true."

"I..."

He couldn't tell her what he was thinking. As befuddled and muddled as it was, the problem was his own to work out. He would not worry her with the whole truth of it — she was already in peril enough.

"Roy. I *was* a fool — but I don't have to be one any

more. I *know* the danger we're in here. I know what you've risked to help me."

No, you sure don't, he thought. But he only said, "Anyone woulda done the same."

She smiled, looked right into his eyes, and shook her head. Then slowly, Miss Charlotte leaned forward. Her lips didn't go straight toward his, but off to the side some — and she kissed him, not quite on the cheek, not quite on the mouth, but just a little on both.

And that intimate second seemed both too long and too short.

Roy closed his eyes, his breath caught in his throat, and he thought he might die in that moment. Almost wished that he could.

When he finally opened his eyes, she was back where she'd started, looking down at him, eyes shining and smiling.

"Roy." It still affected him deeply, how she said his name. That was a hitch in his giddy-up too, but a nice sort of problem to have. Then she added, "I'm not a fool, Roy, and I know there's a chance we'll both die soon."

Well, that sure brought him back down to earth.

"Miss—"

"No, Roy, listen to me, please. I know the danger we're in, and I know Joe Brand won't allow me to leave here, not ever. He told me as much that first night, and I've been terrified since."

"I won't let—"

"I know, Roy, I know. But I also know what that means

— the truth of it. I won't live here as a slave, I'll die before I let that happen, and that's what I've been trying to say."

"Miss Charlotte—"

This time she pressed a finger against his lips to quiet him. She left it there the whole time she spoke, and it sure made him quiver. Her voice came out quiet, but strong, so very strong. "You won the auction, Roy, and that's all we have. Maybe it's all we'll *ever* have. If I'm to die, then so be it. But you used all your money to help me, and the prize was a week of married life. I ... I care for you, Roy. I might nearly have saved us from this as we traveled in the stagecoach. I very nearly came out and told you ... how I felt. I wanted you to ask me then, Roy, but I think I know why you didn't."

She removed her finger from his lips then, though it lingered nearby a long second.

When he spoke, it came out not quite right. "I'm a selfish man, that's all." His voice had wavered some when he said it. For a man good at acting, it seemed like his emotions had caused all his skills to desert him.

"No, Roy," she said. "That's not true. I thought it was then, but I've had all this time alone in my room now to think. The truth is, you were too noble a man to cheat Mister *Tanner* out of the wife he expected. *Mister Tanner indeed* — he never even existed."

"I'm sorry, Miss."

"Do you love me, Roy?"

The full strength of the question left him feeling weak, even if just for a moment.

"Do you not know the answer, Miss Charlotte?"

"I know it." She caressed his face with her fingers, the forefinger touching the corner of his lip as it followed a path to his chin.

"I *do* love you, Miss Charlotte. But I can't be ... I mean, I need to focus on gettin' you outta here alive, not on—"

"I know you'll try, Roy, my love. But as I said, the foolishness is gone from me now, my naivety replaced with a knowledge, a matter-of-factness of how the world is. And I *know*, Roy, I *know*. I'm *never* walking out of this saloon."

"Miss—"

"The auction was for one week of marriage. Give me that week, Roy. Please. I'm to be denied a long life — denied children, and growing old with my loving husband. So give me this wonderful week, a first week of marriage that's all we can make it. Give me that, Roy, my darling. Let me live — just that much."

She was just about breaking Roy's heart — worst part was, he knew it was true, what she'd said. He sniffed, wiped a hand across his eye, wiped the wetness off on his shirt.

"I'll get us out of here yet, Miss Charlotte Hawke. Will you marry me then, once we're free?"

"Yes, Roy." She wiped the tears away from her own eyes, then wiped his eyes as well.

"Alright then," he said. "Don't know how yet, but I'll get us outta this. In the meantime—"

"Tell me stories, Roy."

"What?"

"Tell me stories," she said, and she climbed across him to the other side of the bed, and lay herself down beside him. "We're to be married soon, and I'd like to know all about you. Before we..."

The words hung in the air, as death tends to — and neither of them spoke a few seconds. She lay facing him, but he lay still on his back looking up at the ceiling.

Then she said, "Tell me the minikin story. Tell me how the gift of a gun to a boy could somehow be just the right thing. Tell me *why,* Roy. And tell me about your grandfather, *all* about him — there was love in your eyes when you spoke of him. And rather than piling worry on worry, perhaps stories are just what we need now."

He turned his head to face her, said nothing, just looked in her eyes. Felt like his heart might break open, and his soul leak out all the way through him and into the world.

"This is all we get, Roy. Don't waste it hoping for more. Please?" Her voice was softer than ever — tiny silver bells that played a most beautiful tune. "Tell me all about your life, so I may *know* who I love. Tell me true, Roy, my darling. Please tell me."

CHAPTER 39
MINIKIN

In the low flickering light of the room, Roy reached over and picked the tiny Sharps up from the little bedside table. Turned it in his hands, studied the engraving a moment, as if he could read something in the patterns.

"It was a gun precious to him," he told Miss Charlotte, "and his heart was broke just as mine was. True Philadelphia Deringers are sold mostly in pairs, but not these Sharps, as they're more reliable — rimfire cartridge makes it so, partly. But also, they fire four shots."

"I don't know what a rimfire cartridge *is,* Roy."

"Doesn't matter, Miss. What does matter, this one's half of a pair — there's a perfect match for it somewhere, same fancy engraving on the silver, all done special order, Grampa's own design. He had two sons, you see? The two guns were to be for their wives."

Miss Charlotte lay beside Roy, pulled the blanket up to her neck, watched him close without speaking.

He suddenly sat bolt upright, and her eyes went wide in alarm as she looked up at him. She had never shared a bed with a man, and despite the growing trust she had for him, his suddenness of movement had spooked her.

"Sorry, Miss. I ... Miss Charlotte, it occurred to me sudden that the telling of this story could put us both in mortal danger."

"But Roy, how could it possibly get any—"

"Promise me you'll never speak a word of it, no matter what happens in the course of this coming week. Promise me now."

"I promise, Roy."

She looked impossibly beautiful, like some storybook angel, way her hair spread out over the pillow, framing her face. He looked away from her, placed the derringer back on the little bedside table and went on.

"I won't say names, Miss, not of people or places. But I'll tell you the whole story true. Elder of Grampa's two sons was to marry my mother — this here was to be her own gun. But my mother ... my mother was murdered."

"Oh, Roy." She clasped his forearm in her hands, but he ignored it, spoke almost like she weren't even there.

"Grampa's son got murdered too — and me, I seen the whole thing, I was seven years old."

He lay back again now, turned to face her, his own eyes just inches from hers. He thought nothing of the strange look she wore, for the story itself was a sad one. But he was mistaken about that — for her look was one of puzzlement instead. Puzzlement at him shedding no tears as he spoke of that terrible moment.

"We lived in a place much like this one," he said then. "More like this one than I can say. My dear mother ... she worked there, same way the cats here do."

"That's..."

"It was fine, Miss. My Ma loved me good, and I was a happy little tyke. No shortage of women to care for me neither. It was maybe gonna get even better, once we left. My Ma was to marry a real fine feller called ... my Ma was to marry Grampa's son. But the very day we was to leave, someone murdered them both, like I said. I wanted to kill that man, natural enough — but I was just a small boy, all I had was a slingshot, and weren't yet much good even with that."

"I..."

"It was all so damn sad, the crying all went on for days. All them poor lovely whores, with broken hearts for my mother. It was some outpouring of grief, that first week or two. Guess it ruined their own hopes as well, when hers ended that terrible way."

"I'm sorry, Roy."

"Ain't your fault, Miss." He ran fingers through her hair, then went on. "Anyway, we buried my Ma and Mister ... her beau. The Town Marshal wrote a letter to Grampa, informed him what happened. He came there to visit the grave of his son, and to see where he died, hear the story straight from those who were witnesses to it. Important to do that, he reckoned. Anyway, ended up he never left."

"He stayed and raised you?"

"Him and the ladies together, I guess. I was havin' some bad dreams to start with." Roy stopped, looked about as if someone else might be in the room, then went on even quieter. "My mother shot the killer's finger off, you see? Proper original Deringer, she had. Great big forty-one slug, makes a mess of whatever it hits. Blowed that damn finger right off of him. End of it was there on the floor, you could tell what it was by the fingernail — damn fingernail needed some cutting, and had dirt all underneath it."

Miss Charlotte had looked keen on romance before, but she looked different now. Mix of fearful and fascinated maybe, with some green-at-the-gills thrown in.

"The minikin story, Roy?"

"Sorry, Miss," he said. "I'll stick to the easy parts now, and leave out the gore — I wasn't hardly thinking of who I was telling it to, but went somewhere inside myself as I spoke it, I guess. Been a long time."

"It's alright, Roy, I don't mind, you can tell me anything at all."

"I left out who it was that done the killing — it was the feller who owned the saloon. He tried to say it was self defense, but I'd seen the whole thing, and others heard what happened from the next room. Town Marshal came to arrest him — but he got away, went on the run."

Roy smiled thinly then at Miss Charlotte, didn't touch her, no matter how much he needed to. "I guess it'd been maybe two weeks, and the bad dreams were making me scream myself awake. Grampa was due to go back home that day, and maybe that made it worse — for me I mean — he looked like his son I guess, and it sparked something in me, the fear of him leaving. Like maybe it was me and him who'd die this time. He'd already told me I should call him Grampa, and I was close attached to him by then."

"That's understandable."

"Woke up screaming like a devil that mornin', and Grampa rushed in and picked me up from my bed. Held me close to him and said, 'It's alright, little Roy, I'll protect you.' And I said, 'Don't leave me, Grampa.' And he said, 'Roy, I ain't goin' nowhere.' Then he tells me he knows how to fix them damn frightful dreams, and he tells me get dressed, and we go out into the street, and he tells me to wait there and watch a minute."

"Whatever did he do, Roy?"

"He climbs straight up that building like a damn circus monkey, that's what, and I can still see it now. Seventy years of age the man was, and could barely see six feet in front of him. But he climbed right on up and he tore down that sign — red painted sign with a big yellow star on it, and the words *Lucky Starr Saloon, Prop Big Jim Starr.*"

Sudden as death, Roy stopped speaking, swung himself out of bed, grabbed the derringer and stood there all crazy-wide-eyed, pointing that little gun at the door.

Miss Charlotte had sat bolt upright when he did it.

"Roy?"

Her voice was so soft, and seemed so far away in that moment.

"It's alright, Roy, he's not here, it's just us." She patted the bed then beside her, for him to return, come back to her.

He looked at her, then back to the door, then at her again. He turned, put down the gun, lay back down, looked up into her sweet gentle face. He whispered now. "I should not have said the name. Please forget you ever heard it. The voicing of that name in public ... would mean instant death. Promise me now."

"I promise, Roy. Now tell me the rest of the story."

He sighed deeply, rubbed his tired eyes, then he smiled. "Grampa tore that sign off of the building, threw it down into the street, and the cats all got up from their beds to see what he was doing. All cheered when they seen what he'd done — why, you'd have thought he was walking a tightrope, way they all cheered. Then he set that damn sign up in the middle of the street, leaned it up against somethin', I don't remember what."

"Then?"

"Then he took that there little gun out, and said, 'Roy. This was to be a gift to your Ma when she married my boy. It's yours now, this here gun, no one else's. Long as you carry this gun, you will always be safe. See the pattern of engraving? That's what's called magical runes. Any bad man ever comes, the magic will stop him in his tracks. Won't just blow off a finger, gun like this. It'll kill bad men dead every time.' Then he showed me how to use it."

"He had you shoot at the sign, didn't he, Roy? Didn't he?"

"Yes, Miss, that's just what he did. Town Marshal came along and told us not to do it — somethin' about the Town Statutes. But Grampa just stared at him, never said a word, and the Marshal, he looked at us strange, then he nodded, and walked right away. I put four bullets into that sign. Couldn't miss from three feet away, I guess — but I sure believed him right then. Believed that little gun there was magic, and no one ever could hurt me again, or hurt the people I loved. Then Grampa looked down at me and smiled a most wonderful smile. I can see it now still. And he said, 'A minikin gun for a minikin boy. Fiery little explosions of magic the both of you. Now let's go have ourselves breakfast, and no frightful dreams ever again.' And that's just about how it went."

CHAPTER 40
MISS BIRD-HAT

That first night, Roy and Charlotte together, they told a whole lot of stories.

Wasn't all they did — they were in love.

It was a beautiful thing for the both of them, way they snuggled together that night, telling stories and listening each to the other, and growing in their understanding of just who they were.

When Roy finally took her in his arms, it was unlike anything he'd known before. Was not just a physical thing, as it had been with other women, but a spiritual thing, a blessing on both of their lives as the love they felt found expression in movement and closeness and touch.

He had tried to avoid it, tried to assure her that he would yet find a way they could marry in a church first. But Charlotte Hawke was a strong woman, and in the end she had her way, for her reasoning made perfect sense.

Thing was, the both of them knew they might not live out the week — and the way Charlotte figured it, the Lord would not want them to wait, for He would surely not wish them to die unfulfilled.

They was fulfilled alright. They fulfilled each other first time about three in the morning — then again about four, then again from five until almost six, with a lot more patience that time, and a little less urgency.

In their eyes they surely were married. Didn't need no Preacher to explain to their Maker how they felt, and what their intentions were. Charlotte put it simplest and best: "It's you and me, Roy, the rest of our lives, whether that's long or short. I don't wish to miss out on anything — I consider us married right now, and I promise you, I'll love you always."

She had told him by then about her own life — the joys and the tragedies of it. She had led a precious happy life until a year ago, when her mother had died unexpectedly. A small child, a stranger, had tried to run across the street, and would have been hit by a wagon if she hadn't stepped forward to grab him — she had saved the child, but lost her own footing in doing so. The hoof of the horse hit her head as she stumbled, and the doctor said that she would not even have felt it, it was over so quickly.

Charlotte's father, a furniture maker, had been a mostly temperate man up 'til then, but had fallen to drinking when his wife died. The gambling had started soon after, and before long he had frittered their savings away, and their lives were in ruins.

Then two months ago, he'd been found in an alleyway, shot. Charlotte's work as a seamstress had ended when the factory burned down, and as hard as she tried to find new work, it wasn't easy.

The day she buried her father, more terrible news had arrived in the form of a letter. It turned out he had gambled their house away too.

The man who now owned it said she'd have to leave — he seemed a kind fellow, but needed the house for his family, he told her when she went to see him. He mentioned he personally knew a respectable man — a Mister Tanner of Deadwood — who had asked him to look out for a sensible, hardworking wife with a good head for numbers.

It had all happened so quickly, and now, here she was.

As for Roy, he told many stories — but he never once mentioned the biggest problem he had. That being, that Joe Brand was Big Jim Starr — the man who'd murdered his mother was here in this building.

He decided, after a time, to stop thinking of that.

For that first night, Roy gave himself to Charlotte completely. For just those few hours, he stopped trying to figure a way to escape the trouble they found themselves in. And by morning, he no longer called her Miss Charlotte — but only Charlotte, or Darling. Or every so often Miss Bird-Hat, which she quite enjoyed.

And then it was morning, and they were both famished, and he knew he must leave her alone while he went downstairs.

He dressed and promised he'd be quick as he could, and would bring her back a fine breakfast. She wrapped the blanket around her and told him to hurry, and she picked up the chair, to put it against the door how he'd taught her back in Rawhide Buttes.

It seemed so long ago now, but was just a few days.

"Show me," he said. "Show me you remember how to rig it."

She showed him, and she had it just right. *Clever girl.* It was enough to slow a man down, and make quite a noise — and she knew to scream too, and not to hold back, if it came to it.

CHAPTER 41

CODE OF THE WEST

"Hurry back," Charlotte said as she unlocked the door for Roy to leave.

"I'll knock before I unlock it," he told her, "just in case someone has a spare key, and tries to get in. Don't take the chair away unless you hear this knock exactly."

He rapped out a little tune against the door with a finger: *one, one, one-two, one-two, one.*

"Got it?" he said. "Do it back."

She did it just right, then he kissed her goodbye and he left. Listened as she rigged the chair, then he walked toward the stairs.

He was only to the landing when words floated up to his ears.

"Eleven-eleven," called Fleet Darrow from where he sat eating his breakfast. "I'd hear an estimation of its value."

Joe Brand was at the same table with him, down in that

front corner. "Eleven? What are you on about, Fleet? Ain't but eight-thirty yet."

When Brand spoke, Roy wondered why he hadn't been sure all along. The head was clean-shaved and bald, but the voice was all Big Jim Starr's, its timbre unmistakeable to Roy as he walked down the stairs.

"Just asking the Kid if he thinks it was worth it," said Darrow. "First night's over and done — simple math is, it cost him eleven-hundred and eleven dollars. Well, Kid? I see you're wobbling some on them little legs. Is she broke proper yet or still need some work?"

Roy walked across the room to them and stood by the table. It was the first time he'd seen Joe Brand since he'd shaken his hand — and it was all he could do not to kill him right now. But instead, he worked hard at his acting.

"Aw, Mister Darrow," he said, making sure to look plenty embarrassed. "You know I ain't gonna tell."

"Clear enough got his money's worth," said Brand. "Look at the size of his smile. Reckon he rode the leather right off of her saddle."

"Mister Brand, we're both mighty hungry right now. Gonna go get us some bacon and eggs and some flapjacks, I hope they make good ones. And coffee too, of course. Want me to bring you back anything while I'm over there?"

"Write it down, give it to the barkeep, and either him or one of the whores'll go get it. Do the same every time."

"I don't mind going my—"

"I don't want you leaving the building, Kid." Brand got to his feet then, looked down at Roy. Though older now, he was still a huge man, and no mistake he was dangerous.

"For your own good, I'm saying, Kid, and the welfare of the whore — I mean, *your wife.*" Then he chuckled at his own joke. "Some of the men around town'll be resentful, you winning the auction. Most especially any you gambled against while winnin' the money to pay for it. They'll behave fine in here, so you're alright to come down the stairs, drink and gamble if you like. But outside, we got less control, if you see what I'm gettin' at."

"Yessir, Mister Brand," Roy answered. "I see what you're sayin', but I reckon I'd be alright."

Joe Brand looked down his nose at Roy then. "Problem is, you're kind of a derringer, Kid. No power, and lacking in size. If you was the size of me or Fleet here, for instance, then maybe I'd let you run free — but it's too much of a risk, you bein' such a runt."

"Well, alright then, I guess. And thanks for lookin' out for me, Mister Brand. West's a wild place, ain't it?"

"Entertaining though," said Fleet Darrow.

"Sure is that," said Roy. Then he went across to the bar, wrote down his order, and gave the barkeep the money to go get the food.

The barkeep was perhaps only Roy's age, but a neat little man, immaculately dressed, and not one oiled hair out of place. "Come a bit earlier tomorrow if you can, please," he said politely. Then he nodded toward Brand and Darrow and added, "That way I can get it when I go to get theirs."

Roy waited at the bar and watched him head for the door — but as the man took his first step, Joe Brand touched Fleet Darrow's arm then pointed at the barkeep. Darrow shook his head in distaste, but Brand was insistent. Once he moved, Darrow wasted no time. Quick as a bullet, he intercepted the neat little man and threw him up against the wall by the doorway.

Fleet Darrow lifted that poor feller up by the throat — and the choking noises he made were unpleasant at least. He was a short man, but his feet were so far off the floor now, he was seeing the world from a height unaccustomed. Darrow's eyes were perhaps just four inches from his own, which bulged something fearful as he choked, and the hue of his skin turned all sorts of worrisome colors.

"You'll go get it," Darrow told him, as quiet and pleasant as if they were very good friends, "any time it suits the Kid. He's our special guest — ain't he, Boss?"

Darrow turned toward Brand, but by then he was reading his newspaper. Didn't even look up. Disrespectful, him being the instigator and all, and Roy could see Darrow didn't like it.

Still, Fleet Darrow was a man who always did what he was paid to, like it or not.

"Be *nice* to our guest," Darrow told the poor little man then. He lowered him gently to the floor, readjusted his collar, licked two fingers and smoothed the man's mustache, then, as kind as a schoolmarm on a child's first day, said, "Well, go on then, Mac."

Barkeep nodded right fearful at Darrow, then kept his head down as he scurried on out the front doors to go get the order.

"Ain't easy, keepin' the help in line," said Darrow, as he walked across to the bar to talk with Roy while he waited.

"But a man needs a hobby, I guess." Then he glanced again toward Brand, clearly not happy.

Roy had to work some things out, and that meant bringing up risky subjects to get information — to bring the coffee to the boil, so to speak. Things had to change and keep changing if he yet hoped to save Charlotte's life when he killed Joe Brand. Killing Brand was one thing — knowing which others would step into his place was another.

"Is that the same thing you done to Mister Curly?" Roy asked Darrow then.

"Aw, Kid, you're a riot," Darrow said. "Question like that can get a man killed, do you really not know that?"

"Sorry, Mister Darrow," he said. Then, as if confiding a secret, he quietly added, "I'm just some afraid of what Mister Curly might do to me, when he comes back from Deadwood. I was kinda hoping he won't come in here with you bein' present, I guess."

"'Course he'll come in here!" Darrow laughed a little and slapped Roy one on the shoulder. "Listen, I never touched Curly, Kid. Why, the very thought of such a thing! He's a personal friend — and a man don't do such as that to old friends, no he don't."

"But I thought—"

"No, Kid," said Darrow, curling his long lean shape back against the bar. He did not look at Roy, but instead inspected each of his fingernails, one at a time, as he spoke. His hands were as soft and perfectly shaped as a woman's, feminine even in their movement. "There's certain codes of honor that must be adhered to," he said, "or society is wont to break down. Me and Curly been friends a long time. We'd never raise a hand to each other, or a gun for that matter. Why, I'd quit on any man that'd ask me to do so, as Mister Brand knows well enough."

Roy's thoughts flashed back to Curly killing that friend of his brother's during the second robbery, and he wondered if the same code applied. "But if you didn't do it..."

"I only stood by and made sure the boss's orders got followed," said Fleet Darrow. "It was them useless orange-headed spooneys delivered the message — and between you and me, it puckered me some to see the pleasure they took in it. It was a most distasteful entertainment for me. But then, a man don't always get to choose his own work."

"But would that not have angrified Curly toward you as well, Mister Darrow?"

"Not for a moment, Kid. And if you're worried for your own skin, you shouldn't be. Ain't your fault Curly earned what he earned, and ain't your fault he got paid. He won't hold a grudge, I assure you. Curly's a man who owns his mistakes, Kid. He won't touch you unless it's in a professional capacity. You bein' now more-or-less broke, his interest in you will have waned."

"So I've nothing to be afraid of?"

"I wouldn't go that far," said Darrow, still admiring his beautiful hands. "This is an unlawful Territory, Curly's a man for hire, and you're not his friend the way I am. Ain't no part of the code to prevent him beating or killing you — but he won't do it for sport, or for petty revenge over what weren't your fault, but his own."

"Sounds an interesting code, Mister Darrow."

"It's a good code, and that's why it works. If it weren't for that code, there'd be none of us sorta men left, we'd have all killed each other by now."

"Oh, look, here's my food," said Roy as the barkeep skulked in through the front doors. "It was nice talkin', Mister Darrow. I'll think some on that Western code — it's a fascination to me, and I thank you for the sharing of it."

"No problem, Kid. Come down when you wiggled your bean enough, we'll play us some cards and continue your education."

CHAPTER 42
SIMPLE JOYS

As he walked back upstairs with their breakfast, Roy understood that his life, at least for the moment, would have to be lived in two halves — and that's how it went.

Upstairs, he and Charlotte told each other stories, joked and laughed and grew closer in every way. They made the most of their every living moment together, knew each thing they did to be precious.

Indeed, the threat of their imminent deaths made their lives perhaps sweeter.

The joy to be had from the sharing of food; of watching your love brush her hair; or of brushing it for her — these moments were everything to them. For of course, the making of love is not confined to what happens only behind closed doors in the night.

These things and more they enjoyed. No man or God could have rightfully accused Roy or Charlotte of wasting a single loving moment.

And when their love went to the intimate, in the very best moments, it seemed that they flew, and then she cried like a bird — quietly and softly, with a great strength of spirit, her wondrous voice was transformed. And in those moments of floating, of soaring, of emptiness filled up with fullness, Roy *knew her,* and now understood what love might become for a man and a woman together.

And he wanted more for her — more than one half-beautiful week.

In between times together, they also had times apart. Each moment was precious, but it had to be done. Somehow, it was Roy who must save her — and the burden of it lay on him heavy whenever he left her.

He saw how the joy drained from her face, whenever he left their room. She tried not to show how it hurt — fixed a smile on her face every time, but it was a falsity. And if she'd known what Roy knew, she could not have let him go at all.

But he knew the straight of it — knew that each time he put on his socks and his shop-mades and walked out that door and left her, there was a chance he would not come back.

It verily plagued him, the thought of it, each time he stepped into the corridor. He thought of how it would be for her when it all finally went down.

She will hear a few gunshots;

she will know;

it will break her soft heart.

As hard as it was for Roy, the thought of that, it was a thing he accepted.

But he knew now, for Charlotte to be free, he would have to kill Fleet Darrow too, and not just Joe Brand.

When he went down to get them some lunch, Brand wasn't around — but Fleet Darrow was waiting, and Roy spent awhile with him, played a few hands of poker, allowed Darrow to win twenty dollars.

Men speak looser when they're happy, and not much makes 'em happier than winning.

It was something Roy's Grampa had taught him.

Each time Roy came back he checked there was no one to hear it, then rapped that little tune on the door with a finger: *one, one, one-two, one-two, one.*

If he could have seen how her face looked then, he'd have known how much she worried for him while he was gone. Her look wasn't only happiness, it was relief too. For although Charlotte did not know all the details of what troubled Roy, she sensed there was something more to it — something he couldn't tell her.

When Roy went down to get supper, once again, there was no sign of Brand, but Darrow was waiting.

Again, just the two of them played, and the stakes stayed quite low. This time Roy won the first hand, but lost forty dollars to Darrow by the time the meal arrived.

Darrow laughed at him and said, "Drains the sense from a man, too much of a good thing. You won't have a pot to piss in by the end of the week, Kid."

"Just settin' you up for a big one, Mister Darrow," Roy said. And while the pair of them laughed, Roy felt a growing uneasiness, knowing that the big one would not be a poker hand, but something of far more importance.

Roy went downstairs again just after nine. Before yesterday's auction, he had arranged for Everett to meet him then, and bring extra money just in case he might need it.

Roy had worried that he might not get the chance to speak privately with Everett. Way he figured it, Sunday night would be quiet, even more so after such a big turnout on Saturday.

Seemed like he'd got that wrong. Place was near full up again, and it took Roy a couple of minutes just to find Ev and Hank in the crowd. Finally found them down one end of the bar, next in line to be served.

"There you both are," he said, shaking each of them by the hand in turn. "This place always so busy on the Sabbath?"

"Hank'd be the authority on that one," said Everett, his head turning this way and that as he looked for a particular woman he'd acquainted himself with the previous night.

"Just about double what's normal," Hank said. "Lots of faces more usually seen down at the Strike It Lucky. Reckon Joe Brand'll be happy. Seems like some enjoyed it here so much last night they switched. Might be some of 'em enjoyed the *No Guns* policy, now they spent some time in it."

As they stepped up to order some drinks, Everett leaned in close and, real quiet, said, "Here's your thousand." And he transferred it into Roy's hand, right there by the bar.

Roy coughed into his other hand while deftly placing the money into the pocket of his britches.

"See your friends are here, Kid," came the voice of Fleet Darrow behind them. Roy spun around quick, saw the gunfighter's quizzical expression — that languid smile and one slightly raised eyebrow told Roy that Darrow had seen the money change hands.

"Aw, Mister Darrow, you made me jump," Roy said with an eager smile. "Good news! My friend Everett says he'll stake me so I can build up a bank again playin' poker. Looks like you'll be in trouble now!" Then he turned to the barkeep and said, "One for Mister Darrow too, please."

"Reckon your lucky streak's over, Kid. In my opinion, woman's the great ruination of man — and you got that whipped look on your face, like the last of your sense has been drained. What about you two boys? He look to you like he's hid under the bustle too long?"

Neither Everett or Hank looked too happy to be noticed by Darrow, but they made a fair fist of covering it up.

"I said the same thing, Mister Darrow," said Hank. "But my brother here reckons young Roy to be a contrary feller, of a type who works best by opposites. That's why he wants to stake him, and why I stayed out." Then he turned to Roy and said, "Sorry, Roy."

"Funny," said Darrow. "Figured you two boys lookin' the same woulda had the same thoughts — but they reckon a man learns a new thing every day, so maybe that's mine. You two are a fine entertainment to look at, bein' so much identical. What's different about you, your looks I mean?"

"No difference at all," Everett said. "That's why I always wear a brown shirt, so folks know who I am. I tried partin' my hair on the right instead, but I got right confused — every time I looked in the mirror I kept thinkin' it was Hank I was lookin' at."

Darrow laughed that easy laugh of his and said, "Must be some sorta difference."

"Well," said Hank, "I shouldn't *really* tell folk about it — but I do got bigger privates than he does."

"That's a damn lie," said Everett, "and you best take it back, you ugly cuss."

"Fine entertainment alright, I can see just why the Kid likes you. Why don't the both of you come along and play a few hands, test out if he's yet got some sense left?"

'Begging your pardon, Mister Darrow," said Hank, "but we never gamble ourselves. We inherited our looks from our Pa, and his never-ending bad luck as well. Family curse, I put it down to."

"The looks or the bad luck?"

"Well, both, Mister Darrow. Ain't neither one

agreeable to us. But we made a pact on one thing before we came West, that bein' never to gamble."

"That's just fine then, boys," Darrow told him, "and a fair enough pact, I'll respect it. You both'll sit by and watch then instead. Come on, let's go, time's a'wasting."

"Yessir, Mister Darrow," said Everett, as they all moved off together to go find a game. "Be a pleasure to watch awhile. Although when a certain lady comes by, I might head upstairs, if that's alright with you."

"Glad to hear you got one vice at least," said Fleet Darrow. "I was beginnin' to worry."

CHAPTER 44
THE GREAT MATCH AGAINST TIME

Way things went, Joe Brand came downstairs right when Roy, Ev, Hank, and Fleet Darrow went looking for a table.

Darrow saw him coming and said, "Wait up, boys, I'll see what the Boss wants."

Joe Brand was accompanied by the two orange-headed fools who had beaten Curly. They walked one each side, and a path cleared before them. Well heeled all three, as was Fleet Darrow. The others all wore two revolvers, but their boss carried only the one.

"Figured I'd play me some cards," said Joe Brand, "it being the Sabbath and all."

"Cards is the Boss's main religion," Darrow said to Roy with a laugh. "We best join his congregation, Kid." Then he turned to Everett and Hank and said, "You boys are excused for now, Boss don't like strangers too close."

"Yessir, Mister Darrow," said Hank, but Everett only

nodded politely. Then the pair of them shrank away into the crowd, plenty relieved by the looks.

"Come on, Kid, the Boss'll sure test you out," said Fleet Darrow, as he fell in with Brand and the others. "He can always pick a man's bluff, it's damn near unearthly."

Roy followed behind, and they all made their way to that front corner table Joe Brand and Fleet Darrow always favored when eating their meals. It was right by the stage, and had a view of the whole room.

Sheriff Hosea Grimes was already sitting there, a cigar in his mouth and a painted cat on his lap. Despite the crowded nature of the room, no one else was sat at that table.

Brand nodded to the girl and said, "Ain't poke time, but poker time now — *for him*. But you, go make me some money." She jumped off the Sheriff's lap like she'd been bit. Took a step out of her way as she left, Roy noticed, in order to avoid the orange-haired fools. Even if she hadn't steered around them, the afeared look on her face told the story. As for those two, they didn't sit, just stood close by Brand's side and watched the room.

The Sheriff moved to a different seat without being asked. Brand and Darrow took the best seats, of course, the Sheriff the next best, and Roy had his back to the room.

"How's your *wife*, Kid?" Joe Brand said as he shuffled the cards.

"She's just fine, Mister Brand, it's nice of you to—"

"I sure hope you're enjoyin' her, Kid," said Fleet Darrow. "You paid more for her than this whole damn place is worth."

Joe Brand scowled at him and said, "You might be a top man with a gun—"

"*THE* top man," Darrow corrected him.

"Alright then, maybe even that," said Joe Brand, "but Fleet, you're a terrible bad judge of real estate prices. Still, the Kid paid a big price for a whore, that much I'll grant you. What's the most you ever paid for one, Fleet?"

Brand took a box of cigars out, placed it on the table, opened it up and took one. Then he motioned for all present to help themselves. Grimes reached in, greedy-like, and grabbed the cigar nearest to him. But Fleet Darrow, he took his time, chose one carefully and took a long sniff at it, before answering Brand's question.

Spoke wistfully too, Darrow did. "I paid a hundred one time, Boss, fancy place back in Boston when I was nineteen. Worth every damn penny she was. Finely boned as a bird, with hair black as a man's final moment."

"Sounds like a damn poem," Brand grunted.

"French she was," said Darrow, staring off into the nothingness, "and spoke only that language. I'd have paid just to hear the woman talk. I close my eyes and think of her still, when I have to make do with a plain one."

Brand dealt the cards, then looked beside him and said, "What about you two Deputies?"

Brand had just the previous day decided it'd look better if he had Grimes deputize his other two protectors. The Madden brothers were in their early twenties, both with uncombed orange hair and in need of a bath — they were known to be good with their fists and fast on the draw, though famously unable to shoot straight. They'd beaten an innocent kid to death down in Kansas a year ago — just for sport — and were proud that they'd done it.

Though overly vicious and stupid, they were good at following orders, and that was what mattered to Brand — one deadly gunman was enough, and he had Fleet Darrow for that.

The Deputies sorta looked at each other now, dumbstruck — they were accustomed to orders, but completely unused to questions. But after a bit, one said, "Paid five dollar this one time. I forgot it bein' free on account I worked here, but she woon't give it back once I paid. Reckoned herself rough treated, and..."

He looked at Brand a mite guilty, and shut his cake hole then.

Other one wrinkled his nose, sorta sniffed and said, "Took on this job so I'd git it free. Never paid but two dollars afore that. All'ays got what I pay for."

"Lively minds," said Fleet Darrow. He blew a smoke ring toward the Deputies, then a smaller one right through the first, while they watched, slack-jawed.

Brand shook his head slowly, waved the Deputies away and said, "Best leave us now you two. We need a pair of real life geniuses to watch over the Faro and Dice, make sure no one cheats."

"No one *else* you mean, Boss," Darrow said with that smile of his, but Brand only ignored him.

The Deputies left without a word.

Brand watched them walk away before saying, "What about you, Hosea? I bet you spent a pretty penny once or twice."

"I surely did once," said the Sheriff, looking gravely at each man in turn. "Cost me almost as much as the kid here. Five-thousand at least."

"That's corral dust if ever I heard it," said Fleet Darrow, and raised his bet.

"It ain't," Grimes retorted. "I'm sound on the goose'n you know it, Fleet."

"Go on then."

"Late fifties, it was, Santa Barbara," said the Sheriff. "I wasn't much past a kid then. Seventeen, and mostly fool for my age, I'll admit that now, with hindsight. Wedded this woman for her beauty, and she turned out to be a damn whore, just as all women are."

"No argument there," said Joe Brand.

"Kept sayin' she had her monthlies. Ended up, I was with her but once — and that once only when I forced the issue at gunpoint, three weeks into our marriage."

"Always the gentleman," Darrow said scornfully, and threw down his cards.

"Next day her real husband showed up, and he was Jack Powers. He wanted my ranch for a hideout during troubles he knew might be coming, and sent her ahead of time to find one."

Fleet Darrow seemed impressed for once. "That the real Jack Powers, the horseman?"

"Same feller as won The Great Match Against Time, ain't no lie."

Roy didn't say anything, just showed his two pair and scooped up the ninety dollar pot.

"I never believed Powers done that," said Brand. "Had to be some sorta cheat."

"It was sound on the goose," said Sheriff Hosea Grimes. "Whole thing seen by these two eyes, all done on the Pioneer Racecourse. Greatest thing I ever saw."

"Six hours, forty-three minutes," said Darrow, and he whistled through his teeth as he shuffled the cards. "A hunnert-and-fifty mile, using twenty-four mustangs. Owned most of 'em himself. Long straights and tight bends, way I read all about it?"

"True, every word," said Grimes. "He'd do a mile or two on each horse, dismount and run twenty yards to the next one so as to stretch out his legs. Never took no other break than that, other than drinking some water, one time each hour."

"What of food?"

"Took a bite from an apple each time he dismounted, keep his strength up, then the horses got what was left."

"Hard man, I heard," said Darrow as he dealt. "And you, just a kid at the time by your own damn admission, forced yourself on his wife — and yet you live to tell us the tale?

"True as I sit here before you," said Sheriff Hosea Grimes, and he ran a hand over the back of his neck, some uneasy. "I never knew then just how lucky I was. He laughed about it, you know, when I told him it was my first time, and didn't take but a few moments."

"Wish I'd been there for *that* entertainment," Darrow said with amusement. "You confessing it, not the forcing itself — that bit's downright distasteful, and I'd reckon you forfeit your life the moment you done it."

Roy could see the way Darrow's eyes narrowed, and was glad he wasn't in the Sheriff's shoes at this moment.

"Take it easy now, Fleet," said Grimes, nervous-like. "Ol' Jack Powers didn't mind, so neither should you. He let me off with the forcing — agreed I had the right to one poke on account of I went through a marriage. Kindly allowed me to leave in one piece — after signing over my ranch and stock, worth five-thousand, that my Grandpa had left me."

Darrow shook his head slowly and asked, "Powers let you keep your horse and your guns?"

"He did," said the Sheriff.

"Man can't be fairer'n that," Darrow said. "I say we all drink to Jack Powers' deeds, the good, the bad, the indifferent."

Even Roy accepted the glass Fleet Darrow poured for him from Joe Brand's private bottle. Four glasses were raised and four solemn shots downed, before the poker game continued.

Then Darrow's eyes smiled as he said, "Was she worth the five-thousand for that once, despite the short length of the encounter?"

"Maybe she was, thinkin' back on it," Sheriff Grimes answered, rubbing his chin. "It maybe helped build my nature how it is — I sorta like when they fight it, you see, and I still bear some scars on my back where she fought me so hard."

"Ain't right to do that," said Darrow, "and if she'd a'been mine you'd be dead and gone rotten by now. Still, looks like you got the boastin' rights for high payment, except of course for the Kid here."

But Joe Brand said, "Not so fast, boys, I got the winnin' story right here. And the unfairness of it'll make you wanna kill the next damn whore you run into."

CHAPTER 45
"YOU'RE BLUFFING, KID"

Roy was the only one at the table who didn't look up at Joe Brand. *Surely he won't tell it,* he thought. *Don't show too much interest.*

"You can't beat five-thousand, Boss, surely," said Darrow, as they all put down their cards. Roy won that second pot too, eighty dollars this time.

Brand took his time, puffed his cigar back to life before speaking. Them cigars stunk something awful, and Roy coughed whenever they blew smoke in his direction.

Finally Brand told his story. "I lost everything once, on account of a damn worthless woman. A good business I had, small saloon with four working whores in a quiet little town, and no trouble."

"You got ten workin' here, ain't you?" said Grimes as he dealt the next round. "By the numbers, she maybe done you a favor." He shut up quick when Brand shot a hard look at him.

"She was one of my own damn whores," said Brand, his

voice more gravel than ever. "Looked mighty fine when she arrived, and I partook of her plenty."

Weren't easy for Roy to keep calm, but he looked at his cards and breathed slowly. Went through the motions of the poker game, just like nothing else mattered.

Joe Brand bet a hundred after looking at his cards, then went on with his story. "A few months in, her belly was growin'. I told her to get rid of it, but she kept on insistin' it was mine. Cryin' and carryin' on, and men just won't pay for a woman when she's actin' that way. Told me she'd kill her damn self if I didn't let her keep it."

"There's some fellers pay extra for a run at one that's with child," said Grimes. "Specialists, that's where the money is."

"I'm the one told you 'bout that, you damn fool," said Brand. "And it's true enough, she had two regulars came in most days, and I charged 'em triple the usual price. One was the Mayor — they're always good business, town officials. Anyways, she told me she loved me, all that stuff they say when they're desperate, and I let her keep the damn thing. I was just in my thirties by then, hadn't nearly learned how big their lies could become."

He's the only damn liar. Why, I should...

Roy felt like his ears burned, felt like it was spreading to his face. He thought of the derringer in his pocket, but a voice came into his mind — *Don't bet your life 'til you have to* — and he left that derringer alone. Didn't say nothing at all, just met Brand's bet and raised him another two-hundred. It was a fool thing for Roy to do, him having only a pair of Sevens, but his thoughts weren't running too straight.

"You're bluffing, Kid," said Brand, after studying Roy's face a moment. Then he matched the bet, and so did the others, and they all put their cards down.

Funny thing, Brand had been bluffing too — pair of Tens — and it was Sheriff Grimes took the pot with three Kings.

"You're done for, Kid," said Darrow. "Boss has worked out your tell. Too much wigglin' the bean'll ruin a man, and you can't say I never warned you."

Roy shrugged his shoulders, collected the cards and shuffled. "I'm just tired," he said. "Might go get some sleep after this one last hand, if that's alright with you gents."

"*Gents,*" said Fleet Darrow, like as if the word was new to him. "Ain't been accused of that one this past ten years … but I'll take it."

"Sure, Kid," said Brand. "You young'uns need your sleep, after all."

Hosea Grimes looked at Joe Brand then and said, "So you got a kid out there or not?"

"Got dozens I'd reckon," Brand boasted as Roy dealt the cards. "But that whore's child weren't one of 'em, and I shoulda put the damn thing in a sack and throwed it in the river. No way it was mine — never seen such a scrawny kid in all my damn days."

"Might be the Kid here," said Hosea Grimes.

"His name's right," said Brand, "coincidental. Maybe even his age, thereabouts."

"There you go then," said Grimes. "Meet your Pa, Kid."

They all laughed it up at that one, and Roy forced himself to smile along with the joke.

"I been called a bastard many times," said Roy then, "and oft enough wished it were true. Unfortunate truth is, I got a Pa." He sounded right disappointed when he said that bit, and right angry when he said the next. "Never done a thing for me but whip me and talk about manners, worse than any damn preacher. Same size as me he is — and I reckon I'd trade him for Mister Brand if I could. Ain't easy bein' so little."

"You ain't little, Kid," said Darrow, betting a hundred. "Just maybe not quite full size — what are you, five-seven?"

"Almost five-foot-eight, Mister Darrow. But it ain't height that bothers me, it's muscle. Lack of it anyhow. Why, look at Mister Curly, he's shorter even than me, but a big strong feller not to mess with."

"Deputies'd disagree on that point," said Darrow, raising one eyebrow as he looked at Joe Brand accusingly.

"That had to be done, Fleet," said Brand, "and you well know it. Curly made a mistake, and he'll make sure he does better next time. Anyway, the Kid here's a giant compared to the scrawny pup that whore whelped back then. On close consideration though, that pup might well be Mac the barkeep, just look at him there. Damn derringer can't barely see over the bar."

They all turned toward the bar to look. Mac looked like how a squirrel might look if it took to frequenting a tonsorial parlor and wearing a small shirt and tie.

"You never said how it was she cost you so much," said Grimes, after throwing in his hand.

"Tried to leave me," said Joe Brand, absentmindedly running his gloved forefinger over where his pinkie finger should have been. "Convinced some fool customer she'd make a good wife, then had that feller try to kill me. Shot me right through the belly in my own damn place, and missed every damn thing but guts. Damn Army Colt it was. I shot the both of 'em, self defense, but the Sheriff was crooked, and tried to arrest me on murder. I went on the run with nothin' but the cash from my safe, and ain't never been back."

Roy listened to the lies, stayed away from his derringer, raised his bet another four-hundred.

Darrow whistled through his teeth and looked at Joe Brand.

Brand looked close at Roy, said, "Bluffin' again, that won't work, Kid," and threw in his money.

Grimes was already out, but Darrow smiled and said, "Good enough for me."

Brand had a full house, and a smile like he'd cheated the hangman.

Darrow threw down his three Jacks and rolled his eyes at his foolishness.

Roy looked from one to the other, then put down his four Twos.

"Damn Kid," grunted Brand.

"Always told you, Boss," said Fleet Darrow, his voice filled with musical laughter, "you gotta watch out for the little'uns. Ha! Twos! You're a fine entertainment, Kid."

Joe Brand's face grew darker by degrees, but he did not say a word.

Roy looked as happy and excited as he could manage, scooped up almost sixteen-hundred dollars, thanked them all for the game, and walked away through the crowd. As he went back upstairs to Charlotte, the thing uppermost in his mind was how angered Joe Brand had looked at losing that hand.

I should not have done that, he thought.

But it was too late.

CHAPTER 46
WHO TO TRUST

Roy checked there was no one nearby, tapped out the secret knock on the door, and waited for Charlotte to move the chair before he unlocked it.

He went through the doorway, turned quickly, closed and locked the door behind him. She rushed across, met him there by the door.

"I've made a bad mistake," he whispered in her ear as he held her.

Charlotte looked up into his eyes, studied him so hard he wondered if she could read all his thoughts. Then she said, "It'll be alright, Roy. You'll see. Now come to bed and tell me, it might not be so bad as you think, once we talk it all through."

Somehow, up to now, it had been as if their private cocoon made them safe, immune to the dangers around them — as if time was *not* marching forward to swallow them up, end their lives.

But that illusion was lost now, and becoming only more so — leaking away like the lifeblood of a man in his dying.

They snuggled together in their bed, and a whole lot of truth spilled on out of him. At first he told her only of the card game — the way he had angered Joe Brand by beating him in that way.

"But surely he's used to losing sometimes," she said. "I don't see what you did that's so bad."

"It was not the winning, but the manner in which I went about it. Our situation here is precarious, dear Charlotte. I should be losing to him a little, keeping his mood relaxed, to buy us more time. But I made a rash move, tried to bluff him and lost."

"Wait, you said you won. So which is it?"

"I won the *following* hand, and for too much money. And he took it personal. When I lost how I did, he thought he'd found how to read me — a man's *tell* is his greatest weakness in poker, and he thought he'd seen mine. So the following hand, when he saw it again, Joe Brand was sure I was bluffing."

"And you weren't?"

"No. Not that. I wanted to take all his money. Worse, I had murderous intent toward him — in part, *that's* what he saw. I wasn't thinking straight, and he saw it, thought that look was my tell. But what he mostly saw ... I was rattled. Rattled beyond what I've ever been before."

"But surely—"

"Charlotte. Listen, there's things I've not told you."

"Bad things," she said, placing her hand against his cheek, smoothing what soft fur there was there.

"Yes," he said. But his voice sounded so small, so defeated, he could not accept it as his own — and right then, Roy remembered who he was, why he was here, and what he had sought and prepared for all of these years. And doing so, he rallied his strength.

The next words Roy spoke were not weak — he sounded and felt like himself again.

"But not *all* bad, dear Charlotte, not all. There are things in our favor, ways yet we might win this battle. Can you help me, my love? Help me to think, and to plan, and survive this together?"

"You know I can, and I *will*.

And he did not doubt she was telling the truth, for her own voice, though soft in its way, held strength and faith in it — and too, a straightness and goodness there could be no doubting.

"We have an ally," he whispered into her ear. "The man who stood behind me at the auction."

"But he drove up the price, bid against you. Surely—"

"A ruse, I believe. I met the man once before, down in Reno. He beat me at cards, then invited me to dine with him. He spoke straight back then, not a single strange word in his speech. And we made a deal, never to gamble against each other again. He's a quiet one, like I am, you see. Wins small, doesn't get noticed, plays it always quiet and consistent."

"But here?"

"Introduced himself with a different name, Daniel Rowntree — played cards against me, one hand. Filled my head with all sorts of strange words while we played. Dealt me four damn Aces, then let some stranger take his money, *and* mine — and the darndest thing, he made messages out of it all."

"He spoke to you, I remember. When you won the auction. I was worried he was going to shoot you right then, when I saw him lean in so close. What did he tell you, Roy?"

He had never seen her look more worried.

"Told me, *'Go shake his hand, and don't risk your life 'til you have to.'* His exact words. Ain't somethin' easy forgot in the circumstance. And also, he mentioned the sevens. Something about me having listened to him, by bidding the number I did."

"Seven-thousand, seven-hundred and seventy-seven dollars. But what did it mean, Roy?"

"That's just it. I don't really know. He'd dealt four sevens to the miner he let take our money. But I don't find no meaning in that."

"Forget the numbers for now then — do you think the other thing's simple? *Don't risk your life 'til you have to* — it means he plans to help you, yes?"

"Reckon so," said Roy. Then he sat up, blew out the lamp, watched the crack of light under the door a few moments before going on in a whisper. "But not only that, something bigger. See, he told me to go shake Brand's hand. I'd planned on it anyway, for a reason."

"Oh my Lord," Charlotte whispered. "He's him. He's missing a finger, he's the man who..."

Her voice trailed off into breathlessness, as if the horror of the truth overtook her, and she could not speak it.

"Yes," Roy told her, his whispering closer and quieter than ever before. "Joe Brand *is* Big Jim Starr, the man I saw murder my mother."

They lay there then a long time, holding each other, not speaking. Yet in those moments, there was such a loudness — the rushing of blood and the thumping of hearts and the endless roaring blackness of death as it threatened to overwhelm them in all of its power.

Then they heard him outside, Joe Brand himself, Big Jim Starr, talking loudly and laughing as he went to his bed.

And their thoughts, both Roy's and Charlotte's, contained fearful things. For the truth of their lives was now this: they were trapped in his lair. If he had but an inkling of who Roy might be, they would likely be dead before morning.

It was Roy who finally spoke. "I believe he doesn't know. He told the story, right there downstairs, the story of how he killed her. Full of lies to make himself look good — but he told the story. That's how I got rattled, him speaking of my mother's death in that way. And I can't let it happen again — not if we're to survive."

"Are you certain, Roy? Certain he can't guess it's you." Her voice was breathless with the braveness it took just to speak.

"I'd have seen it. I think. Besides, he'd have killed me right there at the table, and had the Sheriff cover it up."

Again they went quiet a good while. Then Charlotte

said, "This Rowntree, what did he say? How can the sevens possibly matter? What was he trying to tell you?"

"I've shook sticks at that east west north and south, and am puzzled most plaguily by it. All I know is this. When I was in Cheyenne, I sent a telegraph to my Grampa. When Grampa wired me back, he told me to go look up Deadwood way. Told me which stage to catch, and to check all the overnights thorough."

"But I don't understand—"

"He's trained me from the start. I have lived only to kill this man." He sensed Charlotte's horror, but went on. "I'm sorry, but that was true. True 'til I met you."

"If only we'd—"

"But we didn't, Charlotte. We're *here*. This is *it*. And we're in it up to our ears. Grampa said two other things. Told me he thought this was it, and to expect help."

"You think he meant Daniel Rowntree." There was doubt in her voice.

"I thought he just meant to have faith, way a Sin-buster would say it — *Expect help when you need it*. We are on the side of Rightness and Goodness after all."

"I know you are, Roy."

"It struck me funny though — Grampa never was much for prayer. But he's old now, and I figured maybe when you get to eighty-five, knowin' what's on its way might set you to readin' a prayerbook."

"But now?"

"Rowntree told me he was my ally. Told me to shake Joe Brand's hand. I reckon now, maybe that was a message, or why else would he say it? Maybe Grampa ain't prayerful at all, but was just bein' practical at twenty-five cents a word."

Charlotte thought about that for a bit while Roy waited. Sometimes we all need some quiet while we work out our workings.

Then she said, "I'm worried, Roy. What if Rowntree's against you? He could be. Why would he not just tell you straight, if he was here to help you?"

"There's always other folks around. Place like this, you never quite know who to trust. And if Joe Brand even suspected..."

"Alright. But what if you *are* wrong about him? Couldn't he be working for Brand? He could. You *know* he could. I'm sorry, Roy, I just—"

"It's alright, we're thinking it through. Each taking an opposite side, that's how to hear which side sounds right. It's come down to this. You're imprisoned, and I can't get you out on my own."

"But *you* could escape!"

"No." He kissed her then, tender and loving and slow. Then he said, "You know I can't leave you here. And you know too, I have to kill him. I can't walk away. Best chance we got's Daniel Rowntree, and he's where I'm placing my bet."

Her voice came out desperate then. "But he's a gambler, Roy. *A gambler!* How can we possibly trust him?"

"I'm a gambler," he said. He sat up. Then out loud now, not a whisper, he said, "Do you trust me?"

The words hung in the air like the past and the future colliding.

"Yes," she finally said. And if there had been doubt before, it was all gone now. "Yes, of course I do, Roy. I trust you completely."

"Well, that's it then," he said. "I trust Daniel Rowntree."

CHAPTER 47
A NERVOUS WAIT

The next morning, there was no sign of Brand downstairs when Roy went down to get breakfast.

Fleet Darrow was there, but seemed troubled somehow. Didn't speak much to Roy anyway, just sat there reading the newspaper, the way Joe Brand normally did.

That worried Roy, of course. Such a change didn't mean nothing good. And it also reminded Roy of something, Darrow sitting there like Brand often did — to save Charlotte, Roy would have to kill Darrow as well, not just Brand.

Mac the barkeep brought the food, and Roy thanked him. He'd been sure to pay Mac something extra, secret-like, ever since that first day. Perhaps Mac would later help him in some important way — but even if he couldn't, or wouldn't, he had not deserved to be thrown up against a wall and threatened by Fleet Darrow that day.

Roy called out a goodbye to Darrow, who ignored him

completely. Then he went back upstairs and ate breakfast with Charlotte, and they quietly went through all Rowntree's actions and words again. Tried to make heads and tails of it all.

Most of it didn't make sense.

But some maybe did:

'Shoot, Luke, or give up the gun.' — Those words seemed like they might be the signal for getting things started. Seemed clear enough now, that Rowntree would shoot the next time, not give up the gun.

"Leastways I hope that's it," said Roy. "Might just be about poker."

"I don't think so," said Charlotte. "Not from how you told it to me. There's only two things the phrase can mean, taken literally. He means it as a sign to start shooting."

Rowntree had made one other thing *overly* clear — he would shoot for the Jack, every time from now on.

"Whatever that means," said Roy.

Charlotte smiled. "Surely the Jack means a person. Perhaps he means *that* literally too — that he'll shoot at the person called Jack. What's the Sheriff's first name?"

"No," said Roy. "Ain't no one here of that name. But I'll try to ask Everett and Hank about that tonight. Could be someone's nickname, now you say it. Like how they call me The Kid."

Roy heard some boots coming down the corridor then, but whoever it was, they was taking care to step softly. He put a finger up to his lips.

Sounded like two of them, neither one speaking as they went by. They didn't go into the bathroom either. Wasn't likely anyway, as Brand frowned on others using his private quincy — but under the circumstances, Roy and Charlotte were using it, and Darrow was a man who mostly did whatever he chose to.

Seemed to Roy like this business was meant to be hidden away from him.

And that's just the sorta business I wish to know about.

He pointed for Charlotte to stay put, went swiftly and quietly to the door, unlocked and opened it, as if going across to use the quincy.

Whoever it was had been too quick — Brand's office door was just closing. They'd not had to wait. Whoever it was had been expected.

Roy crossed the hall, didn't quite close the bathroom door behind him, but left it open an inch or two. Used the quincy while he was in there, and kept an ear out. Nothing else he could do. Brand had made it clear that even one step toward his rooms would be taken as an attack. 'Nothing personal,' he'd said, 'but a man in my position has to shoot first and ask questions later. Not one step past your own door, Kid.' Roy knew better than to test it.

Instead, he went the other direction, looked down from the top of the stairs. One orange-haired Deputy was watching him from a seat at the bar.

Roy walked down the stairs, asked Mac for a bottle of good whiskey, and asked if Misters Darrow or Brand was around.

"Ain't none o' your damn bidness," said the Deputy through a mouthful of rotting teeth. "I got my eyes on that whore o' your'n. I's gonna git her for free, not payin' like you."

Roy thanked Mac and paid him for the bottle, completely ignoring the Deputy. Then he went back to Charlotte, waited nervously inside the door, listening out for whoever it was to come back.

It would prove to be a long nervous wait.

CHAPTER 48
"I WILL GUTSHOOT THAT BOY..."

Inside Joe Brand's office, Daniel Rowntree leaned back in a chair, smoked a cigar, and made clear all his demands.

"Peabody's mine to kill, and no one else touches so much as one hair on his head."

"Then you'll give me a year," said Joe Brand.

"Two months," said Rowntree. He put the cigar in his mouth and produced a deck of cards out of nowhere and commenced to shuffle them fancier than was usually wise.

He had the tricks alright, and he showed them off — hands maybe twelve inches apart, cards flying in curves and in straight lines at once, and never once going nowhere they shouldn't.

"A fine entertainment," said Fleet Darrow, "but how do we know you're as good at bringing in the money? I've met gunmen that good with the tricks — but when it mattered, I littered the ground with them. Card-players ain't so different, I'd bet."

Rowntree kept up the intricate shuffling, his eyes moving from Darrow's to Brand's then back again — and he dealt without looking once at the cards, then picked his own up from the table. "Then let's see."

The other men picked up their cards and took a look — Joe Brand had four Aces, Fleet Darrow a straight flush of Spades, the highest card a Jack.

"Impressive," said Brand. "They don't feel like marked cards."

"They're not," Rowntree said with a smile. "Standard deck."

"Give me nine months," Brand told him, "and you get the Kid, way you want him. Sheriff'll cover it up proper, it'll be self defense."

"I don't suppose you'd both like to bet against this hand I got?" said Darrow.

"I would," said Rowntree, and he put down his own cards, face up. King high straight flush — Diamonds.

"A fine entertainment," said Darrow.

"Two months," said Daniel Rowntree. "You'll make a lot of money in two months, Mister Brand. Word will spread, they'll come from all around to try me out. It'll draw a crowd oftentimes too, when the bigger boys come. I'll make it a real show, the final month."

Joe Brand had been looking for someone like Rowntree — and he knew now for certain, the man was better than he'd ever let on before. Truth was, Brand was ready to make a deal on any terms the gambler named. He'd been mighty pleased when Rowntree sent a message he had a business proposition to put to him. Still, Brand would do the best deal he could. He rubbed his chin, studied Rowntree's face. "What's the grudge? And why not just kill the Kid on the trail somewhere?"

Rowntree stared at him, shaking his head, then looked down at the table. It was a long silence. Then it got longer.

"Six months," Brand eventually said.

Rowntree didn't even look up.

"Damn card players," said Fleet Darrow. "If they was as good with guns as cards we'd never know when they was gonna shoot."

"Some of us *can* shoot," said Rowntree, looking up at Darrow. "Don't take that wrong, it wasn't a challenge — I know my own limitations. But I'm handy with a derringer."

"Derringer!" Darrow spat the word with disgust, turned and looked out the window. Such trifles were beneath real gunfighters. He had never touched a damn *lady-pistol* in his life.

"No interest in competing then, Mister Darrow?" said Rowntree. "I'm planning a contest, you see. Been planning that boy's death a long time. I believe you'll find it quite ... entertaining."

A smile grew all over Fleet Darrow's face. "Hows about we all agree on three months, Boss? On condition he tells us the story, of course, and lets us in on the plan."

Brand's eyes narrowed a little. "Three months then — but I get sixty percent. And this damn story had better be worth it."

Daniel Rowntree shook his head, only the once but he meant it. "Three months, fifty percent — *and* I get exclusive use of his damn little *Queen* he's so mashed with."

"Sixty-forty," said Brand, "and one poke a day at the whore."

"The whole three months, exclusive to me, and in writing," said Rowntree. "The girl's the most important part, and not up for negotiation. I plan to show him how things will be once he's gone, you see? I plan to see the despair in the young pup's damn face when I show him our contract — when he sees she's *mine* for three months."

"He sure does think high of that wagtail," said Darrow.

"And no one else touches him," said Rowntree, thumping his hand on the table. He pointed at Brand, then at Darrow, and quietly added, "No one, in any way — or the whole deal's off."

Brand said, "But if you're plannin' to kill him any—"

"I will *gutshoot* that boy," growled Rowntree, almost under his breath, "and I know the right path for the bullet to kill him, but slowly. Then I'll pay the Doctor to keep him alive as long as he possibly can. His suffering will be mine to observe. His dying days will be spent watching me — and how I treat his *pretty little Queen*."

Fleet Darrow whistled through his teeth and said, "Thought I was a cold one."

"The terms are agreed," said Joe Brand. "You work my poker table three months, you get forty percent and the use of the whore, and you get away with killing the Kid however you want."

"Fifty percent," said Rowntree, "and no story."

"Fifty it is," said Fleet Darrow. "But you'll tell us the story — that's not negotiable neither. Come on, Boss, what's the use of money if not for such prime entertainment?"

"Fifty it is then," said Brand. "Now tell Fleet the damn story so he'll shut the hell up."

Daniel Rowntree told them the story then. Fleet Darrow hung on every word, enjoyed it immensely — but Joe Brand, he wrote out the contract as he listened. Time had become of the essence, for Curly would be back soon from Deadwood, and if there was a shipment of gold, plans must be made for the stage to be robbed. Robber's Roost this time, Brand had decided.

Rowntree told them that Roy was older than he looked; that he grew that fluff on his face to seem younger; that his name was not Peabody, but Price; that he was a damn site more shrewd than he ever let on; and that he'd have picked Curly's marked deck before it was even unwrapped.

Brand swallowed a good slug of whiskey. "So he's good as you, maybe?"

"He's nothing more than a Seven," Rowntree retorted, and he held his head high. "And I — I'm a damn King."

"He sure got Curly a good one," said Brand, "and he's a fair hand at poker."

"The marked deck is Peabody's favorite tool," said Rowntree. "Curly played right into his hands by trying to use it."

"Kid had me fooled all ends up," said Darrow. "Seemed a nice sorta kid. So you're sure then? Couldn't be mistaken identity?"

"Oh, I've followed his career real close," Rowntree told them. "I know *all* about him. And the way he's attached to that whore, he's not even thinking straight. Now I've finally found him, he'll get what he earned — and I'm ready to dish out some justice."

"I'm more one for cash myself," said Joe Brand. "Justice seems overrated to me, but each to his own."

Rowntree told them then *why* he wanted Roy to die and to suffer. "Two years ago in Colorado Springs, Roy *Price* tricked my brother out of everything he owned, playing poker. Matt was a fool, but he didn't deserve that."

Darrow cocked his head to one side. "Lost everything, you say?"

"Matt didn't trust banks the way I do. Carried everything on him in a money belt. The damn Kid got the lot — not just that, but his horse and his saddle and the derringer he carried as well."

"Man bets and loses that way," said Fleet Darrow, "some might say it's his own fault."

Rowntree looked at him coldly. "It was the manner of how it was done. This so-called *Kid* had been there the whole week — I myself was away. He won a little from everyone else, but *always* lost to my brother. Matt was saving for a particular ranch, and almost had enough for the purchase. Planned to marry his sweetheart once he had a home to take her to. That *nice sorta Kid* of yours scooped Matt in with his treachery — you've all seen how he acts, like some innocent kid on a lucky streak."

"He sure enough made fools of us yesterday," said Darrow, and Brand shot him a hard look.

But Rowntree appeared not to notice, just went on with the story. "He made like it was personal to him — that he just *had* to win a big hand against Matt, and couldn't leave

Colorado Springs 'til he did so, or his luck would never return. He raised the stakes up and up, dealt Matt four damn Queens — then beat him with Kings."

"Marked deck?" Darrow asked.

"Marked deck. Matt kept his cards, took them home, four Queens and a damn Seven. That filthy rotten *Kid* left town right away — on my brother's horse. Worst thing was, I played poker against him the very next night, Denver City, not knowing who he was or what had happened."

"What matters most is, who won?" said Darrow with a smile.

"That isn't funny, Mister Darrow. The Kid had told everyone he was headed for Pueblo, was even seen to ride south out of town. But he'd doubled back to the north, camped by Monument Creek, caught the Denver stage from there the next morning. I did beat him that night, up in Denver — took three lousy hundred back from him — and while I was sitting there doing it, my young brother was dying from the bullet he'd put in his own head."

"Oh," said Darrow. "Now I see why you want your revenge. Won't he remember your brother, recognize who you are by your name?"

"Rowntree ain't my name, no more than Peabody's his. And my brother was much younger, we don't look alike. Different fathers. *Peabody* has no idea who I really am. Besides, he won't even know what Matt did after he left. Or what trouble and heartbreak he caused — but he'll know it all before he dies, and have time to think on it."

"Well," said Darrow, "at least a shot to the head would have ended your brother's life quickly."

"Poor Matt hadn't even done that right," Rowntree said coldly. "He lingered on almost two days. The grief of it broke my poor mother, and she passed herself the next month. Just stopped eating and faded away. So whatever happens, nobody else touches that Kid — he's all mine, no matter what. Make it clear to your men."

CHAPTER 49
ALL BUSTED UP

Roy had his ear against the wall, *felt* Brand's office door open more than heard it.

They kept their steps quiet again too.

Roy nodded to Charlotte, counted to four, unlocked the door, opened it up to walk out. Fleet Darrow may not have noticed that Roy looked surprised, but Daniel Rowntree had no trouble reading it.

The pair were almost to Roy's door when he'd opened it, and they had to stop as he stepped out in front of them and turned to lock the door behind himself.

He looked at one then the other, and said, "Sorry, I didn't hear you coming, Mister Darrow."

"That's alright, Kid. You and Daniel Rowntree here met at the auction, I guess."

"Before it," said Rowntree with a smile. "We played a hand together. If I'd won, perhaps I'd have been in that room now instead."

"You shoulda gone for the Jacks, Mister Rowntree. Sure glad you didn't."

"Next time, Kid," said Rowntree. "Next time."

"You comin' downstairs, Kid?" said Darrow. "Rowntree's got plans for a game. Another fine entertainment, in fact. The Boss has agreed on a contest for your lady's second week."

Roy felt the smile drain from his face. "A contest? What sort of a contest?"

"Come along with us, Kid," said Fleet Darrow. "It was Rowntree's idea, we can all have a drink while he tells you about it."

"Alright," Roy said. And the three of them moved away together — they weren't trying to stay quiet now, he noticed.

As they came to the top of the stairs, Roy noticed Curly drinking at the bar — and his brother, Big-Nose, was with him.

Roy stopped in his tracks, but Fleet Darrow — one step down already — turned and said, "I told you before, Kid, don't worry none about Curly. Come on, let's go have that drink."

Curly watched them the whole way, and as they came to the bottom of the stairs, he nodded a greeting and said, "Fleet. Good to see you. You too, Kid, how you been? I hear you been prosperin' since I left. Who's your friend?"

"He ain't really my—"

Darrow interrupted Roy quick. "Business acquaintance of the Boss's, Curly. Mister Rowntree, meet Curly Brown."

Rowntree went to shake hands, but Curly said, "Sorry,

Rowntree, I'm busted up, can't use my hand. Nice to meet you though, any friend of the Boss's is a friend to me too."

"Who's *your* friend there, Curly?" said Darrow with an amused look. "He looks some familiar — I just can't quite place him though.

"Just some feller called Smith," Curly said with a laugh.

"Fleet," said Big-Nose with a nod and a rough sorta smile.

"Smith was it?" said Darrow. "Better than Brown I guess. Feller called Brown with a bounty on him, I heard. Your brother, ain't it, Curly, that Brown feller?"

"So I heard," Curly said with a laugh. "But I ain't seen my brother in years. Boss ready to see us, Fleet?"

"He said you can go on up without me," said Darrow. "He's waiting. Take up a bottle of the good stuff, I noticed his was low."

Mac the barkeep placed two bottles on the counter without being asked. Big-Nose picked one up without a word, then he and Curly nodded at Darrow and moved off up the stairs.

Roy noticed that Curly was still having trouble walking. Grimaced at each step he took, and it was slow going, him leaning on the railing, and putting both feet on each step.

"Busted ribs, my guess," said Darrow, his eyes narrow with annoyance. "Told the Boss them damn pups overdone it." Then he grabbed the other bottle and walked across to the front corner table, Rowntree and Roy right behind him.

"It's unlocked, I ain't got all day," called Joe Brand, soon as Big-Nose knocked at the door.

The brothers Brown took off their hats and walked into Joe Brand's office. Big-Nose closed the door quietly behind himself, followed Curly across the room, put the whiskey bottle on the desk and waited.

"Sit," Brand growled. Then, as they did so, he scowled at the clearly uncomfortable Curly and said, "What the hell's wrong with you?"

"Busted ribs, Boss. Sorry." He kept his head down when he said it.

Brand poured out three whiskeys. "Something happen in Deadwood, or did the Maddens do that to you here?"

"It was from here, Boss. My own fault, I know it," said Curly, then he poured the shot of whiskey straight down his gullet.

"Yes it was your own damn fault," said Joe Brand. "I swear, you two boys is *trying* to outlive your usefulness.

One with busted ribs, the other with a price on his head that keeps him away from Wyoming!"

"But you told us to kill that feller, Boss," said Big-Nose.

"Don't remember telling you to get yourselves seen when you done it," growled Brand. "So who's guarding the stage from now on?"

"Now don't get wrathy, Boss, please," Curly said, "it'll all work out fine the next run. Seen Doc Bevins in Deadwood — he bandaged me tight, but reckoned two ribs to be broke. Bumps and ruts just about busted me halfways apart, just gettin' to Deadwood and back. You know I ain't weak or a shirker, but there's worse trails south, and I just couldn't manage the pain."

"My question was, who the hell—?"

"Sorry, Boss. I suggested a feller to take my place just this one trip. Miner needin' a stake, and everyone's happy for me to take the job back the followin' week."

"So your damn fool big brother here can't rob you this time — *again!*"

"Sorry, Boss," said Curly.

"Sorry, you say? Yet the pair of you fail me again."

"Weren't my fault, Boss, that last time," said Big-Nose. "It was that damn Kid. I *owe* him, way he killed Floyd, shot him clean through the eye. Fluke or not, he's mine to kill, and ain't no one better get in my—"

"You the Boss now, are you? Brand spoke quietly, but with menace. *"Well, are you?"* His mean little eyes had just about closed when he said it, and Big-Nose visibly flinched.

"No, Sir," he said. "I just thought—"

Brand threw his still half-full whiskey glass at Big-

Nose, who ducked just in time. The glass smashed when it hit the heavy log wall behind him.

Then Brand sat and stared at the brothers a few moments, first one then the other, before speaking, even quieter this time, and slowly.

"Do I pay you to *think?*"

"No, Boss," said Big-Nose.

"What ... *do* ... I pay you for?"

Big-Nose hesitated a moment. He shot a glance toward Curly, whose head shook, the tiniest of shakes. Then Big-Nose managed to say, "To follow your orders, Boss."

"That's right," Brand said, as if speaking to a simpleton. "Remember that, and let's not have no trouble again, hmmm?"

"Yes, Sir, Mister Brand."

Brand turned to face Curly again. "Gold shipment on the stage?"

"Not much to speak of this time, Boss," Curly said. "Which means next week's should be big."

"Lucky for you."

Curly eyed the whiskey bottle, but didn't dare reach for it. "Yessir, Boss. You want we should do somethin' else while we wait for next week?"

"I'll let you know," said Brand. "In the meantime, just try not to make me no trouble."

"Yessir. I mean, nosir. I mean..."

Brand's already beady eyes narrowed then. "You ain't thinking to take no revenge on the Maddens, you boys?"

"Should be *you* that does that, Boss," said Big-Nose. Then he lowered his head and said, "Didn't mean..."

"See, that sounds like you been thinkin' again," said Brand. Then he laughed and said, "Leave the thinkin' to me, boys, you ain't suited. Now pour us some drinks, Mister *Smith,* you look like you could use one."

The mood lightened then, and Curly said, "I got nothin' against the Maddens, personal. They just followed orders, Boss, and I know I earned what they gave. They should be taught not to break bones when it's one of their own gang, that's all. But it wouldn't be right, such a lesson coming from me. Not as long as I'm working for you, Boss."

"Well," said Brand, "I ain't happy about it, and I'll have a word with the fools. Fleet weren't happy neither, but I'd best not let him deal with it, we'd just have to bury 'em."

The three men drank and laughed a little then, and Brand finally told them how he'd had the idea for the auction, and dragged a whole lot of money out of the Kid, for a week with the new whore Curly delivered.

"That was some clever and forward thinkin', Boss," Curly said.

"It gets better," said Brand. "Turns out the Kid's a professional poker player. On the one hand, it makes *you* look even stupider, getting out a marked deck for him to read. On the other hand, he'd have beaten you anyway — and he fooled Fleet as well."

"Did the Kid tell you that himself, 'bout him bein' a sharp?"

"No, ya damn fool, 'course he didn't. Was that Rowntree feller just went downstairs with Fleet — he's a sharp too. Turns out he's been lookin' all over for the Kid, got a score to settle. Been planning it all a good while."

Curly threw down his fourth whiskey and laughed. "Bet you got a plan to profit by it somehow, Boss, ain't you?"

"Just about didn't need one," Brand said. "Rowntree's planned it himself, and its workings suit me just fine. Our new friend Rowntree drags what's left of the Kid's money out of him, then he kills him, slow and painful, for revenge." He looked hard at Big-Nose then and said, "You got any problems with that?"

"Nosir, Boss," Big-Nose replied with a smile. "Just happy he's planned him to suffer."

"Good," said Brand. "Because if anyone else touches one hair on the Kid's head, Rowntree won't honor our agreement. Agreement being, he works the poker table here for three months. Things that man can't do with cards ain't hardly worth doing."

"Glad it worked out, Boss," said Curly. "We any part of the plan? I mean, it'd just be nice to see the Kid get what's coming to him. He *did* kill Floyd, after all."

"Thought you hated Floyd," said Brand.

"I did," Curly replied. "But my brother here didn't — and family's gotta count for somethin', don't it? Umm, Boss. I had to pay Doc Bevins for my treatment. Any chance of—?"

"I'm not a damn charity," said Joe Brand. "You're off the payroll for now, the both of you. Can't pay you just to sit 'round lookin' ugly, can I? Now shut up and listen, and I'll tell you what Rowntree's got planned so you don't muck it up."

CHAPTER 51
FOUR JACKS

Downstairs, under Fleet Darrow's ever-watchful gaze, Rowntree had been telling Roy of the plan. Not the extra parts he'd told Joe Brand, of course — the part about Roy getting gutshot weren't mentioned at all.

"It's simple enough, Peabody," Rowntree explained. "I reconsidered my position. Decided I still wanted a week with your ... *Queen* ... and suggested a contest of sorts for her second week here."

Darrow laughed some and said, "Amount of time the Kid spends up in that room, there might not be much left of her after a week."

Roy ignored him and said, "So the contest is cards, I guess? And anyone can enter? Me included?" He heard a sort of whine in his voice at the end, but he didn't really care.

"Sure, you'll be invited," said Rowntree. "But not everyone. It's only by invitation, to be held after breakfast tomorrow, so you'd best be ready."

"Tomorrow?" said Roy, alarmed. "But I got the whole rest of the week."

"You'll get your whole week, Kid," said Darrow, clearly relishing the show. "Though I'm guessing you won't much enjoy it, thinkin' of how Rowntree here's gonna use your girl hard when he gets her."

Roy looked into Daniel Rowntree's eyes. "You really think you got what it takes?"

Rowntree looked back at him, his eyes just about dancing with mirth. "Might not be me takes the prize. With the right allies, any man could win."

"Maybe so, Mister Rowntree, but poker levels things up, I always reckoned."

"Maybe not level enough," Rowntree said. "Let's play a hand, Mister Peabody."

"I need to get back upstairs," said Roy, and he stood as if to leave.

"Might as well stay awhile," said Rowntree. "You've not heard about the rest of the contest. Hate to see you arrive unprepared."

Roy sat back down and watched Rowntree commence to shuffle fancy — fancy as he'd ever seen. Fancier even than Roy could shuffle himself.

"That's neat tricks alright, Mister Rowntree," said Roy. "You mean to put fat in my fire, but a lucky streak goes a long way, and I reckon I'm on the best one I ever had. So how's about just bein' straight, and tell me *how* I'm gonna win the extra week with Miss Charlotte?"

Rowntree dealt as he spoke, and he watched Roy's eyes

the whole time. "Well, young Peabody, you've got confidence anyway. I like that, you're going to need it. So, here's what you're up against. It's all to Mister Brand's satisfaction, and all on his whim — so don't try to change it, he knows his own mind. He'll be competing against us too, by the way. And so will our friend, Mister Darrow here. They're the two big guns."

"Ol' Silver Sam too if he wants," Fleet Darrow said with a laugh. "On account of him being an underbidder before, and fine entertainment besides."

Roy picked up his cards and looked at them. Three Aces, a Two and a Seven. "Anyone else invited?"

"The Sheriff, of course," said Rowntree. "He made a bid too, remember? He's not heard of this yet, but I'm certain he'll want in."

Fleet Darrow looked at his cards and said, "We gambling on this hand or what? Just for interest's sake, I mean. Not that I got much. Honest."

"Alright then," said Roy. "I'll bet twenty, and take two cards please. So, no one else in the contest? How many hands do we play? I'm sure Mister Brand plans to profit, so how much is the buy in?"

His head spun from the possibilities — *was* Rowntree yet to be trusted? He seemed somehow different than before.

What if it ain't an act?

"I'll just take one card," Darrow said, "and raise you a hundred for sport."

Rowntree met the bet but didn't raise, and he threw away one card himself. "Just that one other feller who bid at the auction, I believe. Thousand dollar buy in. Each man deals one hand then the poker round is over."

Roy looked at Rowntree, then at Darrow, who looked more amused than ever. "The *poker* round? But what else—?"

"Shootin' contest, Kid," said Fleet Darrow with glee. "You reckon poker's a leveler, but it ain't got nothin' on guns. Guns is what truly levels things, man to man, in the West."

"But I can't—"

"Come on, Kid," said Darrow. "You're on a lucky streak, remember? Contest tomorrow'll be *all* sorts of fun, I wouldn't reckon. Only wish we could put it on the stage, make a show for the public."

"It has to be private," Rowntree said in a hurry. "Mister Brand doesn't want people thinking it's okay to fire guns in his place."

Roy looked hard at Rowntree, then directed his question to Darrow. "What are the rules then?"

Darrow's eyes danced the whole time he answered. "Target'll be set up at the end of the room. One free shot for each entrant. Then each extra shot costs five-hundred. Most points takes the girl for the week. Don't you just love a good novelty?"

"To be clear," Rowntree said, as he dealt out the extras, "each man starts the contest with a thousand. He can't buy extra shots at the targets by bringing in extra money — he has to win that money from the poker game."

"But I can't shoot worth a damn," Roy said, and his brow was creased deep as he looked at his extras. Rowntree had dealt him a Two and a Seven — same as he'd thrown away. "I don't even own a proper six-gun," he whined.

"Lady-pistols," said Darrow, with a slight disgust in his tone. "Sure you own one of *them,* Kid." He'd smiled a sneaky one at Rowntree when he said that. Then he added, "Think I'll raise another hundred."

Rowntree said, "What I think our friend Mister Darrow means, is that most men who play poker carry a derringer for personal protection — and usually know how to use it. You *do* have one, Mister Peabody?"

"I have one," said Roy. "But that thing is tiny — ain't no use at all past four feet."

"Well, I hope *that's* a bluff," Rowntree said, "or it won't be much of a contest. Rules can't be changed now, they've been set and all written down. We'll toe a line ten feet from the target, so those with long arms will shoot just over seven-and-a-half."

"Fancy my own chances, maybe," Darrow said happily. Then he demonstrated the prodigious length of his arms by reaching one out across the table, and playfully scratching Roy's cheek with two perfectly manicured fingernails. "Just need to work out how to shoot a damn lady-pistol. Ain't never lowered myself to touch one before — but it can't be too hard to master for a feller like me. You in or out, Rowntree?"

Rowntree said, "Out," and put down his cards, one at a time, all face up and spread so they could see 'em. First four he put down were Spades — the Nine and Ten, the Queen and King — then right in the middle, he placed the blood-red Five of Hearts to ruin things.

"Shootin' for a particular Jack?" said Roy. "Seems like terrible long odds to me."

Rowntree threw his hands up in front of him and said, "Just wasn't my day. But it'll come."

Darrow looked like the cat that got the cream when he said, "What you got there, Kid?"

"Three Aces, Mister Darrow," Roy said as he placed them on the table for viewing. "That enough?"

Fleet Darrow smiled and put his own cards on the table. "Four Jacks."

Rowntree faked puzzlement a moment. Then he openly winked at Fleet Darrow and said, "Now however did that happen? Why, I wanted that Jack for myself. Must have made some unlucky mistake."

"They say luck's a lady," said Fleet Darrow with a big hearty laugh, "but I reckon she's mostly a beautiful, fickle damn whore. Can't think badly of her a moment though — for she's ever been a fine entertainment."

Daniel Rowntree's lilting voice and spurious smile were both clearly meant to mock Roy. "One Ace short, Peabody? Unlucky today — maybe you'll get it the next time." Then he laughed it up good and added, "Only way you'll get that Ace is to deal it yourself. Best get upstairs and practice, tomorrow's the day."

CHAPTER 52
TOMORROW'S THE DAY

Thing about men, is each one turns out to be two. Even the man who shows himself the hardest and toughest and most uncompromising in all his public dealings, might well, at home, be the most henpecked and worn down feller ever to say the words, "Yes, dear," and climb out of bed in the cold dark night to go mend a rattling pane — just so his "dear" will stop nagging him.

Point being, only those closest to us, might ever truly see what we are.

Roy, like all others, was a man of two parts. There was the true part, good and straight and open as a corral gate with a remuda still but halfway through it. He mostly kept that part a secret. Then there was the side he cultivated in public — the "acting" side, you might call it.

That side of Roy — the acting side — was who he took back upstairs to Charlotte on this one occasion.

It wasn't that he didn't want her help. Maybe he even *needed* it. But that great responsibility he had always felt around women was weighing upon him more heavily than ever before.

Ever since he was seven years old, Roy Stone had been a protector of women. He just couldn't help it. For some men, that sorta thing comes as simple as breathing.

He thought about that on his way up the stairs. Took a few minutes extra on the quincy before going to Charlotte — thought it through some more while he sat.

This is my own problem, mostly. Her problem too, in a way, but it's mine to fix. I'll explain things to her in good time. But first, I'll think on it myself, with no female influence, no ladylike irrationalism, no womanly emotion to affect my straight thinking.

Five minutes later, he still wasn't getting nowhere — but he knew it just would not do to sit there on that quincy all day.

He walked out, crossed the corridor, knocked the secret knock on the door, waited for Charlotte to move the chair. It was a comfortable ritual now, but it would not happen many more times.

We'll be free, or I'll be dead.

He unlocked the door, set his best acting mask on his face, and went in.

"You were gone a long time, Roy," she said, and she kissed him. "I was worried about you."

"Just been playing poker and yammering downstairs."

It hurt him to think.

She will hear a few gunshots;
she will know;
it will break her soft heart.

"What's wrong, Roy? That was Daniel Rowntree you went with, I heard the other man say his name. I'm not a fool, Roy. Something's wrong, I can tell."

"No it ain't, I'm just tired from tryin' to think. I need to go outside awhile, ride a fast horse or somethin', just breathe and be free I guess. I ain't suited to being stuck inside this place like a woman."

"And I *am?* I belong here, do I? Well, Roy *Whatever-Your-Name-Is,* you're free to go off and leave me whenever you like!"

She tried to storm off in a huff — but there's only so much stormin' and huffin' any person can manage in a ten-foot by twelve-foot room. After two stampy steps she'd got to the bed, and then she was just about done, so she threw herself down and cried.

Weren't expecting that, he thought.

Truth was, her little tantrum only served to make him wrathy at the edges. He knew he was meant to go comfort her, but he didn't have time for none of that now — this was serious doings going on, and he had to protect her!

Damn womanly feelings! Just what a man needs in a tight moment ain't it!

"I got the squirts, I'll be in the damn quincy," he growled. Then he turned and walked out the door, locked her in with her tears and her foolishness.

Didn't help none, of course. Never does. Always was a

problem with women, their need to cry and carry on, right when you need 'em to be straight and strong and bounce thoughts off without 'em interrupting.

He didn't really have the squirts. Didn't even take down his britches before he sat down — might need to leave anytime.

Fifteen minutes later, he was still sat there on that quincy, and his thoughts were about clear as mud with cow-chips all through it.

I'd kick a dog if I had one, he thought. But he knew that wasn't true, and he laughed at the silliness of the thought. *I never kicked a dog in my life.*

I'm treating Charlotte like that though.

His dang legs were gone numb from sitting on that fool indoor thunder-box too long, and by the time he got the blood moving in his legs again, he had to wait longer anyway — Curly and Big-Nose were finished, and were coming down the corridor.

He put an ear against the door and listened while they went past — didn't hear nothing useful — then he went back in to his darling.

"I'm sorry," he told her right off, and she jumped right up from the bed, ran to him and kissed him, before he even had the chance to lock the door.

"I know it's hard," she said, caressing his cheek. "And I shouldn't have said anything. But I know by your face now when something's gone wrong, and I just want to help, darling Roy. Whatever you need me to do, please just tell me."

Roy was a lot stronger than he looked. He swept her right off her feet and threw her over his shoulder, then he turned and locked the door, before carrying her across the room. He laughed as he threw her in the air and she fell to the bed.

She was a sight alright, still being short on proper clothes, and her landing on the mattress that way had set her flesh to all sorts of bouncing and jiggling.

"Listen up then, Miss Bird-Hat," he said, wiggling his eyebrows for fun. "Best thing you can do for me now is to help me clear out my wrong thinking. Know of any way you might do that?"

Then he jumped on the bed right beside her, and she squealed with laughter — then they cleared out their thinking together, best possible way they could think of.

And when they were done they lay there in each other's arms, and Roy thought it all through, his mind clear now.

"With the right allies, any man could win."

"Maybe you'll get that Ace next time."

"Only way you'll get the Ace is to deal it yourself."

"Get upstairs and practice."

"Tomorrow's the day."

"Tomorrow's the day." Roy had said it very quietly, just thinking, but it had slipped out of him. Then he realized he'd done it, and he looked at Charlotte's face.

Her eyes told a tale of worry, but her smile spoke of confidence in him.

"I'm sorry," he said. "Didn't mean to speak it out loud."

"It's alright, Roy," she told him. "I knew it was coming.

I'll be quiet again, let you think." And she looked at him with such trust, he knew he could do it, knew he could save her from harm — and knew he would give his own life for her, if he had to.

Tomorrow's the day.

CHAPTER 53
"HE CALLED ME QUEEN"

In the end, Roy never spoke no more to Charlotte of the cards, or of what Rowntree said, or of what any of it might mean. Not until their last moments together anyway — he would leave it 'til right before he went off to kill, or be killed, or both.

All that, because he'd decided it didn't much matter. Either way, his best chance was about to present itself — most likely his only chance. He would kill Joe Brand with his derringer during the contest.

If Rowntree was truly his ally, he would help when it come to the scratch. All Roy could do was to listen to Rowntree — to trust him, or maybe learn not to.

Roy's only trips downstairs in that final twenty-four hours was to go and get meals — plus one trip at night to say his goodbyes to Everett and Hank. They were there, just like he expected. And once again, Fleet Darrow was right there as well, all on top of them the whole time. No chance to speak quietly, no chance even to pass a note.

Don't matter, Roy decided. *Everett's got my last letters to send, and the money I left there to carry out what I want done.*

It was a relief, all that being in place, and Everett being a man he could trust — but it didn't make leaving his darling no easier, for what would likely be the last time.

He had told her of the contest. It was only right that she knew — so that she could prepare herself for the news that must surely come.

They had stated their feelings and said their *goodbyes* and *I-love-yous* — not just said them, but brought them to life, made them physical in ways that were beautiful and lasting. They were joined forever somehow, in all ways that mattered.

He dressed slowly, deliberately. Rubbed his left boot for luck. He had told her the meaning of that.

She sat now on the bed they had shared, looked up into Roy's loving eyes.

"I believe that I carry your child," she told him, and she rubbed her belly when she said it. Her eyes danced with his, and she said, "You come back to us, Roy."

"He called you my Queen," said Roy, cupping her chin and cheek in his hand, half-strong and half-gentle. "Rowntree said it, I mean, and he's right. "You're my Queen, my dear darling Charlotte."

"Queen Bird-Hat," she said, her voice as thin as her smile.

"Yes," he answered. But his own voice did not weaken — for he must be strong, and always *believe* he would win.

"Queen Bird-Hat," he said with a laugh. "I'll be back in an hour or two, don't you fret or worry."

Then a strange look came upon Charlotte's face, and quietly yet urgently, she said, "Roy, wait! He called me Queen."

"Yes, but—"

"I was right, Roy. The Jack. Don't you see? He said he'll shoot for the Jack. We're all cards in the pack, every one, don't you see? The Jack will be Darrow, I'm guessing. But *listen* to Rowntree, Roy, listen! *Oh, Roy, please!* Listen to him, trust him, do whatever he says. He's your ally, you were right, it's all true!"

"Alright," he said. "Our money's on Rowntree." And he smiled, leaned down and kissed her, one long last lingering kiss of the finest lips he'd ever tasted. He stood then and said, "Time I gave you my name."

Then Roy turned, walked to the door and unlocked it, opened it up and walked through. Looked both ways to make sure there was no one nearby to hear him. Turned and stood there in that doorway, said, "I love you, Charlotte Stone."

And he closed that door for the last time, and then he was gone.

They were all there already.

Waiting.

Roy walked down the stairs, took it all in. The front saloon doors were locked tight, and the shutters all drawn. Every lamp lit, just like night time.

No sunlight would shine on this final hour of reckoning.

He'd expected less men to be there, and his heart sank — but only a little.

I'll still get it done.

He *knew* he would kill Joe Brand. The problem was his own survival, once it was done.

It was one huge round wood table in the middle of the room, and the players were already in their seats. Strangest thing, not a woman to be seen — which showed the integrity of the poker game was to be taken serious.

No distractions.

Mac the barkeep turned his head and nodded to Roy.

He mouthed the words *"Good luck"* as he nodded, but no sound came from his lips.

The piano player was there too. Sat up straight at the piano he was, all clean and pressed and ready, as if it was night-time, and the whole saloon full of gamblers and drinkers and whoremongers. It occurred to Roy then that he did not know that man's name, had not ever met him, and perhaps never would. He smiled at the feller and put that out of his mind.

It no longer mattered.

It occurred to Roy then, that the place had the air of a funeral — rather than a contest and a merriment, the way the auction had done.

He pushed *that* thought away from him too.

Of course, it was Joe Brand who spoke first. He'd waited 'til Roy came to the bottom of the stairs, then he turned from his place at the head of the table and said, "Look, boys, it's the Kid, finally blessed us with his presence. You're five minutes late, Kid. Just partook of a last poke for luck, I expect."

Most of them laughed. Not Daniel Rowntree.

"Sorry, Mister Brand," said Roy as he crossed to the table. "I didn't expect quite so many players. Thought the game wouldn't take long, or I'd have made sure to be early."

"Got your thousand, Kid? Take a seat and put it in front of you, Mac'll change it for chips."

"Yessir, Mister Brand, I got it alright." He took the only available seat, placed his thousand on the table, and Mac took it quick, put three stacks of colored chips in its place. Roy was seated directly opposite Joe Brand. Too far to shoot under the table anyways. And worse, Roy had Curly sitting one side of him, and Big-Nose sitting the other side.

"Kid," said Curly with a quiet nod.

"You know most of the boys," said Joe Brand, who got to his feet now. "But I'll make introductions anyway, so we're all on friendly terms."

"Friendly fellers, we surely all are," said Fleet Darrow, and he even sorta looked like he meant it.

"You all know Fleet Darrow," said Brand, putting his gloved right hand on the gunfighter's shoulder. "Next to him's Deputy Levi Madden, then—"

"Naw, I'm Lucius, Boss," said the orange-headed fool, which earned him a real unfriendly look.

"You're Levi if I say you are, Deputy," Brand said. "Now what's your name?"

"I'm Lu ... naw wait, I'm..." Orange-haired fool sat there with his left eye all screwed up and his right eye looking across at his brother for guidance. Thing was though, Levi was the clever one — too clever to say a word anyways, right now when it might get him shot.

Joe Brand shook his head and said, "I best not confuse the boy further, he'll forget who he works for." Then he pointed at him again and said, "That's Lucius Madden. Next beside him's Curly Brown, down the end there Roy Peabody. Next beside him's ... Mister *Smith,* I believe, is that right, Sir?"

"That's me alright," Big-Nose said with a chuckle, and most of them laughed it up good.

"I notice a resemblance to my friend Curly Brown

there," said Fleet Darrow then. "Cousins perhaps, Mister Smith?"

"Could be," said Big-Nose. "I got cousins all over, I reckon."

"Next to Mister Smith," Brand went on, "is ol' Silver Sam. You got a last name, Sam?"

"Reckon I did have at one time," said the old man. "But I sold it for money to drink with."

Fleet Darrow busted out laughing and said, "You won't never need drinkin' money again, Sam, not while I'm alive to buy for you. You're a fine entertainment alright, and a good feller with it."

Old Sam made a fancy gesture with his old wrinkled hand, half like a bow and half like a wave, and said, "Thank you, good Sir — but it shan't be needed. I plan to win this day and expire most pleasantly drained within the week, naked as the day I was born, and lying exhausted on the soft milky chest of that lovely young woman upstairs."

"A fine entertainment," Darrow repeated. "I hope you succeed in your plan."

"Next to Sam," said Brand then, "we got Deputy Levi Madden — this one knows who he is, he's the clever one, right, boy?"

"Yessir, Mister Boss, Sir."

"See? Clever as a sheep, that one. Then we got Daniel Rowntree next to him, who we all can thank for the idea of today's entertainment."

There were some murmurs of, "Thanks, Mister," from the Deputies.

But Brand quickly told them, "Shut your cake holes, you damn fools, you can thank him after he takes a year's wages from each of you. And finally, here at my left, you all know our upstanding Sheriff, Hosea Grimes. Now some of you boys I've had to make loans to so you could play — let's be clear, if you've anything left when we're done, it comes straight back to me."

"Weren't thet a gift?" said Lucius Madden, but Brand just ignored him and went on.

"Rules has been writ out by Rowntree, and is nailed up on the wall in plain sight right there, boys."

"But I cain't make hids nor tails of thim scratch marks," said Lucius.

"Calm down and shut it, I'll tell 'em out loud too — but only one time, so listen up good. We each deal one hand of poker. First two cards you deal goes face up in the middle — them two's community cards, then each man gets dealt three face down. Twenty dollar ante, then two rounds of betting like usual."

It was Lucius didn't get it, of course. "Can anyone take them first two?"

Roy noticed Joe Brand's hand move then to his gun — the big pearl-handled revolver. "One more word from you, Lucius, there'll be one less player alive to take part in this game."

"Poor gump can't help it, Boss," said Curly. "He only ever played poker round here, where it's generally always four men, and no need of community cards." Then he turned to the orange-haired spooney and said, "It's alright, young Lucius, I'll help you to learn as we go."

Lucius looked to his brother, who nodded it was okay, then he made a small wave of thanks to Curly.

Brand removed his hand from his six-gun. "May I finish now, please? Thank you. Way it works, even if a man's out of money, he still deals when it's his turn, then throws in his hand, sight unseen. The ten-thousand dollars on this table is the only money can be used in the game. At the end of ten hands of poker, each man in turn gets one free shot at the targets. Even if he's broke — one free shot, every man. All shots after that one cost five-hundred dollars. If you got money, you *must* use the money to take shots — no holdin' onto the money. Man who takes the most shots might not win, but the more money you got the more chances you get to score points. Man who hits any part of the postage stamp scores ten. Red ring around it's worth seven. Anywhere in the white ring is four. A single point if you hit the target anywhere outside that. All clear enough?"

Right away, Roy said, "What if it's a tie, Mister Brand?"

Brand was silent a moment, then looked partway left and said, "Rowntree?"

"Once saw that happen," said Rowntree. "California. The two men swapped pistols and took one more shot with each other's."

"That'll do then," said Brand. "You little whores all bring your lady-pistols? Well, keep 'em hid in your bustles, 'cause first we's playin' some poker."

CHAPTER 55

IN HONOR OF WILD BILL
HICKOCK

I t was Hosea Grimes who dealt first.

"Music," growled Brand, and that fine clean piano feller started out down the heavier end of the instrument. It sure sounded fearful to Roy, first minute or two anyway.

While the Sheriff was shuffling, Daniel Rowntree explained — for the benefit of those less experienced — that with ten players, a hand might be won with not much of nothing at all.

"Two pair's a good hand, and even three Twos will generally win you big money. Lots of times, men'll have the same hand, and then it comes down to high card. And as always, a good bluff sometimes beats a good hand. Only last week the Sheriff here tried to raise me two-hundred, and scared me right off — dang bluffer beat me with a damn pair of twos."

Grimes laughed as he dealt out the cards. "What *did* you have when you folded that night?"

"Had me a straight," Rowntree answered, and they all busted out laughing, especially Grimes.

For such a high stakes game, it was played with a high degree of merriment. The somber mood of the room when Roy first arrived hadn't lasted much past the initial dealing of cards. At that point, the novelty of the contest seemed finally to take over. Mac kept the drinks up to the men, the piano feller switched to playing good lively tunes — and soon, it seemed like most of the men round that table were only there for enjoyment.

No one had much that first hand. There was some bluffing, of course. Fleet Darrow won it with two pair, but the pot had stayed quite small, the way opening hands often do.

Got interesting the next hand, when Rowntree dealt. They were using ten brand new decks so no one could complain — all ten stayed unwrapped, in full view the whole time on the table, until each was about to be used.

The two face cards Rowntree dealt were an Ace and an Eight.

As Rowntree dealt the rest of the cards, Fleet Darrow remarked, "They say Hickok had Aces and Eights when that yellow murderer sneaked up behind him. Cost me my fair chance at the man."

"Heard that too," said Silver Sam. "They's callin' it the Dead Man's Hand now. Seen it wrote big and black, took up half the front page of the Chronicle."

"Fabrication to sell newspapers," said Brand. He looked at his three cards, then the two face cards in the middle, then his own three again. "Any fool believes that, you best believe this here's a bluff, and I'll happily take all your money." And he put a hundred dollar chip in the center.

"You'll get your turn, Mister Brand," said Rowntree, and pushed the chip back toward the saloon owner's pile. "Bets must be made strictly in order, lest there be confusion."

Joe Brand was unused to being told what to do. He was the boss, and was pretty much accustomed to doing whatever he wanted, whenever he chose. Fleet Darrow pushed those boundaries at times, but he didn't mind too much — no one else was game to, and it reinforced their perception of Darrow's power, and therefore his own by extension. His mouth tightened now as he looked at Rowntree, but he only laughed. "I know it, Rowntree," he said. "Just makin' sure these boys all think I'm runnin' a bluff. Hurry up and bet, Deputy, we ain't got all the damn day."

"I think I believe it," said Darrow, "about Wild Bill. If they only hoped to sell papers, they'd have made the hand a better one. Four of a kind or a flush. Be a much better story, you see?"

As the betting started up on this hand, the talking went on.

"It should rightly have been a handful of Kings," Rowntree said. And there was something in his tone that made Roy sit up and listen. "I've never met a real King — but I played against Wild Bill several times, and he seemed like a true King to me. Often chased Kings too, in the game."

"I played him some too," Silver Sam said. "Over in

Deadwood mostly — he never liked Custer City, for reasons I won't be repeating. Dang bluffer Bill was though, tell you that much. I once throwed in three Tens, and he won the thousand dollar pot with a dang pair o' Kings."

"You see?" Rowntree said with a laugh. Then he looked off into the *used-to-be,* someplace away in the distance, and added, "Bill beat me with four Kings one time, and he looked his happiest then. Fulfilled, almost, how I'd put it. I was never so glad to lose money. He was a finer man than will be remembered, most likely. *A drink to Wild Bill!"*

Sheriff Hosea Grimes leaned back, turned to his left, spat tobacco juice onto the floor. "Fine man? Hickok weren't half so game as they tell it, and not half the man he's made out to be."

Hard to say which came first — the opening wide of several men's eyes and mouths, or the loud click of Silver Sam's pistol as he cocked its hammer and pointed it.

All them things happened right quick.

"I been havin' some strife with my hearin'," said old Silver Sam, barely containing his rage. "What's that you say, Grimes? Best you speak *real* clear — old man like me's mighty shaky, and the trigger on this ancient gun can't maybe be trusted."

CHAPTER 56

DEAD MAN'S HAND

Sheriff Hosea Grimes had never figured himself facing danger from an ancient drunk with a derringer. Yet here he was, staring down the barrel of the palm-size pistol — and from three feet away, that forty-one barrel looked to him like a cannon.

He looked down at Silver Sam's left hand, then up at the man's face, then he swallowed. The Sheriff's thoughts were clear enough to any man who could even passably read another man's eyes.

And them thoughts wasn't brave.

"Easy, Sam," he said, his voice the weak whine of a man preparing a lie. "I only said, *He was a fine man.* And agreed too, that Hickok was as good as what others just said."

Silver Sam's old eyes had a fine conversation with the Sheriff's then, before Sam's mouth come right out and said, "Seems like an irony to me, way you're fillin' your britches right now after sayin' what you said about Bill. Why, I reckon in your situation, young Bill woulda filled me with hot lead by now and gone right back to his card game. Yet you sit there disgracing yourself and that damn badge you wear. Well?"

"Well what, Sam? I was only—"

"The well what is," said Silver Sam with a slow smile, "are you goin' to reach for your gun, Sheriff Damn Full-Britches Grimes? Or instead, make apologies to Bill?"

Words spilled outta Grimes so quick you could bare understand 'em. "I'm sorry, Sam, I'm sorry."

"Not me! Apologize to Bill, ya damn piece of—"

"Bill, Bill, I meant Bill! I'm sorry, Wild Bill Hickok, disrespecting your good name in such manner. Please, Sam, I didn't mean nothin' by it, it was talk, that's all, only talk, I—"

"Shut up now, Sheriff," said old Sam. "You done talked enough. Think best we *all* drink to Bill now, as this fine feller Rowntree suggested." But he kept the gun pointed.

"You can put the toy gun away, Sam," said Darrow. "If the Sheriff behaves badly toward you I'll blow his damn disrespectful head off his shoulders myself." And he smiled coldly at Grimes.

If Hosea Grimes had ever had the respect of any man present, he'd sure lost it by now. His words about Wild Bill had been bad enough — but the whining way he'd backed down, that was inexcusable.

All present put down their cards — or in Silver Sam's case, his gun. Then they all raised a glass and drank to Wild Bill. Even Joe Brand — who in truth, respected no one, either living or dead — was not game to leave his glass on the table.

There's some things just ain't an option, if a man hopes to keep up his breathing.

"To Wild Bill," said Fleet Darrow again, after putting down his glass, empty. "We'll sort out who's fastest when I get down below. It's either Bill, or it's me, or it's Old Scratch himself, and it ought be a hot competition." Then he raised an extra fifty and said, "So. Bill's the King you say, Rowntree? What am I then, the Ace?"

"I'd surely call you the Jack, Mister Darrow," said Rowntree.

He IS the Jack, Charlotte was right, thought Roy, and somehow, he kept his face blank as excitement roared through him. *Rowntree will shoot for the Jack. That's just what he said that first night here, and been showin' me ever since.*

Darrow seemed a little taken aback. "Only the Jack? How could that be?"

"You, Mister Darrow," said Rowntree, "are the Jack, a Prince among men. Straight and handsome and tall, a man of discernment and intelligence — but deadly and dangerous with it. The sort of man gets the job done, stays forever young, makes a difference to history. Admired and feared by all men, loved and desired by *almost* all women. I'm surprised you never thought of it before."

"Maybe he's got better things to think about," growled Brand, much to Darrow's amusement. "Like this game we're playing, for one thing." And he flicked that hundred dollar chip to the center of the table.

"Well, perhaps *he* does," said Rowntree, fixing Brand in his gaze as he dealt out the extras. "But as a poker player, such thoughts are how I make my living. You see, Mister Brand, I know you have at least one Ace in your hand. Now how could I possibly know that?"

Brand smiled coldly. "Cheatin' maybe? You marked one of my cards? Maybe somehow you know what you dealt."

"Maybe that last one," said Rowntree. "I've heard tell such things are possible. But in this case I'd have known anyway, no matter who dealt. Because I know *you*. Not just you — other men too. But certainly *you*. Thing is, you'd only raise that much if you had Aces. I don't know everything about you, Mister Brand, but that much I do know."

Rowntree's sure pushing it, thought Roy.

"Superstitious nonsense," said Brand, glaring at Rowntree. "Leave me out of all that. I ain't built what I got from superstitions and hunches."

"That's true," said Darrow. "The Boss don't scare easy along such lines. He's as like to bet thirteen on the wheel as any other number."

"Perhaps, Mister Darrow," said Rowntree. "But even if *he* doesn't know it, Mister Brand *is* the Ace. Just as you are the Jack, and aspire to collect them — just as Wild Bill was a *King*, so that's what he went for, whenever he found opportunity. Each person's a card, whether they know it or not. Your Boss is the Ace. He relates to the Ace, and resents anyone else collecting them. If I was to beat Mister Brand with four Aces, he'd take it as a personal affront."

Rowntree dealt me four Aces, that one hand we played here, before he said all that cryptic talk.

"Best send the Aces all my way," said Darrow with a smile. "I take care of all the Boss's most important business, I'm sure he'd want me to look after 'em."

In the end, Joe Brand won the hand with Aces and Eights. Didn't seem to alarm *him* none, he was just happy to win. But when Fleet Darrow saw the cards, he shifted sideways in his seat, creating a few extra inches of distance between himself and his boss.

Levi Madden dealt next, and then Silver Sam, and then Big-Nose. Roy won pretty big and lost small, and collected his thoughts as he played. Today wasn't created by Rowntree for winning at poker, or shooting at targets — maybe not even about saving Miss Charlotte Hawke, though it still seemed a faint possibility. Daniel Rowntree, whoever he was, had set this all up for a reason.

Roy thought back on all Rowntree's words, cast most of them aside, cleared his head some.

Surely, he's the unexpected ally.

Roy knew Rowntree had given him Joe Brand to shoot at. Knew Rowntree would shoot at Fleet Darrow. But the when and the how was the problem.

When? How will I know when it's time?

Then it was Roy's turn to deal, and he gave it his full concentration, made sure he'd win.

Be foolish not to win my own deal, this situation.

But as Roy shuffled, he heard Fleet Darrow say, "What about the Kid here, Rowntree? What's he, a Ten? Or now I remember, I reckon yesterday you called him a Seven — said he weren't much at all. I recall that correct?"

Roy stopped shuffling a moment, looked at Darrow, then at Rowntree.

"Kid's a Seven, you got that part right." Rowntree was staring hard at Darrow, who just looked amused.

"Mister Rowntree's correct there, I guess," Roy said. "Seven's maybe too kind. And I might not be much, but my lucky streak's runnin' still, by the look of the chips."

It was true. Roy had won the largest pot, and lost only a little on the others.

"Kid's a Seven for sure," Rowntree stated clearly again. And this time, he looked into Roy's eyes. "You don't much notice a Seven, never think of him being a danger — but the Seven's an underrated card. Win more than they lose, or they help out at least. And though only medium size, a Seven's more or less made in the shape of a gun. And maybe that's what he is — maybe the Kid here's the gun, and the rest of us just *think* we're better."

Well, you couldn't blame all them fellers for laughing. For a man with busted up ribs, Curly sure laughed it up big. Wasn't just him though, it was most everybody else too. All except Silver Sam, and Daniel Rowntree himself.

Fleet Darrow slapped his own thigh and said, "You kill me, Rowntree, you're a fine entertainment. Kid's a gun — that's the best one I ever heard." Then he made a mock pistol with his perfectly manicured right hand, pointed it at Roy and made a sort of a *"POP"* sound, as he used his middle finger as its trigger.

"You may laugh," said Daniel Rowntree, "but remember, he beat us *all* at the auction. All sevens then, true to his nature — seventy-seven-hundred, and seventy-seven dollars. Man like that, he knows when to take a risk. Why, he'll bet his whole life when he has to — if conditions are right."

It was like a damn echo in time, and Rowntree's words — from both then and now — filled up Roy's mind like a choir.

'Don't bet your life 'til you have to,' was what Rowntree had said.

I'll know when, Roy decided. *I just have to watch for the signal — it'll be Sevens.*

CHAPTER 57
THE COLT AND THE RIDER

It maybe unnerved them all some, Rowntree's talk about Sevens and Roy — for when the face cards he dealt were a Seven and an Ace, nobody much bet against him.

He won the hand alright, but the pot stayed small — won it with three Aces, it turned out.

They all looked at Brand, but it didn't seem like he took it too personal. He just laughed and said, "So much for Sevens."

By the end of the ten hands of poker, it was Rowntree and Roy who had scooped up most of the money. The Deputies were both broke — lost their whole thousand, and so did the Sheriff.

Joe Brand lost all his too, pretty much, but he didn't care. Every penny was coming back to him, by special arrangement with Rowntree — the whore being his, and the contest being only a ruse for Rowntree to kill the damn Kid.

The four that were broke at the end would get just one shot each at the targets, and though they were glad to be part of the fun, none of them held out any hope of winning the prize. It was widely accepted that Fleet Darrow would shoot the stamp right out of the target, despite never having fired a derringer 'til the previous day. He had been first to go speak to the gunsmith, and bought himself what he considered the finest possible weapon for the circumstance.

He showed it off now, and Roy noticed that Darrow's opinions on derringers had changed some. He was *proud* of the tiny weapon he'd bought, that was clear by how he held it, and showed it off to the others.

"Looks just like a real gun, don't it?" said Darrow.

True enough, it did. Of all the derringers there, that five-shot revolver of Darrow's most looked the part. It was gold and silver plated, had fancy engraving done new at the factory, the nicest pearl grips you ever did see, and to top it all off, an octagonal barrel that really set it apart.

"Damn, just look at that thing," said Sheriff Grimes. "Looks nicer than these double-barrel Remingtons he sold the rest of us. Still, ours take a forty-one rimfire. That thing you got's smaller, and won't have enough power, Fleet."

"Thirty-two's plenty," Darrow said sagely. "It's a Remington too — the Rider it's called, and ain't so much smaller'n my Colts. Three inch barrel to their four-and-three-quarter. Got a proper trigger too, not that nonsense you boys got on yours. And I like the sound of 'em together — a Colt and a Rider. It don't get no better than that."

Thing was, Fleet Darrow still had six-hundred dollars, so he'd be getting two shots. "Twenty points might about be enough," Darrow said as they all milled around, while Mac and the piano feller put bottles of whiskey and clean glasses out on the bar.

Silver Sam too, had earned an extra shot in the contest. He had managed his money pretty well, and ended up with just over nine-hundred. Not quite enough for a third shot though. He had his own pocket-pistol, an original Philadelphia Deringer — they'd all seen its business end already, especially Hosea Grimes. That pistol looked nearly as old as Silver Sam's horse, but he reckoned the gun a spring chicken compared to the animal. "That fine gray is older'n some of these here local hills," he told them all proudly.

Big-Nose and Curly had done pretty well, both having profited almost three-hundred. Each of them had three shots coming — but neither man liked his chances, hearing 'em talk.

"Damn fool thing disappears in yer hand," Curly said. Sitting on his huge meaty palm, it looked even smaller than it was. "How's a man meant to aim it and squeeze on the trigger at once if he's got man-size hands? You got the same problem with yer privates, ain't you, Lucius?"

Lucius Madden didn't quite get the joke, and nobody explained him — so he scratched his head, slumped down in a chair, went back to drinking more whiskey. His almost-as-stupid brother did the same.

They were useless for anything but violence, those Maddens — and even in that they lacked subtlety. Always overdid it, and had cruelly, needlessly, broken too many innocents' bones.

Regarding the uselessness of tiny guns, Big-Nose agreed with Curly. "Ain't even got proper sights, the fool things. Be more chance if we throwed 'em at the damn target."

When Roy counted his chips, he had just under twenty-nine-hundred dollars. Rowntree? He had edged Roy out, but only by fifty dollars.

"You each get six shots," said Fleet Darrow. "But the boasting rights are with Rowntree."

Rowntree played it down though. "Boasting rights go to most points once the shooting's all done." Then as an afterthought he added, "Though if anyone hits the stamp, they'll sure get my applause. Hard enough to hit anywhere on the targets from ten feet with these guns — but life wasn't meant to be easy."

"It also weren't meant to be long," said Silver Sam, a bit sadly. "So my old bones keep tellin' me. Tolerably numbing the pain's why I drink how I do."

That was when Mac the barkeep called, "Coffins are ready, Mister Brand. You want us to go out front and keep folks away now?"

CHAPTER 58

NO ORDINARY PURSE GUN

C *offins?*

It wasn't a comfortable thought. But when Roy spun around to where Mac had spoken from, he saw what it was about.

Two brand new coffins, built solid — one oversize and one smaller, both of them as yet unused — were stood against the wall. Not down where the stage was, as expected, but at the opposite end of the room.

On each coffin, a full size outline of a man had been painted. One man a bit over six feet, the other maybe five-eight like Roy.

"Now *that's* a nice touch," said Fleet Darrow. "Always helps to shoot at a man."

Made for some nervous laughter, that did — mostly from Hosea Grimes. He sounded none too settled when he said, "Small one looks like he's based on the Kid."

"Big one's you, Hosea, I'd reckon," said Joe Brand. "Just look at that belly."

Most laughed along with Brand then, but not a one of them spoke — for there was not a man present who didn't believe he was wrong. The bigger one could only be Joe Brand himself, at least of those men who were present.

Me or him'll end up inside one, thought Roy. *Most likely both, if I'm honest.*

Rowntree himself had painted the targets on earlier that very morning — the Roy sized coffin was on the left. On that one, round circles, red inside white, had been painted on the head and the belly. On the bigger one, the colorful circles were on the areas of chest and privates.

And though one body was clearly much bigger than the other, each of the painted rings were of the same size.

Joe Brand had not allowed a line to be painted on his floor, so a rug, eight feet by ten, had been put in place by Mac instead.

"Any shooter's toes touch the rug, they's fair game to be shot right off," said Brand, caressing his pearl-handled six-gun with his gloved right hand.

Brand wasn't the only man packing a full sized revolver today. Fleet Darrow wore his, and so did the Sheriff and Deputies. Although today, Darrow only carried one of his Colts, having allowed his new Rider a place in his left side holster. "Had it modified last night," he'd explained, "to accept the small gun. I'll still carry my Colt on my right side, natural enough — I never was much left-handed."

For reasons unknown to Roy, neither Curly nor his brother were armed — aside from their derringers, of course. And the Deputies had reputations for being bad shots.

All of that was important. Roy knew this would not be easy, and the danger immense. But Roy knew, if he kept his Sharps full, he'd get four shots when the time came — three if it commenced right after he'd shot at the target. He assumed too, that Rowntree would not bring a pocket knife to a gunfight — the gambler would be well armed, Roy was dang sure of that.

If Roy and Rowntree could kill Brand and Darrow with their first shots, they might yet get out of this alive — perhaps even completely unharmed. Thing is, the resolve of the troops is often broken, when they see their leaders expire in front of their eyes.

Besides all of which, the other men in attendance were unlikely to shoot well with derringers. As for Roy, he had a special liking for them. And not just that either — his little Sharps was properly maintained and accurate; it was fitted with usable sights; could kill at up to fifteen feet; its small caliber did not ruin the shot with its recoil the way those big forty-ones did; and most of all, in Roy's hands it shot perfectly straight, for he'd practiced with it most days these past fifteen years.

In short, that beautifully made four-shot Sharps was surely no ordinary purse gun. Even if it weren't really magic; even if those strange special rune mark engravings didn't actually help; and even if it was small — it was a gun to be reckoned with. And today, it would fulfill its purpose, Roy truly believed that.

The odds of Roy himself surviving still weren't too good — but any chance, no matter how slim, was better than no chance at all. He was a gambler, he accepted those odds, and today, he *would* bet his life.

"You're up first, Sheriff Grimes," said Rowntree. "Each man takes one shot at a time, same order as we dealt in the poker game."

Grimes took his derringer from his pocket, turned to Rowntree and asked, "But which one do I shoot at?"

"Any target you choose to," the gambler answered. "Remember, a point for anywhere within the outline. Four points for the white band; seven for the red; ten for any part of the stamp. The line always counts as a hit."

Sheriff Hosea Grimes took his time. "Gutshot's the right shot, I reckon."

He stood himself in front of the left side coffin; put his lead toe near the rug; closed his left eye; raised the gun; aimed it at the Roy-sized target's belly.

Made a fair old crack for such a small pistol, noise of it filled up the room as the smell of the smoke filled their nostrils — those closest to Grimes flinched a little, then as they moved forward past him to examine the target, just about everyone laughed.

His shot had gone straight, but too low.

"Should at least be points for the stones," said Fleet Darrow.

"There are — on the other target," Rowntree answered. "Should have taken more care in deciding which man to shoot at. Write it up, Sam. Zero for your friend Grimes."

Silver Sam wore a wide toothy grin as he picked up the chalk with his gnarly old fingers. He wrote a fat zero beside the Sheriff's name on the blackboard and said, "Wild Bill shot better'n that while wearin' a blindfold."

Grimes was brimming with anger, but his gaze went from Sam across to Darrow, who smiled and raised up his eyebrows, as if he was making a dare. Then Grimes turned and walked away without saying a word.

"Time for the lady-pistol specialist," Darrow said, and Daniel Rowntree took a four-shot Sharps from his pocket.

Right weapon, thought Roy. *Can he use it?*

Way Roy saw things, he had a lot riding on Rowntree's ability to shoot straight.

Darrow craned his neck for a better look at the pistol. "What is that thing?"

Rowntree kept the gun palmed and said, "Sharps twenty-two."

Joe Brand sure scoffed at that. "Ha! From ten feet? A damn twenty-two? Thought you knew what you were doin', Rowntree."

"Less than eight feet, hand to target," said Rowntree, toeing the line in front of the larger of the coffins. "It only has to hit, not to kill. But even this little gun can kill from three feet. Anyone care to ask how I know?"

Nobody answered — although Fleet Darrow smiled and nodded respectfully. He understood guns, and men too, much better than Brand did.

Rowntree aimed low — clearly, he was aimed at the privates. The Sharps wasn't half so loud as Grimes' forty-one Remington, but it made a satisfying pop.

"Thought you'd be able to shoot straight," said Darrow, surprised, after moving past the smoke to see where

Rowntree's shot hit. "Just about missed the coffin completely."

Roy moved forward with the others, looked at where the projectile had hit. He did *not* look at Joe Brand, as he turned and walked away to stand alone.

"Missed the circle, but still scored a point," Rowntree said, looking satisfied. "Means I'm winning so far. I'll admit though, more luck than good shooting, I'll need to do better."

"Clever aiming, I reckon," observed Curly thoughtfully, then he jabbed a stubby finger repeatedly toward the target. "This body's painted bigger for one thing, and the hands also bein' at that height gives good area to score if yer shot ain't too straight."

Rowntree never looked at Brand either. He just nodded his agreement at Curly, turned away from him and the others, and walked back past them all to where Silver Sam was doing the scoring. But just before he went by Roy, he winked a sly one right at him.

He had shot at the target that was drawn Joe Brand's size — and he had shot the right hand's pinkie finger.

That sure weren't only luck. This Rowntree feller can shoot.

CHAPTER 59
A FINE TRIBUTE

L evi Madden was so drunk he had to be stood up facing the target, and the gun put into his hand so he could fire it. Nearly shot his own brother's damn foot off when he finally did.

Big-Nose just shook his head, grabbed them both by the back of their collars and dragged them across to some chairs. Said, "Sit, you pair'a buffoons, and sober the hell up. Me bein' off Mister Brand's payroll for now, I reckon you and me's maybe got business later."

Lucius tried looking at him hard, but by then Big-Nose had gone back to watch the rest of the shooting. As for Joe Brand, he just looked at Big-Nose and shrugged his huge shoulders — even he knew by now, them Maddens weren't no use at all.

Silver Sam took the lead with four points then, his shot having been aimed at the bigger target's chest.

"Well I'll be a drunken monkey," said Fleet Darrow. "Didn't think you could even see somethin' ten feet away."

And when he shook old Silver Sam's hand, the old man looked rightly proud.

As for Sheriff Grimes, he just loosened his collar a little and looked the other way.

Big-Nose was next. Missed the coffin completely, put the shot into the log wall about two feet to the left. "Damn thing's useless," he said with a rough laugh. "Let's do this with Winchesters tomorrow, at about fifty yards. Then we'll see who can shoot and who can't."

Next it was Roy's turn. He knew it didn't make no sense to start up the gunfight just yet — Rowntree would want to wait 'til everyone grew more relaxed, got invested in the contest, and maybe had less bullets in their derringers. He shot at the smaller target, the one same size as he was — aimed at the belly, but pulled slightly up and left as he fired. Bullet hit halfway between the belly and the upper arm — about two inches from where he'd meant it to hit. Not too bad for a late-changing jerk-shot, and he knew he'd do better next time. He had practiced a lot at switching his shot to the side, sometimes by several feet — but a change of height was always too hard to judge.

"Damn," he said right away. "Damn zero to start. Dammit, damn dammit damn."

"I've heard you more eloquent, Kid," said Fleet Darrow, eyebrows raised in amusement.

"And this Kid shot Floyd through the eye," Big-Nose said in disgust. "His luck sure was runnin' *that* day, but I reckon his streak's over now."

Roy only smiled a weak one, stepped to the back, went

off and stood by himself, just shaking his head some and mumbling.

Curly's shot was no better than his brother's, then it was mutually decided not to allow Lucius Madden to shoot until he'd sobered up some.

After that it was Fleet Darrow's turn. He didn't even go near the line. Stood about a foot back behind it, square in front of the smaller of the coffins, left that Remington Rider where it was inside the left holster.

He looked over at the coffin to his right, then to the left one in front of him, then he turned his head and his body further that way, so he could see Roy, and he smiled.

As Fleet Darrow smiled, he spoke. "What say you, Kid? Shall we make this one for Wild Bill?"

"Sure, Mister Darrow," Roy answered, "one for Wild—"

Fleet Darrow still wore the smile as he spun, unlimbered the gun from the holster with his left hand, and shot the stamp from the belly of the smaller size target. And in the same flowing motion, before anyone knew he had done it, a second shot came right behind it, and Fleet Darrow said, "Dammit, I missed." And he holstered that beautiful weapon, still heated and deadly and smoking, the gunpowder smell mixing now with the burn of fresh leather in the modified holster.

Took Roy's breath right from him, it did. And he knew right then, he would never see movement as beautiful and fluid and perfect from any other man — not if he lived to a hundred-and-ten, and spent his whole life searching for it.

The others moved forward to marvel at the first shot —

it had gone through the middle of the stamp, in the target on the left coffin's chest.

But Darrow himself ignored that one completely. He went direct to the larger of the coffins, a scowl on his face, and shaking his head in his misery. "Knew I missed," he mumbled, as he studied the target that had been drawn on the head. "Mistake like that is the sort of thing gets a man killed."

Roy had followed him, stood a respectful distance behind, did not say a word.

The praise from a few feet away might as well have been spoken in some far off Territory — Fleet Darrow did not hear their words, nor did he care to.

Finally, he turned to Roy and said, "Seventeen." He shook his head sadly, and added, "Arrogance, that's where I went wrong. Should have used my right hand, I never was much with my left."

A freak of nature, that's what Fleet Darrow was.

Roy *knew* small guns — knew what was possible, and knew too what wasn't.

What Fleet Darrow just did, was more in the nature of magic than true possibility. Shooting derringers just didn't work that way. Took years of hard work to shoot one *somewhere* near straight.

Roy looked at the man then, and he wished that things could be different. He saw this other man for a moment, not as what he was, but what he might have become.

Fleet Darrow's only love was for fine entertainment. Firing pistols as straight and fast as he could, entertained the man like nothing else. He was a natural alright.

What a pity he chose a wrong path.

Roy could aim, he could fire, he could hit within an inch or two every time. But to draw from a holster and shoot *two* targets — *two men, it could have been* — at that speed — *that speed!* — what a magical thing that had been. It was a thing Roy could *never* do, no matter what runes was engraved on his gun; no matter how much of a lucky streak he ever got running.

"I reckon Wild Bill'd be happy with that tribute, Mister Darrow," Roy said, and he truly meant it. "First feller dead, shot through the heart. Second feller dead too, bullet through his eye into his brain. With a derringer, no less, from twelve feet, two shots in half a second!"

"But I missed the damn stamp," Darrow said, and he sounded defeated. "Missed it by almost an inch!"

CHAPTER 60
THE DARK HORSE

"**W**rite it up, Sam," said Rowntree. "Ten points to Mister Darrow."

"Seventeen," Darrow argued, "from two shots."

Daniel Rowntree turned to look at him. Looked some rattled, that was the truth of it. But he stood his ground, followed through. "Rules are clear, Mister Darrow," he said. "One shot each round. The second shot you took doesn't count — impressive as it was. If this was a *formal* competition, you'd be disqualified for shooting out of turn — but we won't stand on ceremony here. I'll be coming to shake your hand, Mister Darrow, you sure as hell shot the stamp. Please write it up, Sam, ten points."

Silver Sam chuckled with glee, said, "Never seen *nothin'* like that before. A fine tribute to Bill, and maybe quick as him, I reckon. Yessir, I thank you for lettin' me see it, Fleet Darrow. Man don't see much new at my age, but that there was newer'n a baby comin' into the world. Ten points it is, Sir — and I'm glad you weren't shootin' at me, as I'd have somewhat missed the enjoyment of it."

It was a hard act to follow for Joe Brand, and he didn't even try. "Hand me your gun," he said to Sheriff Grimes. He took the pistol, lumbered across, took no time aiming, and shot at the smaller of the targets.

"One point for Mister Brand," said Daniel Rowntree.

"Nice shootin', Boss," said Fleet Darrow.

The bullet had hit the chest of the target — might have been four or seven points if he'd aimed at the other one and made the same shot.

"I'll save my best shooting for later," said Brand, with a glance at the orange-haired Deputies, who had fallen asleep in their chairs now, only stirring momentarily whenever someone fired.

Rowntree looked mighty pleased with a four to commence the second round. Someone did the math and reckoned he could still maybe beat Darrow if he kept such scores coming.

"That opening one and five fours'd do it," said Silver Sam.

"I'll give it my best," Rowntree said, as Sam wrote up the score.

Silver Sam shot well again.

Made Fleet Darrow happy alright, the old man doing well. "Who'd have thought of ol' Silver Sam as the dark horse? Seven more points, that's well done, and he's back in the lead. A fine entertainment."

Curly and his brother both missed completely, and Roy scored a single point this time. He took careful aim, flicked it left as he fired — bullet went right where he wanted, in the target's right arm.

When Fleet Darrow's turn came again, he stood well back and faced the wrong way, asked Roy to drop a kerchief from his hand as the signal to fire.

"Left-handed again, Mister Darrow?"

Darrow nodded. "Drop it when ready, Kid." This time, he didn't smile. This time was serious.

When the piece of cloth fluttered to the floor, Darrow spun and he fired, twice this time again. He'd aimed for the lower targets this time — shot clean through the center of both stamps.

What a thing, thought Roy. *What a thing.*

The man Roy called Grampa had spoken of such feats being possible — had trained Roy to believe that one day, with practice, he might even do such himself. But here, confronted with the truth and realness of it, Roy knew that such things were beyond him.

Man like Fleet Darrow is born to such greatness, then he works to improve every day of his life, never-ending.

Except it would *not* be never-ending — every man must come to his end, including Fleet Darrow.

CHAPTER 61
DON'T BET YOUR LIFE 'TIL YOU HAVE TO

"Twenty points altogether," Silver Sam said. "Fleet Darrow has the lead, and just two men might yet take it from him." Then he raised a finger thoughtfully and added, "Mathematically speaking at least, as they each have four shots to come."

The Maddens had stirred in all the excitement of Darrow's last shots, and Lucius demanded his turn. He scowled at anyone who looked at him, and said, "I'll show all you damn skunks how it's done."

Deputy Lucius Madden toed the line, held the pistol out in front of him, and fired. Right between the two coffins it went — missed each by twelve inches or so.

"Next time," he said, "I'll show you all. And not with this damn toy here neither."

"Sure you will, Deputy," Curly replied. "Next time. I'll look forward to it." And he moved up and took his last shot. Went left of the target again, and then he was done.

Big-Nose said, "Might as well let me miss now too, and leave it to the boys who yet have a chance."

All present agreed or ignored it, and Big-Nose took no time at all, missed completely again, and seemed glad to be done. Went back away some, sat down at a table, examined that small gun as if to work out if it had some problem.

All came down to Roy and Rowntree, then on.

Rowntree made another four.

Silver Sam cried, "Rowntree moves to nine points, with three shots yet comin' to him."

Roy took careful aim — shot at the smaller coffin again, but at the higher target this time. He aimed straight, didn't do nothing fancy, and that little twenty-two went right about where the man's top lip would have been, if such features had been drawn on.

"Seven," he cried happily, after he rushed forward to check.

"It's a seven alright," said Darrow. "Nice shootin', Kid."

"Kid's on eight," Silver Sam said as he wrote it up on his blackboard. "Three shots yet to come, still a point behind Rowntree, who's eleven back of Fleet Darrow."

Rowntree shot another four — then Roy missed that left coffin completely. He slapped his left thigh as he let fly a pretty choice cuss word.

"Fleet Darrow the leader on twenty," Silver Sam announced then. "Rowntree thirteen and Peabody eight — both men with two shots to come."

Every man in attendance was engrossed in the contest by now. It was the business end, after all, and large bets had already been made.

Silver Sam stood at his blackboard, back out of the way, several feet to the right. Rowntree and Roy took their turns stepping up to the line for their shots. In between, each waited quietly behind while the other man took his turn — always after reloading.

By now, everyone besides Roy and Rowntree were making bets every shot. Each was closely examined, soon as it hit the target.

Their keenness to see the result of each shot overtook them, just as Roy had hoped it would. They no longer stood back behind — instead, they stood in a ragged sort of line that curved off to the right, starting from just beside the shooter.

The man nearest the coffins, of course, was furthest away from the path of the bullet — but he was only four feet to the right, standing close as he was to that right hand coffin.

And that man was Roy's target, Joe Brand.

From that wall, they stood in order of seniority, with just one exception. Brand was closest to the front, so it was he who got first look at where each bullet had hit. Darrow was beside him, as always — then Lucius and Levi were next. Curly and Big-Nose — who were, after all, off the payroll — stood behind just a little, craning their necks to look over the Deputies' shoulders. And finally, closest to the shooters, and well out of order, was Sheriff Hosea Grimes.

Perhaps he was feeling disgraced after what happened earlier. Or perhaps he preferred to watch from the wider angle. It didn't much matter. He was where he was, and

Roy couldn't change it to his liking — he just had to accept it.

If only it was Brand in that spot, thought Roy. *But he's still within range where he is, and the angle ain't bad.*

Rowntree stepped up for his second-last shot. The man took his time, waited for the betting to stop and the men to go quiet. He took careful aim at the larger of the targets, squeezed the trigger — and sent the bullet low, through a leg.

"Dammit," he cried. "Just one point."

Roy had expected Rowntree to shoot a seven — thought that'd be the signal. Now he wondered if Rowntree's plan was to wait 'til the last, while they all examined the very last shot of the contest.

But he kept his mind open for some other sign, just in case.

Roy stepped up to the line. Took his aim at the larger of the targets, gave Rowntree some time.

Not yet, huh?

Don't bet your life 'til you have to.

Roy aimed at the chest of that target, decided to take his best shot, aimed for the stamp.

He squeezed the trigger smoothly, the little Sharps exploded, the bullet cut through the air, missed the stamp by an inch.

The men all rushed forward, and Darrow, delighted, announced the score, "Seven points!"

The excited men settled their bets, drifted back to their places — same order as before — as Roy moved away and reloaded.

Silver Sam, good and loud, called the scores. "Fleet Darrow, still the leader with twenty. Roy Peabody now on fifteen, with one shot remaining. Daniel Rowntree, also one shot left, on fourteen points. Anyone wants to bet, I've a hundred, I'm backing the Kid."

"I'll take that bet," Sheriff Grimes barked.

"The Kid's good, but too inconsistent," said Darrow. "My hundred says Rowntree improves, wins the day with a seven."

"You're on," said Joe Brand in his mean gravel voice. "Neither one of 'em's got what it takes."

The others made their bets, and Rowntree stepped up, toed the line. "To win, a man needs to be patient," he said, looking worried. "Give me a minute to think, while I choose a target."

CHAPTER 62
"SHOOT, LUKE..."

Roy had never felt more alive. Miss Charlotte, waiting upstairs, came to his mind for a second — her fleshy, feathery softness; her sky-starry voice like the lasting sound of a bell that may never stop ringing; the silken cream of her skin, how it searched for his touch and then yielded, part of her, part of him; and finally, the love and the truth in her soft, deer-like eyes.

All these parts of Charlotte, Roy breathed into himself now — and filled up by her strength and her spirit, he banished the thought of her, cleared her away from his mind. As men have always done, he carried the *essence* of a woman into the battle — but her body, her physical self, and even her memory, he must leave behind, to do what must surely be done.

Concentrate, Roy, be here now, be inside this one moment.

And he did what he told himself to, what he had

trained himself to — trained his mind to do — all these long years.

The room became still and quiet. Roy watched Rowntree then. The man looked at the bigger coffin in front of him, then stepped back.

He'd changed his mind.

He walked back past Roy, wiggled his eyebrows, as if the whole thing was a joke. Then he came back, stood in front of the smaller of the coffins; set himself; took a moment — then fired at the head.

The eager men's faces had been turning from shooter to target, shooter to target, as they'd waited for the shot — but as soon as the derringer spat its flame, those men rushed across, champing at the bit to check the result.

"I win, Fleet, it's only a damn four," Joe Brand announced with derision.

"Dammit," Fleet Darrow said. And for a man who still led the contest, he sounded truly disappointed.

"It's all down to the Kid," Silver Sam cried. "Fleet Darrow has twenty, Daniel Rowntree all done at eighteen. Final shot of the contest! And I'm still backing the Kid, if anyone else wants a piece of it."

"Another hundred," Grimes said with a scowl.

The others made their final bets, as Roy knelt down, touched his left boot for luck, and prepared to step up to the line. There had been no signal.

Maybe I misunderstood. Maybe he's changed his mind. Maybe...

There would never be a better opportunity. If he left it

'til after the shot, other men would get between him and Brand.

Roy settled himself, and decided, this must surely be it — whether Rowntree was with him or not.

This is my time.

Time.

Slow time, take time, be inside this one moment.

Roy moved forward past Rowntree, who ignored him. He watched everyone fall into position, knew this was it, his only chance.

He knew where he would shoot from, had planned it during the contest. He stood firstly in front of the smaller coffin — looked at it, took aim, put the gun down, turned away.

"Kid's nervous," growled Brand. "He's a useless damn derringer, just like I said all along."

Then Silver Sam called, "Give him quiet."

And whether they truly went quiet or they didn't, the sound all melted away, and out of Roy's mind.

And time slowed again ... slowed some more.

He moved forward again, toward the big coffin this time.

Looked around at Daniel Rowntree, just three feet behind him, to his left, forty-five degree angle.

He looked forward to the target, stared a moment, then turned his head to look at Joe Brand; then Fleet Darrow; then down along the line at the others.

Next, back away further, he looked at old Silver Sam, who nodded a slow one, that one nod seeming to take forever.

From there, Roy's gaze went in reverse — back along the line, from Sheriff Hosea Grimes all the way to Joe Brand.

And finally, Roy looked again at the target.

He took a slow measured breath, toed the line, looked down the sights. He aimed at the stamp at the center of the chest of the drawing — same height as the real Joe Brand's chest — as time slowed even more he was hugely, perfectly aware of Joe Brand within range, only ten feet away. The living breathing man he had come there to kill, was exactly, precisely, thirty degrees to the right of the target he aimed at.

Simple shot, Roy. Turn thirty degrees and then fire, from inside this one moment.

He knew what to do — all the years and the practice and training had all come to now, this pinpoint in time, this one shot, this was what it was for.

And then, from the midst of his moment, his peripheral vision warned him that something, somehow, was wrong.

All their eyes are on me, not the target.

He saw their eagerness too: in the shape of their bodies; the way their heads craned toward him; felt the crackle of impending death as it hung in the air.

He felt the air near him move, knew it was Daniel Rowntree, to his left and behind, forty-five degrees still — and though the hairs on the back of Roy's neck did not tingle, he sensed it, the menace of Rowntree's Sharps derringer, as the man raised it up near Roy's head.

He knew what they watched now.

Knew he had to be quick.

In the midst of that moment came a sound, a warning, a signal — and Roy knew then, he knew which words they would be; the words came to his ears as he turned; so slow, so deliberate his movement, as he turned toward Brand; and the words were still coming as the death in the moment unfolded.

With his derringer already raised, almost finally aimed at its target, the voice of Daniel Rowntree rang out. "Shoot, Luke, or give up the—"

But as Roy was completing his turn toward Brand — *all too slow, all too slow* — it was Curly who fired the first shot.

And the shot killed its man.

CHAPTER 63
CHARLOTTE, ALONE

For Charlotte, alone in her room all this time, dread her only companion, it was a most terrible time.

She had never much been one for prayer — her belief on it being, that the Lord had no time for such trifles — but this time, this time she prayed, with all her faith, all her intention, all her good heart and her soul.

The time had gone by so slowly. The saloon was always quiet in the mornings — the soiled doves were all sleeping, there was almost no one downstairs, and there was no music.

But today, it felt different, completely — the piano music had started some minutes after Roy went downstairs. It had seemed ominous to begin with, then gotten faster, happier somehow.

She felt better then, just a little, but an emptiness gnawed at her.

Roy had brought extra food up that morning, but she

couldn't eat anything now. Still, as long as the music kept playing, Charlotte felt soothed somehow.

But just like all other good things, it came to an end. There was quiet for a few minutes, and she knew the poker game must be over — and soon the shooting would start.

When it did, the first shot was a shock that went all the way through her. Wasn't loud — not from where she was. Loud enough to know what it was, then she thought she heard laughing, and the dread coursed all through her, fearing Roy had been killed.

But of course, another shot came soon after, then a minute later another, and so it went on.

She loved Roy, truly she did — but in those long minutes of dread, she hated him too. Hated the fact that she loved him. She could not end her life; could not give up on him; could not stop believing he would save her, and save himself too.

Then she realized the truth — he would sacrifice his own life for hers.

And that was the moment Roy's final gunfight began.

She heard too many gunshots;

she shrieked and she cried.

she did not know for certain;

she threw herself down on the floor, just to be closer to him.

and it broke her soft heart,

when after it, nobody came.

CHAPTER 64
"DO YOU SEE HIM IN ME?"

As Levi Madden crumpled dead to the floor from Curly's bullet, Roy fired at Brand, put his first shot into the man's chest.

Darrow was fast — so incredibly, inhumanly fast — and yet, the way things unfolded, even he was not fast enough.

For the tiniest fraction of a sliver of a moment, he had turned toward the sound of Curly's bullet — even though he was already drawing his Colt, he had taken his eye off the Kid, and off Rowntree's derringer. Rowntree fired that derringer over the Kid's shoulder, and its twenty-two bullet punched through flesh into Fleet Darrow's belly, then a second one followed it — just before Darrow got his shot off.

Fleet Darrow's problem was, he'd turned too far left in response to that very first shot — had to stay his gun hand and reverse it, to fire back at Rowntree. But even as he squeezed the trigger, he was bumped by the falling Joe

Brand, and his shot went awry several inches. But it was Curly's first shot that had saved Rowntree's life.

Big-Nose acted soon as Curly did — he put a bullet through Lucius Madden's head, the vicious orange-haired Deputy arriving in Hell half-a-moment behind his own brother.

As Sheriff Hosea Grimes drew his pistol to kill Roy, old Silver Sam did his bit — from eight feet away, the old man fired the forty-one slug from his ancient Philadelphia Deringer. It flew through the skull of Sheriff Grimes just above his left ear, and lodged itself in his brain pan. Somehow the Sheriff stood there twitching a moment, eyes wide and rapid blinking, then he crashed to the floor on his face.

"Don't shoot, Kid," came Curly's voice through the thick smoke, as he kicked the gun out of Darrow's hand. "We're with you! Tell him, Rowntree, quick!"

"It's true, Roy," cried Rowntree, "don't shoot. The Browns are working for me."

"They all dead?" called Silver Sam. "I just about can't believe it — of Fleet Darrow at least."

"Don't you move," Big-Nose Brown growled from somewhere, as another man gasped and groaned.

Roy stood where he was, gun-smoke filling the air all around him. He was rooted to the spot, unable to make his legs carry him forward to check if Joe Brand was dead.

"You hit, Roy?" It was Rowntree's voice from beside him, and the man gripped his arm now. Then more urgently, he said, "Are you hit?"

Roy focused on Rowntree's worried face. A thin *"No"* was all he could manage.

There was groaning, fast breathing, a gurgling sound coming from where Big-Nose and Curly were.

Where Joe Brand and Fleet Darrow are.

"Drink this, Kid," said Silver Sam, and he handed Roy a shot glass — but it fell through his fingers, landed at his feet without breaking, and the whiskey splashed over his boots.

Roy watched the splash — *slow, so slow* — then fast, so terribly fast, the world speeded up, and Roy looked up, alarmed, looked around, saw the carnage, for the smoke was beginning to clear, float off into the ether.

"Kid. Come here, Kid. Can you?"

It was the voice of Fleet Darrow. Sounded somehow distant and broken — yet there was a love of life, still, in the sound that came from him.

Rowntree gripped Roy by the shoulder, led him forward.

"Brand ain't dead yet," Big-Nose told them as they came closer. "But he ain't worth a damn."

"Never was," said Daniel Rowntree. "The Kid's here, Mister Darrow."

It was like all the rest of Roy's senses came back to him then. He saw Joe Brand sprawled back against the wall, the blood soaking through his shirt in two places, his chest and his belly — and he saw, too, Big-Nose Brown's gun pointed at Joe Brand's head.

Brand was in a bad way for sure, and Roy wanted to speak to him quick — make sure the man knew who he was, and why this had happened — but he felt he owed Fleet Darrow something.

Felt it was important.

Curly propped Fleet Darrow up against an upturned chair, knelt beside him, put the glass that Silver Sam had brought up to Darrow's lips. The dying gunfighter took a sip, murmured his thanks to Curly, as Roy knelt down by Darrow's feet.

"How you doing, Mister Darrow?"

"Well played, Kid," Darrow said. "Well played."

"I'm real sorry, Mister Darrow. Weren't personal with you, and I wish things was different."

Fleet Darrow fixed Roy in his gaze, grunted a little in discomfort, cleared his throat some and said, "Lot to go through, just for a woman. But I truly hope you'll be happy, you and the girl."

Roy felt a pang of guilt — he'd forgotten all about Charlotte 'til Fleet Darrow mentioned her.

She will have heard gunshots;

she...

She's safe where she is, and I'll get to her soon, when I can.

"Thank you, Mister Darrow," Roy said. "But ... it wasn't..." Roy paused a moment, reflected on it. He had to be be truthful, whether he liked the truth of it or not. "It wasn't *all* about the girl, Mister Darrow. There was ... she's not why this happened. Not really."

Darrow smiled. It looked painful that smile, but he smiled. "Then what, Kid? Damn, I just love a good story."

"Hurry, Roy," said Daniel Rowntree, his voice coming

urgent now. "Jim Starr won't last much longer, if you wish to speak to him."

Darrow still looked into Roy's eyes. "Jim Starr? Brand? Plot thickens, huh, Kid? Let me watch the show? That be alright?"

"Sure, Mister Darrow," said Roy, and he squeezed the man's shoulder. "Move him so he can see, can you please, Mister Curly?"

"Damn nurse maid now to my friends," Curly growled. "Who'd ever have thought it, huh, Fleet?"

"You're sure gettin' soft, Curly," Darrow said.

Roy noticed how easily Curly moved Darrow — sure as hell didn't have broken ribs, the way he gently lifted and moved his old friend around. He moved the chair, set Darrow up leaning back against it again, only now the dying gunfighter had a good side-on view of Joe Brand.

Roy knelt down in front of the man he had come there to kill, and he used his words like a weapon. *Big* Jim Starr." Mocked the man with his own name.

The facade of the man was all gone. In a man's dying, all disguise and pretense melts away, and the truth of him is exposed. He was no longer Joe Brand — he was Big Jim Starr, murderer of women and unarmed men. Older, and with less hair. But he was Big Jim once again.

"Damn you, Kid," the dying Big Jim Starr gasped. "You sneaky damn *derringer*." Bloody froth bubbled from his mouth, and his shirt was soaked with his blood. "Always hidin' somewhere."

"I told you I'd kill you, Starr. You shoulda known it was me. That was plain disrespectful, not to know me when I arrived. Stupid as well — you allowed me to hide in plain sight, in your own saloon."

The huge man coughed up more blood, choked on it some, spat it out. "You growed better'n expected. Still a damn runt though." The voice was no longer a spade in wet gravel — it was drowning in muck and in blood, as his life drained away.

"Runt I am," said Roy. "And what does that make you?" He took a moment to let it sink in, before he went on. "You lied to your friends, Starr. Lied about my mother. Left out how she shot off your finger with a derringer, right before you killed her in cold blood."

Roy's hand shot out then, and he tore the glove from the dying man's hand, exposing the truth for all present to see.

"Wasn't no big man with a Colt like you said — it was my own tiny mother who shot off that finger, you poor excuse for a man."

Starr tried to answer, choked on it.

Roy smiled a bitter one and went on. "Shameful, that, for a *big man* like you. Shot by a *woman*. With a purse gun, no less. And now a runt's come and killed you with one. How about this for your grave marker? *Big Jim Starr — Murderer of women — Shot to death by a runt with a derringer — Died with fear in his eyes.*"

"Damn kid." Starr's eyes kept closing now, but he forced them to open. He raised a great effort to speak again, and it came out almost a mumble. Said, "Was good shootin', Kid. Maybe you ... maybe you are ... my son."

Roy laughed in the dying man's face. Laughed a great

belly laugh and said, "No, Mister Starr. My dear mother lied to you about that. She trusted me with the truth though, not a week before you killed her. My father was a shopkeeper. Shot dead in a robbery, a week before she came to your town. He was five feet and six inches tall, and worth a thousand of you."

"Dmmn ... dmnn..." Starr tried again to speak, but he was drowning in his own fluids.

Blood and bile bubbled down his chin.

Down his neck.

Down his shirtfront.

"This all's been somethin' to see," said Fleet Darrow, finding a happiness even in the hour of his dying.

"Ain't over yet," said Daniel Rowntree, and he knelt down too, beside Roy. "Mind, Roy?"

"I sure don't," said Roy then. "Truth is, I'm a mite curious."

Daniel Rowntree leaned forward, gripped Big Jim Starr's face in his hands, his thumbs keeping the man's eyelids from closing. And he said, "Look at *me* while you die, Starr. Look at *me*. Look at my eyes. Do you see it now, Starr? Do you *see* him? Do you see him in me?"

CHAPTER 65
A FINE ENTERTAINMENT

As Big Jim Starr's eyes widened in that final recognition, he looked fearful, tried to turn his gaze away from the man he'd known as Daniel Rowntree.

Rowntree did not allow it — held the face tight, the eyes open. Looked into Starr's eyes as he died.

Then he pushed the big lifeless body away, and he stood as it crumpled to the floor with a rustling thud.

Roy looked close at Rowntree — could not make himself remember, but he *knew*.

Finally, he knew.

"Mister Rowntree," Roy said. "Don't suppose you'd care to show me that Sharps of yours now."

Roy took out his own from his pocket, held it in view of Rowntree, and of Fleet Darrow too — that beautiful tiny Sharps derringer Roy had just killed Joe Brand with.

The tiny gun sat on his palm, showing clearly the runes

that had long ago been engraved on it — '*the magic,*' as Grampa had called it.

"Sure, Roy," Rowntree said, and he wore the faintest of smiles.

He took out the gun, let in lay on his palm, put his hand beside Roy's. The guns — the runes and the magic — were exactly the same.

"You're Grampa's son," Roy said. "You're Reese Scott's younger brother. I ... I thought ... they said you were dead. Grampa showed me the letter."

"Yes, Roy, I'm Dan Scott," he said. "I thought I was dead too, that damn war. I died three times — so they told me, when I finally came through it. Infections, one on the next. Went on for months. Someone made a mistake, sent the letter."

"But Grampa—"

"Your grandpa knows now, Roy, I found him. And yes, just to be clear, I'm Reese's brother. Makes me your uncle, I guess. If it any way matters."

"Matters to me," said Roy, and he sorta looked away, sorta smiled. Then he looked upon the man's face in wonder. He could barely remember Reese Scott — the look of him anyway. Only his kindness, his words, and the happiness the man had brought to Roy and his mother so long ago, all too briefly.

Daniel Rowntree — Dan Scott — looked at Roy and he nodded. "Matters to me too, I guess." Then seeing how Roy studied him, he added, "I don't look like Reese, except for the eyes. Different mothers."

They exchanged one more look, then both turned away

— saw the face of Fleet Darrow beside them, completely enthralled.

"A *fine* entertainment," he said, and he smiled a warm one. And somehow, his eyes had gone soft — perhaps with the progress of his dying, perhaps something else.

From the porch Mac had heard all the gunshots, run for the Doc right away. Doc Delaney took some waking — just like so many others, this doctor had served in the War between the States. He had seen things that filled his dreams with such horrors, he now spent every night searching for the bottom of a deep whiskey bottle, in order to quiet them damn dreams long enough to sleep. Found the bottom of that bottle too, night after night, all these years.

He came now to the door of the saloon. Silver Sam was already waiting, and he opened it soon as he heard the Doc coming. Knew Mac was no fool, and would have gone for him quick.

Knew too, that it would take awhile — old Silver Sam had been through wars of his own, and the real reason he drank how he did was much the same as the Doc's.

Sam had done enough doctoring too, to know there was nothing could be done for Fleet Darrow — nothing but to help him die comfortable.

When the bravest of the painted doves worked up the courage to creep to the top of the stairs, she'd seen who was dying, who wasn't.

She'd gone back, told two trusted others, and the three of them came now. One of these truly did love Fleet Darrow — he'd never really known how she felt, only that she treated him kindly, even more so than others.

When she started her wailing, got hysterical, the Doc gave her a big dose of laudanum, told the other women to look after her, back upstairs. Curly it was, who carried her up.

Even he looked sad then.

Darrow watched it all in good humor. "I'm done for, Doc, ain't I? How long?"

"Maybe a minute, maybe an hour," the Doc answered. "Ruptured something inside — you're bleeding internally. No way to fix it, Mister Darrow. I'm very sorry."

"Don't guess a whiskey would hurt then?"

"That stuff'll kill you," said Doc Delaney. "Though not fast enough for my liking — I've worked away at it some time now. In the circumstances, I'm prescribing one glass for each of us."

Old Silver Sam brought a bottle and some glasses, and he poured one for each man in the room who still lived. "To you, Fleet Darrow," he said. He swallowed his own then picked up Darrow's glass, held it up to the dying man's lips, allowed him a sip.

"You're a fine feller, Sam. Best damn man in Custer City."

Roy drank to Fleet Darrow along with the others. Looked at him and said, "Anything else we can do, Mister Darrow? Write to somebody maybe?"

"No, Kid. Only child, me. Thankful for that at least. I seen my own mother killed too. And I'm genuine sorry, Kid."

"Me too, Mister Darrow. Me too."

"Call me Fleet, will you, Kid? May I call you Roy?"

"That'd be an honor, Mister Darrow. Fleet. Be an honor."

"Difference to you was, I killed my damn father that day, after he killed my Ma." He coughed, motioned for a drink, sipped what Silver Sam offered, then went on. "She was a dear woman. Well, I took it bad, I guess — shot him with his own gun while he slept it off. Dammit, I been killing ever since. Glad you got your man, Kid. Good for you, young Roy. Good for you."

"I'm so sorry, Mister Darrow, I am. I wish..."

"It's alright, Kid, don't be sorry. You and Rowntree here done me fair. No, not Rowntree after all, what was the name? Man should remember the right name of who bedded him down. Please, what was it again?"

The man he'd always called Rowntree gripped Darrow's arm then, looked at him true and spoke clearly. "Dan Scott," he said. "I'm Dan Scott. I'm sorry, but you'd have done your job right and killed Roy here. I promised my Pa I'd protect Roy while he killed his man. Nothing personal against you, Mister Darrow."

"Fleet."

"Fleet. And you call me Dan."

"Dan ... Roy ... the pair of you done me a favor — I been itchin' to get to that showdown, don't y'know? Yessir. Me, Wild Bill, and Old Scratch himself. That'd be worth a payment to see."

"I'd pay to see it, Fleet," said Roy, and all present agreed they would too.

Darrow took one more sip, then he sighed. He was mighty pale by now — it wouldn't be long. "Reckon me and Bill might team up and take the place over," he said. "Yessir, me and Bill, *there's* a team. Like to see Old Scratch try to stop us."

"Reckon that's the plan, Mister Darrow. Fleet."

"Such money as I have, share it out to the whores here. One in particular was a comfort, but they all could use a few dollars. Lord knows they earn it."

"I'll see to it," Roy told him.

"Listen up now, young Roy. I want you to have my Remington Rider — and the Colt in my room upstairs too. And this other Colt here's for you, Daniel Scott. Reckon the both of you earned it."

"Thank you, Fleet," said Roy. "Means a lot."

"To me too," said Dan Scott.

"Near got you, didn't I, Dan?" You could still hear faint touches of laughter in Fleet Darrow's voice. Then it went harsh when he added, "That damn woman-killer Brand ruined my shot when he fell."

"You grazed my arm, still, Fleet. Greatest shooting I ever saw. You won the contest too, if it matters."

"I'll be sure to let Wild Bill know, I got derringer boasting rights."

Fleet Darrow's eyes closed then as he rested, and they all went quiet and waited. It was a long couple of minutes, but nobody so much as murmured, nobody moved. His skin by now was almost like bone, so pale he had become.

Then Fleet Darrow's eyes opened again. "Thanks for comin', Kid," he said, and laughed weakly. "It's sure been a fine entertainment. We shoulda done all this up on the stage ... and charged ... and charged folk..."

His eyes flickered a little and closed again, and they thought he was gone. But he wasn't done yet, and a few seconds later, he got himself going again for the very last time. "Entertainment like this one ... coulda charged folk ... a hundred ... damn dollars."

Then he smiled at Roy, one last smile — and the gunfighter Fleet Darrow died, entertained to the end.

CHAPTER 66
ANOTHER GOOD CUSS

They stayed silent almost a minute after Fleet Darrow died.

"Could have become a great man," Silver Sam said, "with a fairer start to his life."

"True enough," said Roy, and the others all nodded their agreement.

Curly looked at Roy, tried to smile. "What'll you do now, Kid?"

"I ... I don't rightly know, Mister Curly."

"You, Rowntree?" said Curly. "Sorry, it's Scott, ain't it?"

"That's right," said Dan Scott. "I'll get on the next stage to Sidney, and a train after that. I've not seen my father in many a year, and the man's eighty-five, so it's time. Will you come, Roy?"

"I ... yes, Dan. 'Course I will. I want Grampa to see me married up." Roy turned then and looked to the stairs. "I best go ask Charlotte proper."

"Good on you, Kid," Curly said.

"What about you, Mister Curly? You and ... you and Mister Smith plan to stay?"

"We'll talk about that, I guess. I believe Mister *Smith* here prefers honest work. Least when it comes available. He's funny that way."

"Sheriff position's come recently vacant," said Silver Sam, and every head turned to where Hosea Grimes still lay face down dead on the floor. "Previous one spoke ill of Wild Bill Hickok ... but I don't guess Mister Smith would ever behave such."

"Wild Bill was a fine man," Big-Nose said, "and done Sheriffin' work some himself, I believe."

"Think about it, please, Mister Smith," said Doc Delaney "This could be a fine town if the right sort of men did the steering of it."

Roy looked around him. Five men lay dead, and at least four of them had deserved it. His job was finally done. But now that it was, he held strong to the hope he would never have to kill a man again.

"Dan," he said. "When I was real small, I sure loved your brother Reese, and so much wanted for him to be my Pa. He was a good man — made my Ma happy, treated her like she deserved. Then when your own father came there to bury him, well, he saved my whole life I reckon. I love him maybe like you do. Now you come here and done what you done. I ... I just wanna ... it means somethin', Dan, what you done. Reckon I might like to call you Uncle. That be alright?"

"I'd like that, Roy." Dan Scott glanced across to the

stairs, then looked up at the ceiling. "You best get to that girl, she'll be worried."

"One last thing before I go, Uncle. I thought the signal was to be sevens. All that different stuff you said, I never was quite sure what was what. Kept waitin' for you to shoot a seven so we could get started. Then later ... well, you know what happened."

Dan Scott laughed it up good then. "Roy. Every shot I took was my best. I never could shoot that well. I believe Fleet Darrow's the only man I've ever killed — and I fought in that damn rotten war two years. Sevens? Ha! I was lucky just to score fours today, I believe. Not easy, derringers, at the best of times."

"But that first shot, when you shot the finger..."

"Accident. Aimed at the privates. Worst shot I took all day — but I saw the funny side, and the irony. Took it as a sign we were doing the right thing — and of something else too — that maybe there's magic in the runes on these little guns after all." Dan glanced upward at the ceiling. "Get upstairs, Roy, stop delaying it. Don't make that girl wait any longer."

Roy nodded to them all, started walking to the stairs. Then he bounded up them all two by two, put the deaths and the fighting behind him, ran toward his future. Just about flew down the corridor, put the key in the lock, turned it and tried to open the door.

Didn't budge, and he heard Charlotte scream, scream for all she was worth.

He put his shoulder to the door, thinking someone else

was in there — and the chair she had placed against the door shattered all into pieces.

Charlotte was down on the floor, her arms wrapped round the far bedpost. Looked up at him, terror in her eyes as she squirmed, tried to hide.

But as Roy stood framed in the doorway, she saw who it was, and she stared up at him a moment, her body gone slack.

"I forgot to do the knock," he said. "What in tarnation are you crying for?"

She leaped, half-scrambled, half-ran to him. "You damn fool," she cried, her face hard against him, her little fists punching his chest and his arms and his shoulders. "You damn fool, you damn fool, you damn fool."

As he held her, Roy smiled and said, "Cussing now, are we?"

And she said, "I damn well am, aren't I? Oh, Roy, I thought you were dead!"

"Well, we best get you some clothes. We can't go get married with you dressed like that."

And he kissed her the way she deserved, and she kissed him right back.

Cedar Rapids, Iowa.
August 12, 1878

It had been a full year since they'd left Custer City behind. A year of them being home with Grampa — and they were a true family now. Four generations together.

Roy sat in the parlor, letter in hand, watched them all from his chair. They hadn't long finished breakfast. It was always a nice time of day, because it was when they were all there together, with not much to do but be happy.

Charlotte lay back on the sofa, cradling a small precious bundle. Her eyes were closed — but Roy knew her so well by now, he could tell she was really awake. Just enjoying a moment of peace, her face blissful, relaxed.

She had looked the same way when they married in the

little stone church nearby, with all of their family and the whole congregation watching on. Wore the hat with the bird on it too. Roy insisted on that.

Somehow, she's become even prettier since then, he thought. *So pretty, I ache when I look at her.*

Uncle Dan, as usual, was happily arguing with Grampa. Didn't matter what it was about — they just enjoyed the intellectual sparring. The old man was eighty-six now. Could not see three feet in front of him, but seemed just about fitter than ever. Seemed like having all this family around made him want to live on forever — and it seemed like he might.

Roy thought back on that very first moment, when he and Charlotte and Dan had arrived. They'd wired Grampa they were coming, but they hadn't said when.

Sneaked up on him, sort of, they had.

He had turned the old saloon into a dance hall the previous year, so it wasn't open for drinking during the day. He'd been out on the porch, just smoking a pipe as he rocked in his big old chair, and he'd fallen to dozing, perhaps just a minute before.

"Lazier'n ever," Roy had said, and old Clarence Scott had been startled awake, his pipe fell from his mouth and down on the boards of the porch.

"You sure this is him?" Dan had said then. "The man I remember would never let such undesirables as us sneak up on him this way."

"Roy? Dan? Dan, my boy, let me look at you! Oh, my boys. My boys both come home to me now. And who's this here with you? Come close, girl, let me see. Oh my, she's too pretty for you, Roy, I might have to steal her from you!"

Now, old Clarence Scott, in his day, had been some sort of man — a champion boxer, the bravest of soldiers, an Indian fighter of note. Even when he first came, at seventy years old and with his eyes already failing, he was the toughest man in all Iowa — that soon becoming widely accepted as fact, and no man being game to put it to any sort of test.

But when that old man saw his boys, he broke down in tears — showed what a real man is. That being, a man unafraid, even of his own deepest feelings.

He had cried tears of joy, his old eyes being useful for that at least. "My boys," he had said fifty times that first day, if he'd said it even the once.

Grampa had a wife now as well. "Man's a glutton for punishment," he'd said. But the way he looked at Maisie told a more truthful story. Maisie had worked for Big Jim Starr in the old days. She was a fixture there long before Roy was born, and he'd known her his whole life. She had helped raise him, even before his dear mother was murdered — and certainly after. She had been Roy's mother's best friend, and was fifty-four years of age now. He looked at the kind woman, as she in turn watched the friendly argument between father and son.

She looked so very happy.

That day Roy came back, and he found out they'd married, he could not help expressing surprise. And Maisie had said, "Old coot hornswoggled me good. Reckoned he was all done with poking, and just wanted a companion.

Ha! Swore blind and blue he just wanted someone to play checkers with him, and help keep the bed warm and cozy cold nights."

Roy had looked at the old man then — he was still fit and healthy, but he looked his full age, eighty-five. Older even maybe. "No, Maisie," Roy had said. "Surely not. He must be long done with all that."

"You'd a'thought so," Maisie had answered. "Yet somehow, he got his second wind. Two years now it's been, and that wind blows in still, twice every week on the regular. It's a good thing I love the old coot, or I fancy I'd kill him for the liar he is."

"All that true, Father?" Uncle Dan had said then.

But old Clarence Scott only smiled and said, "A gentleman don't discuss such personal issues. But I will advise this — if I was you, Son, I'd find a nice retired cat for a wife. You cain't beat experience, bedroom-wise, and that's a true fact, yours for free."

Roy chuckled at the memory now, and Maisie looked up, caught him watching her, and she smiled.

"You planning to read that letter, Little Roy, or waiting for winter to come, and use it for kindling?"

She had never stopped calling him *Little Roy*. Sometimes he complained, but the truth was, he kinda liked it.

He smiled affectionately at her, opened the letter, commenced reading.

Deer Roy.

First thing. Hank and his new missus says howdy.

He got hitched to Eula. You remember her. Pritty little thing loved Fleet Darrow. Wore black and morned him for months. Hank is a fine Pa to her son and loves them both a lot. She reckons Hank more hansomer than me. But when Hank wore my brown shirt she flat beleeved he was me. She tryed to kiss me and we had to tell her the trooth about us swopp-ing the shirts. Then she made us both sleep in the barn even tho it was her fawlt not ours.

Now Hank seen me write down the howdy, he mite stop his pesterment of me. That be a first.

The pigs bizness is good. Custer City been grow-ing like flees on a dog. And all them new folks got to eat too.

Now old Silver Sam is Mayor, you shood just see him. What a fine site. Wares a stripe suit and tall hat and only half drunk not full drunk except late at nite. Turns out its troo. He rearly is clever when hes not drunk. His gray horse still alive. Mite be sum sort of record for a horse age he reckons.

Him and Curly Brown done what you ~~sugesterd~~ sujesterd. They done what you reckon they shood. Turned the Golden Nugget into a Dance Hall. They was short on whores anyway since me and Hank married the best two they had. Alcie and Eula consenterd to work in the Dance Hall but dont do no extras. Some of the girls do some dont. They all make more money now than before. Even with-out they do enny whore-ing. Men pay good for a dance and behave proper too. They know what Curly wood do. And Curly looks after the ladies all real good. Respecks ladies he does. He did had to kill one feller who got nasty drunk and beat on a woman reel bad.

Sheriff SMITH is a real fine sheriff. Best joke ever is that he had to kill two bad fellers — that aint the joke part — but one feller looked sort of like him. Big nose and ugly and short with big mussels. So he rote that fellers name as Big-Nose Brown and sent in the paper work. They sent him a $200 bounty for kill-ing his own self and now once a week he goes to the boneyard and visits the grave thats got his old name writ up on it.

We all reckon Fleet Darrow would call that a fine entertaynment.

They drink a glass to Fleet Darrow once evry week. And one each to you and your Uncle Dan too. We go in for that evry tuesday. Drink 3 glasses one after the next to pay our respecks. Even tho only Fleet Darrows dead we allways do it. Sumtimes its 4 drinks if Silver Sam speeks of Wild Bill.

Me and Hank still feel bad about lett-ing you pay so much for that horse. Aint no horse with a hole at each end can be worth a thousand dam dollars. But may-bee if hes so good as you say he mite win you a race and win it back. And even I could see how you and that animal felt a belong-ing to each other. So I dont dowt hes with the rite man.

Last not leest, we all was so peskily happyfyed to see the fotograf of your new baby. Evryone in the hole town asks to see it and its bend-ing at its edges now. Hole town allways be grayt-full what you done for us Roy.

Your frend allways,

Everett Ferguson. and Alcie too. and Hank and Eula.

PS.. Also I neer forgot to say Alcie is with child. So I mite be a Pa soon like you.

And may-bee Hank will hav his own too we aint shore on that yet but we hope-ing.

Also Eula's baby now 4 months in age looks a bit like Fleet Darrow now may-bee.

It will be a fine entertaynment if it is Fleet Darrows boy we all reckon.

Roy looked up from the letter.

What a thing. A Fleet Darrow child.

Bully for you, Mister Darrow!

What a fine thing.

He'll surely have a luckier start to life than his father did.

He felt his dear Charlotte's eyes on him, and looked across to the sofa.

"You look so amused, Roy, what is it?"

That voice. That wonderful voice. Is there any sound in the world that might yet match its beauty?

And of course, right then, as if she'd heard his thoughts, their tiny baby woke and started up crying.

"It's a letter from Everett," he said as he stood and crossed the room. "Let me hold her now," he said. "I'll rock her awhile, stop her crying."

"I'm afraid you don't have what she wants right now, Roy," Charlotte said. "She's hungry, my love."

Maisie came over, looked down at the beautiful baby,

turned to Roy with a smile and said, "She's well named. She looks *so* like your mother."

"Angelina," he said. "Stop your grumbling then, baby girl. Can't I just feed her milk from a bottle? I don't like standin' by all the time doin' nothing to help."

"Roy Stone," said Maisie sternly. "Leave your poor wife and baby alone, and go blow out some cobwebs. Go on now," she said, "go ride your horse, Little Roy."

It was what his dear mother had always said, and Maisie had never forgotten. Difference was, he had a real horse now. But the words made a bittersweet memory.

"Go on, Roy," Charlotte said. "Do as Granny tells you."

As he went to the stable, he thought about the new baby Charlotte carried inside her.

Will this one be a boy? He'll be Reese, of course. That'll make Grampa happy, and it's only right.

A half hour later, Roy was out on the trail, the quiet side of town by the river, with that plain little horse he so loved. He was no race horse — Roy had only told Ev and Hank that so they'd take his money — the horse was too little for one thing, he'd never win races, not really. But that sure didn't stop that horse from being something special.

Roy turned the little bay gelding around now, faced back toward Cedar Rapids, held him tight, as if it was the start of a race.

"Won the Preakness last time," he said, in the horse's left ear. "This time it's the Kentucky Derby, and we're going to win, boy."

He wished his dear mother could be there to see him — somehow though, he knew she was, as he reached down near the stirrup, touched his left boot for luck, then sat up and cried, *"GO!"*

As always, that fine horse knew what *GO* meant, they made a great burn of the breeze in that next sixty seconds, flat out with their ears all pinned back, wild and wont, hell for leather. Rolling, roiling thunder of hooves and hot breath, they sliced through the air, like lightning formed into flesh bone and spirit they were. Horse and rider together in one perfect moment, their kindred hearts beating joyful, as they flew under bright morning sun, magic runes in their minds.

That's what we needed — they thought it together as they slowed. Thought it inside and outside their minds, for the pair were connected.

As they slowed to a walk, the horse turned in to take the path down to where sweet grass grew by the river. They would drink, then they'd share an apple. Roy would lay on the grass while his friend grazed.

Horse and rider having blown out the cobwebs, the little horse stopped, Roy stepped down to the ground.

He rubbed the horse on the neck, said, "Good boy, Fleet. That's a fine entertainment alright. Good boy, Fleet, good boy."

The End

ALSO BY J.V. JAMES

WOLF TOWN

Cleve Lawson is a man for minding his business. But when
he witnesses a stranger murdered by road agents, then the
outlaws kill his best friend, Cleve decides it's high time he
stuck his nose in where it don't belong.

As if all that ain't problems enough, he meets a tough yet
beautiful woman who takes a shine to him – and a feller
with fists of iron who takes unkindly to that.

Throw in a murderous road agent gone loco, an unfaithful
dog, a wise-cracking Sheriff, and a range war between
sheep and cattle men, and Cleve's got more troubles than
an unarmed man in the middle of a gunfight.

Available as an eBook and paperback.

FYRE – A WESTERN

What if you went off to fight for what's right, and someone told your sweetheart you'd died? What if that same person told you that she was dead too?

What if that man up and married her? After secretly killing her family? And what if that man was the brother you trusted?

And what if, one day, you came home?

A story of trickery and cunning, of brotherhood and truth, and of war. Of bandits and shootouts and justice, and of doing what's right. Of a tall man who slithered, and a dwarf who stood tall as the clouds, and became Billy's friend.

It's the story of how Billy Ray becomes Billy Fyre – and how, seven long years after being told he'd lost everything, finally, Billy comes home, to fight for what's his.

Available as an eBook and paperback.

Printed in Great Britain
by Amazon

82996769R00222